DIRTY CHARMER

New York Times Bestselling Author

EMMA CHASE

DIRTY
CHARMER

PROLOGUE

Tommy

WHEN I WAS A BOY, THERE WAS A SPINDLY OLD woman who lived down by the docks. Some said she was a witch. Others claimed she'd had "the sight" since she was a girl. Still others believed she'd seen enough, been around long enough to predict things. Despite the whispers, and fire-and-brimstone warnings from the local priest, all the new young mums would make their way over to her rickety shack with their newborns in tow.

To have their futures told.

The story goes she took one look at me and said to my mum, "Drown this one in the river, Maggie."

She wasn't a particularly nice woman.

"He'll be handsome as the devil and twice as charming," she'd said. "But he'll be wild, stubborn and foolhardy—and he'll break your poor dear heart because he won't be livin' long."

My mother never went back to see the old woman after that. *A load of rubbish*, she'd say. Because if anyone is stubborn, it's my mum—and as far as she was concerned, her darling boy was going to live forever.

The kick of it is . . . I'm beginning to think that old woman may've been on to something. Because . . . well . . . there's a good chance I might be dead.

I don't feel dead, though I'm not entirely sure what dead is supposed to feel like.

I remember the fire at the Horny Goat Pub. The charring walls, the smoke thick as black wool scratching at my eyes and filling my lungs. There's no smoke now, only the sharp scent of disinfectant, a crisp, cool softness beneath my head and a bottomless darkness—like outer space if the stars blinked out.

I was looking for Ellie in the pub—I remember that too. Because little Ellie Hammond is the sister of our Duchess Olivia, wife of Prince Nicholas. Because it was my shift, and it was my job to guard her, to keep her safe. Because my duty to the crown is one of the few things in this world I take seriously and even if I didn't, I sure as hell take my best mate, Logan, seriously. And he's sick in love with Ellie though he won't let himself admit it.

And Ellie's a good lass. She brightens a room the way a jewel takes in sunlight and throws out sparkles over anyone close by. Lo deserves a light like that in his life.

Are you there, God? It's me, Tommy.

I know we haven't spoken since my last confession . . . when the blonde with the perfect arse was kneeling in the pew ahead of me. I had to say three Hail Marys and she had to say three Hail Marys, and before we knew it, we were breaking all sorts of Commandments and a few deadly sins at her flat for the rest of the afternoon.

But I'm hoping you'll look past all that, Lord, because I have a favor to ask.

Please . . . let Ellie have made it out alive, even if I didn't. Logan needs her. They need each other.

That's all for now—perhaps I'll be seeing you soon.

Cheers. Nanu-nanu. Amen.

As I sign off with the Almighty, a rush of air dusts over my skin, shifting and moving—like an incoming answer to my prayer. That stinging sanitized smell dissipates and is replaced by something infinitely sweeter.

Apples.

A whole orchard of round, red, ripened apples suddenly surrounds me. I breathe in deeper, hungry for more of the delicious scent.

"God, look at him," a voice murmurs from my left. "Tell me you wouldn't boff his brains out if you had the chance."

The tone that responds is smooth, refined and distinctly feminine.

"Inappropriate, Henrietta."

"Yeah, yeah, I know . . . but still. I would ride him like a shiny new bicycle from here to Scotland and back again."

The silky voice groans, "Etta . . ."

"I bet he knows how to ring a girl's bell too. He's got that look about him. *Ding-ding.*"

I like this Henrietta. She seems like my type of girl. Or angel or demon, depending on what the hell is actually going on. It's probably time I find out.

The polished tone takes a turn towards authoritative. "Hush now, I have to record his vitals for Dr. Milkerson."

It's the kind of voice I wouldn't mind taking orders from—the best kind. *Lower, Tommy. More, Tommy. Harder, Tommy.* The imaginings cause a pleasant, stirring sensation in my groin and apparently, even if I'm dead, my cock is very much alive.

That's comforting.

"Speaking of Milkerson, have you noticed the way he looks at you? I bet he'd give his cutting hand to take a peek at *your* vitals. Maybe you'd have a clue about that if you ever bothered coming out for drinks with us after shift."

"I don't have time for drinks. There's too much to do—too much to learn."

"Oh, for Saint Arnulf's sake, Abby," Henrietta gripes. "Why do you have to be so stuffy all the time?"

"Saint Arnulf?" she asks.

"He's the patron saint of beer, everyone knows that. Heathen."

"All right, that's it—out. You're distracting me," Abby returns crisply. "If you're not going to focus, you need to go."

Henrietta's voice retreats. "You know what does wonders for focus? Letting your hair down once in a while—and your knickers!"

The air around me rustles again, before settling back into a quiet stillness. Then, slowly, the scent of apples returns. But it's even better now. More intense. Closer.

A gentle little sigh floats just beside my ear and the satiny, lilting voice goes low—as soft as the stroke of petal blossoms along my skin.

"I'd never tell Etta this, but she wasn't even a little bit wrong. You are a beautiful man, aren't you?"

And I have to know. I have to see.

I hadn't realized my eyes were closed, until I'm able to drag them open. The light is bright, blinding at first—I squint against the glowing white halo that frames her.

"Mr. Sullivan? You're awake."

She has the face of an angel—high cheekbones, luminous skin, and wide, round, dark green eyes. But her mouth is full and lush, and her hair shines like a golden fire, a mass of deep red, honey and chestnut hues.

There's just something about a redhead. A passion, a spirit, a strength that sets them apart. That makes them unforgettable. Irresistible.

She's too tempting to be angelic.

But still I ask, "Is this heaven?"

"No, you're not in heaven."

I shrug. "I always figured the other spot would be more my scene anyway."

Her rosy lips curve into a smile, and that's blinding too.

"You're not there either."

I shake my head to clear the fog and hoist myself up, coming fully awake. And I look around. It's a hospital room—white walls, sterile chairs, wires connected to a bleeping machine behind me. I touch my chest and arms to make sure they're still there. I wiggle my toes beneath the sheet because while my cock is definitely at the top of the list, it's good to know the rest of me still works too.

"I'm alive?"

She's still close, still smiling.

"Very much so."

Relief floods through me, making my chest feel near to bursting. And without another thought or a second's hesitation, I lean forward and crush my lips against this sinfully stunning girl's mouth.

It's an impulse—a reflex—like that photograph of the American sailor and nurse at the end of WWII. Because when you almost died but didn't, all you want to do is feel alive. And I've never felt more alive than I do in this moment, kissing this lovely lass.

I sweep my mouth across hers, sucking gently, luring her to follow. She's stiff at first, surprised, but she doesn't struggle or pull away. And then after a moment—her muscles yield and her lips go soft and pliant beneath my own. She melts against me, molds our upper bodies together with a breathy, needy moan. My hands delve into the satin of her hair, holding on, tugging her closer, feeling the swell of her breasts tight against my chest. Her hands grasp for my shoulders, digging in, as our heads move and angle together. And our kiss turns hotter. Wetter.

I stroke the tip of my tongue across the seam of her lips, teasing them to part. When they do, I sink right inside the tight, warm cavern. And the taste of her. *Christ*, she tastes like fruit in the Garden of Eden, succulent and forbidden. The desire to suck and lick at more of her pumps through me—to see if the rest is every bit as sweet as her mouth.

I lean back, dragging her with me, over me—fucking those pretty, delicate lips roughly with my tongue—and I groan deep and long when her tongue brushes against mine, mouth-fucking me right back.

It's good—so bloody good—I may not have been dead before, but this kiss just might kill me. My pulse pounds in my ears and the machine is fairly screeching behind me with my wild, racing heart.

I think it's the machine that does it, that breaks the spell. Because as soon as the sound penetrates my own awareness, the woman in my arms tears her mouth away and freezes above me, a look akin to horror sweeping across her face.

Breathing harshly, she scrambles off the bed as if it's swarming with red ants and I'm their king.

"That . . . you . . . that . . . " Her tits rise and fall beneath her light blue top with each quick, panting breath. It's lovely. "That was completely inappropriate!"

"It really was." I nod, pushing a hand through my dark hair. "Want to do it again?"

Her eyes flare, gaping.

"Absolutely not. Never again."

I click my tongue. "Careful. Never's a very long time."

A dainty line appears between her auburn brows as she frowns, lifting her perky nose, crossing her lithe arms—the very picture of prim and proper and posh. My cock twitches at the sight and something else awakens inside me.

The primal part of a man that craves the challenge, the chase, and even more—the conquering.

"You've suffered a serious concussion, Mr. Sullivan."

I shrug. "I feel fantastic."

"And some smoke inhalation. You may be delirious."

"No—this is all me. Delirious would've been not jumping at the chance to kiss you the second I could."

That comment ruffles all her pretty feathers.

"There's no reason to get flustered just because you enjoyed it, pet," I coax her.

"I am not your *pet*, Mr. Sullivan. And I don't get *flustered*. And I certainly did not enjoy" —she wags her hand in my general direction in a flustered sort of way—"*that*."

A grin tugs my lips. "I beg to differ. And your tongue's been in my mouth—I think it's all right to call me Tommy now."

Her eyes darken to a shade near to black with passion or fury—with feeling. And I know that Henrietta was wrong. Apple Blossom isn't stuffy—she just hasn't met a man who knows how to bring out her reckless side.

Not until now—not until me.

She tugs on the lapel of her white coat, straightening her spine.

"I'm leaving."

"Funny. Typically the girls I kiss like to tell me when they're coming." I wink.

Her cheeks flush a deep, dusky pink, and I just bet those pretty petals between her legs flush the same shade when she's really hot for it.

Saying that out loud isn't one of my better choices.

Because right after I do, she slaps me. Hard and fast. With enough force to jerk my head to the side and leave my left cheek pulsing with the sting. It's impressive.

"Ow."

And it's not like I didn't deserve it.

But looking back now, that's really when I should've known.

In that perfect, indelible moment as we stare at each other—my eyes lapping her up and her jade gaze swallowing me whole, as we take each other in. Just a few dozen inches apart, taking and taking each other . . . and already craving more.

CHAPTER ONE

Tommy

"HEY, TOMMY! YOU GOT A CROWBAR WE CAN borrow?" Seamus—a small, sandy-haired boy of about eleven—calls to me from across the street with a few of his lads standing behind him.

I drop the bag of trash in the bin and close the lid. Then I fish the pack of cigarettes from my pocket, slip one between my lips and light up, blowing out smoke as I answer.

"Are you planning to bash someone's skull in with it?"

It's a question that needs to be asked. Because in this neighborhood—it's important to make a name for yourself, to build a reputation, by any means necessary.

Just like in prison.

Seamus grins wickedly. "Nah, not today. A lorry broke down a few blocks over. The driver gave us a fiver to make sure no one pops the back and takes his cargo."

"So, you're going to pop the back and take his cargo," I state, because of course they are.

"Well, sure. It's a Custard Cream and Jaffa Cakes truck. We gotta eat, don't we?"

Fair point.

I tilt my head towards the back gate. "Crowbar's in the shed. Don't touch anything else and make sure you return it or I'll be bashing your skull in."

Seamus agrees with a wave.

I finish my cigarette, crush it out with the heel of my black, shiny dress shoe and head up the walk to the narrow, three-story brick house with bright pink flowers filling the window boxes. We keep our property respectable—even if the rest of the neighborhood is falling to shit.

I step through the dark green door, over the threshold and into chaos.

Otherwise known as a day that ends in *Y*.

Juniper, the one-eyed cat, chases Angus the hedgehog—who should've been named Houdini—down the hallway. The television is blaring in the parlor because Granny's in her rocker and she's been stone-cold deaf for longer than I've been alive. A car backfires outside and Roscoe the bulldog tries to squeeze himself under the sofa but his arse and wagging tail stick out. In the kitchen four of my seven siblings laugh and chat raucously while gearing up for breakfast.

Some people collect stamps or antique teaspoons.

My mum and dad collect mammals.

Hounds, cats . . . for a few years we had a goat named Barney who kept the grass in the rear yard perfectly manicured. And though you wouldn't know it by looking at him, dark-haired, smiling Andy, who's sitting at the end of the table, isn't actually related to any of us. He was best mates with my oldest brother, Arthur, and somewhere along the way my parents just sort of acquired him.

My mother hands me a cup of tea and a bowl of porridge and I eat it while leaning against the counter.

"You're looking sharp, Tommy," my sister Winifred tells me. She and her two boys are home visiting for the next few weeks. They're in from Australia, where her husband is stationed.

I smooth my black tie down the front of my light gray shirt. "Thanks, Win. Me and Lo have a meeting up north with the

Dowager Countess of Bumblebridge. We might be taking her on as a new client."

The fire at The Goat that caused me to get knocked on the head two years ago also knocked some sense into Logan when it came to Ellie Hammond. He confessed his unending love and, of course, she felt the same. But you can't be a guard to the royal family of Wessco and be getting off with their relatives—at least not officially. So, Lo resigned. And then he approached me about starting a business together—private security, drivers, personal bodyguards—that sort of thing.

I'm always up for adventure and mayhem, and running S&S Securities has been filled with that.

"Oooh, the old angry bee herself," Andy jokes, referring to the Dowager Countess.

"I heard she sleeps in her jewels," Janey says. "The whole bit— earrings, bracelets, a diamond choker."

"I heard she eats her young," my mother teases.

"I heard she does vampire facials with actual blood just like Kim Kardashian," Fiona chimes in.

Winnie makes a gagging face. "Whose blood does she use?"

Fiona rolls her eyes at the ignorance. "Her own blood, of course."

"Not even seven in the morning and we're already discussing bloodshed," my oldest sister, Bridget, says as she breezes through the back door, carrying my one-year-old niece, Rose, on her hip. "Such lovely breakfast conversation."

My mum takes Rosie, giving her a piece of toast to gnaw on, and Bridget pours herself a cup of tea, sipping it with a tired sigh, while rubbing her firm, bulging belly.

Doing what I do, it's important to be aware, observant. To take note of small details that the average person would miss—because the devil, and most times the danger, is in the details.

The marks scattered down Bridget's arm—finger-size bruises—immediately catch my attention.

"How'd they get there?" I ask her.

She glances down like she's just noticing them, then rolls her hazel eyes heavenward.

"Desmond had one too many at the pub last night. We had it out when he got home."

"He grabbed you?" I ask evenly.

"Only after I smacked him upside the head first. I bruise easy these days, Tommy—it's nothing."

Sullivans don't come small but the girls in my family tend to veer towards petite—delicate boned. Bridget's husband is in masonry; he works with stone and concrete all day and he's got the muscles to show for it. And she's six months pregnant.

"Right." I nod, schooling my features.

That's part of the job too. To not give anything away, any hint of what you may be thinking or feeling—or planning. I'm very good at my job.

But that doesn't fool my mother. While the rest of the clan engages in conversation, she comes up beside me, speaking low. "Leave it alone, Tommy. What goes on between a husband and a wife is no one's business but theirs."

My mum is a good woman—but she's not a *soft* woman. She's not passive or subtle. Her kindness and love comes with an overbearing, steel-tipped edge. The kind of nurturing that says you'd damn well better let her mother you or she'll make you live to regret it.

Which is why I'll never understand her ridiculous "it's between a husband and wife" crock-of-shit stance. My sweet sister has bruises on her arm—and I'm supposed to be all right with that?

Not in this lifetime.

"I mean it, Tommy," she warns.

"Yeah, Mum." I give her my easy, boyhood grin. "I know you do."

When you're a part of a large family, siblings pair up into factions—it's the only way to survive. Janey is the most badass of my sisters—if she's ever interested in being a bodyguard, Lo and I would hire her on the spot.

Janey's eyes meet mine and she lifts the serrated knife she's using to slice bread, quirking a brow. I nod in return. And just like that, our plan is in place. Later this evening, me and Janey will swing by Katy's Pub to communicate to Desmond that if Bridget ends up with another mark, Janey will cut his balls off with that bread knife and I'll make him swallow them.

"Hey, Tommy," Bridget says, "I meant to tell you, I saw a flat for rent over near the hospital. Seems like a nice place, with views of the water."

None of my siblings flew the cuckoo's nest until they got married. Living here was fine when I was working on Prince Nicholas's security team—we were traveling more often than not. But now that I'm here full-time it's a bit crowded for comfort. Stifling. I'm a manspreader—I like my space.

"I'll give it a look."

Andy squeezes out from around the table and heads off to his job at the automobile plant. No sooner is he out the door than my younger brother Lionel comes charging down the stairs, late for his class at uni. When he moves to nab the last slice of ham, my mother slaps his hand away.

"That's for your dad. If you oversleep, you starve."

It's the law of the jungle around here.

Still, when Lionel grabs his rucksack off the counter I see Mum slip him a sandwich and a banana, because she's not quite as hard as she wants us to think she is.

A few minutes after Lionel's exit, my dad comes through the perpetually revolving door. For as long as I can remember, Dad's worked the graveyard shift at the power plant.

Like Homer Simpson.

He sinks down into his chair at the table, kissing my mother's cheek when she slides his warmed plate and tea in front of him.

"Thank you, love." He chews on a bite of ham and gazes around at us, his balding head gleaming beneath the white glow of the kitchen ceiling light. "How are my angels today?"

Between the two of them, Dad's the softie. The pushover. Growing up, if one of us deserved the belt—and with eight of us around, someone *always* deserved the belt—he'd take us back behind the shed and give us one, single smack. But he'd look so stricken afterward, the guilt alone kept us well-behaved for days.

Though I still can't tell if he calls us his angels sincerely or not. I mean, Satan was an angel once too.

There's a knock on the back door and a moment later Logan St. James steps through it, wearing his own dapper dark suit.

My sisters greet him warmly and my dad says, "Logan, how are you, son?"

When God was passing out families Logan was dealt a rotten hand, so my parents have tried to fill that space for him.

"I'm well, Mr. Sullivan," Logan says and smiles—something he does a lot more of these days.

"Do you want a bite to eat, Lo?" my mum asks. "There's some porridge left."

"I'm fine, thank you."

"Are you coming to supper on Sunday?" she asks. "I'm making my roast."

In the summer, Mum likes to do Sunday dinners up big— friends, family and half the block are invited.

"I'll have to check with Ellie."

"Smart man," Winnie says with a grin.

"On top of Finn teething, she's been feeling poorly lately," Logan explains. "I'll let Tommy know if we can make it."

Finnegan is Logan and Ellie's nine-month-old son. He's the spitting image of his father, with his mother's energetic zest for life.

I slip my suit jacket on. "We've got to get on the road."

"Well, good luck today, boys." My father stands and pats our backs. "Make us proud."

Logan goes out the front door to the car, but before I can follow him, Fiona comes sneaking down the stairs with a huge bouquet of roses in her arms.

"Tommy." She glances towards the kitchen to make sure the coast is clear. "I need you to get rid of these for me."

I pluck the card out from between the stems.

"Who the hell is Martin MacTavish and why the fuck is he sending you flowers?"

Flowers are an instrument of seduction—a tool wicked boys use to charm good girls into debauchery. I should know; I've sent lots of flowers to lots of girls. And debauchery is fun.

But knowing my baby sister is getting flowers and having to contemplate that she may be doing God knows what with fuck knows who? That's *not* fun.

"Shhh! Keep your voice down," she whisper-yells. "If I wanted to answer those sorts of questions, I'd deal with Mum."

"Then go on and deal with Mum." I call her bluff. "Let me know how that works out for you."

Her face collapses into a mask of pathetic pleading, and her big, sad doe eyes stab me straight through the heart. "Pleeeasse, Tommy. You know how she can be. I need your help. Please, please?"

As the youngest of many, Fiona's superpower is finding a person's soft spot and exploiting it. It's near impossible to tell her no.

"All right, all right," I relent with a sigh. "Give them here."

"You're the best big brother ever!" She kisses my cheek, passes me the flowers and bounces away.

Outside on the stoop, I hand the roses to Logan.

"Give these to Ellie, would you?"

"Okay." He stares at the bouquet curiously. "Why are you giving my wife flowers?"

I shake my head. "Because God is punishing me. And I need to get a place of my own, that's why."

We make it halfway to the car before an excited, high-pitched voice calls from over the bushes on the side of the property.

"Hello there, Tommy—hi! Hey, Logan."

Melanie Thistle has lived next door my entire life. When we were twelve I kissed her at the top of the Ferris wheel during the Autumn Pass festival, and she's been keen on me ever since.

"Hi, Mellie," I return.

Lo lifts his chin. "Melanie."

She waves vigorously and smiles so broadly, I can almost see her back molars.

"How's school treating you?" I ask, even though I shouldn't.

But it's automatic at this point—chatting women up is what I do.

Don't get me wrong, the Thistles are a good lot and Mellie is a sweet girl studying to be a veterinary assistant, but she has this desperately infatuated way about her that's off-putting. Now and then she gets this fanatical look in her eyes—and I know she'd sneak in my room and stare at me while I slept if she thought she could get away with it. Gives me the willies.

"School's going well. Yesterday we learned about snakes—boa constrictors to be exact. They're fascinating creatures. The way they wrap themselves around and around and around whatever they de-sire . . . so it can never get away. Then they just *squeeze* the life right out of it!"

She demonstrates by wrapping her hands around her own neck, and squeezing—hard.

"And that thing they do with their tongue—it's like this . . ."

Melanie flicks her tongue in and out of her mouth. Then she does it again, trying to look sultry. And failing.

"It's really sexy, don't you think?"

Logan squints wordlessly. And I slip on my dark aviator sunglasses.

"Right. Okay, then." I hook my thumb towards the car. "We need to head out. There's an appointment. Waiting."

"Oh, of course. Don't let me keep you."

But before we can make a break for it, keep us is what she does.

"Your mum invited me to supper this Sunday."

Of course she did. As far as my mother is concerned, Melanie would be the perfect daughter-in-law. Someone she could remake in her own image—like a clone. A mini-mum.

As Ellie would say . . . yikes.

"Will you be there?"

I rub the back of my neck. "It depends on work. We've been hammered with business lately. You know—clients and training the new hires."

"Yes, it's wonderful how well you're doing. Truly."

For a moment, I feel genuinely proud. Because Lo and I *are* doing well. A couple of nobodies from nowhere—who would've thought it?

Then Melanie keeps speaking.

"And you know my door's always open. If you ever want to drop by—we can discuss the boa constrictors some more."

And she's back to flicking her tongue.

"'Bye, Mellie." I turn and don't stop until I reach the car.

Logan's behind the wheel and once we're down the block, he comments, "So . . . Melanie's still carrying a torch for you, eh?"

"More like the Great Fire of London, yeah." I chuckle.

"She's probably just nervous around you." Logan laughs. "Jittery. Ellie says she used to be like that with me back in the day. This one time, she tripped over her own feet and almost bashed her head on the kitchen counter—would've knocked herself clean out if I hadn't caught her." He shakes his head. "I think you should give Melanie a chance, take her for dinner, see how it goes."

Logan St. James is giving me dating advice.

I push my sunglasses down the bridge of my nose, stare at him, and voice the only logical conclusion.

"My mum got to you, didn't she?"

He laughs again, turning the car onto the main road out of town.

"No, she didn't get to me."

His voice goes softer. Sentimental.

"It's just . . . having Ellie and Finn, a family . . . being settled. It's a good thing, Tommy. It's really good."

I nod, because I know for Lo it's not just a *good* thing—it's everything.

"And if you look past the temporary insanity and whatever she was trying to do with her tongue, Melanie's a nice girl."

I tend to go for women with a bit of a wild side. Feisty. A girl who can handle herself, stand up for herself. When something comes easy—and for me, women have always come easy—it's a challenge that grabs you by the balls. Holds your attention. Heats your interest.

I look back at Logan. "Exactly. When have you ever known me to like *nice* girls?"

CHAPTER TWO

Abby

*T*IC-TOC

One of the drawbacks of being born into an extraordinary family is average can feel like utter failure. When you're Lois Lane surrounded by a household of Supermen it can be rather . . . intimidating. Disheartening.

Or motivating, depending on your outlook.

Tic-toc

I come from a long line of remarkable people. Perfect people. People who seem like they were manufactured on a shiny assembly line of grand accomplishments.

Tic-toc

Take my father for example—Montgomery Felix Haddock, the 10th Earl of Bumblebridge—seated at the far end of the dining table, reading the morning edition of the *Wessconian Times*, his distinguished brow drawn low in concentration. Many would have been satisfied with their inherited title, but not my father, not in this family.

Tic-toc

He went on to become a world-renowned barrister specializing in international law and human rights. He's also the founding partner of Haddock & Lipton, the most esteemed law firm in Wessco.

Tic-toc

Mother—Antoinette Bellamy-Haddock—seated to Father's right, wearing her oval mother-of-pearl reading glasses, was awarded the Nobel Prize in Physics before the age of twenty. Twice.

She's now the Head Chair of the Bellamy-Haddock School of Physics and Chemistry at Wilfordshire University.

Tic-toc

Beside mother is my eldest brother, Sterling—a three-time gold medal triathlon Olympian and Rhodes Scholar. His wife, Gertrude, recently developed the cure for Ebola and their ten-year-old twin daughters, Estelle and Helena, are musical prodigies in violin and cello, respectively.

Tic-toc

Seated across from Sterling's family is my sister, Athena—an international supermodel and mathematician who managed to solve the previously unsolvable Collatz Conjecture in-between photo shoots.

And I'm not even joking.

Her husband, Jasper, sipping his tea and checking the market fluctuations on his phone, is a self-made billionaire and Governor of the Bank of Wessco.

Tic-toc

There's an empty seat beside Jasper where my brother Luke would be sitting if he were here. Several years ago, Luke was on his way to becoming the youngest chess master in the history of the game. But then he ... stopped.

Tic-toc

Now he travels, returning home occasionally—but he's very good about sending photos from all his trips to the family group chat.

Tic-toc

In the seat of honor is my grandmother, the Dowager Countess of Bumblebridge. Her blouse is silk and dark green, matching the color of her eyes—the same shade as my own. The diamond bracelet around her slender wrist sparkles in the midmorning sun streaming through the arched windows, as she fills in the pages of her leather-bound organizer with perfect penmanship.

Tic-toc

Though my grandfather passed away years ago and there is "Dowager" in front of her title, Grandmother is still very much the head of the Haddocks. Because my father's commitments take him out of the country, she casts the votes for the family's seat in the House of Lords.

Tic-toc

Grandmother's accomplishments are . . . *us*. She's the glue that holds us together, the force that pushes us onward and ever upward, the fuel behind our desire to bring recognition to the family name.

Tic-toc

And then, there's me.

I graduated from one of the most prestigious universities in the country—but not early. I went on to attend an elite medical school and graduated with honors—but not as valedictorian. I'm the duck in a sea of swans. There's nothing remarkable or extraordinary about me—though it's not for lack of trying.

Tic-toc

"How are you progressing in your residency program, Abigail?"

Saturday brunch at the Bumblebridge estate is a quiet, reserved time for the family. A period of self-reflection and study. To refresh our focus, and prepare and plan for the week ahead. So, my grandmother's inquiry is not an attempt at pleasant conversation—it's a request for a status update.

Tic-toc

"Things are progressing well," I reply. "This afternoon I'll be scrubbing in on a laparoscopic cholecystectomy."

I'm a surgical resident at Highgrove Hospital, with a focus in cardiovascular specialty. I gesture to the open medical journal in front of me, though I already know every step by heart. I record myself reading aloud and play it at night as I go to sleep to reinforce the information. "It's an honor for a third year to be selected to assist in such a procedure."

Tic-toc

"I see." My grandmother nods. "It's a six-year program, is that correct?"

I take a drink of water to moisten my suddenly parched throat. "That's right."

"Mmm," she hums. "And you'll actually require *all* that time to get through it?"

Every pair of eyes at the table turns to me. Even Estelle and Helena stare. Creepily. Like those little REDRUM girls in *The Shining.*

Tic-toc

And the damned clickety-clack of the grandfather clock in the corner sounds louder than ever. More distracting.

Tic-toc, tic-toc, tic-toc

Can't they hear it too?

"I'm doing everything I can to accelerate my way through the program; however, it does seem that I'll need the full six, yes."

She nods—not appearing disappointed exactly, but none too pleased either.

Tic-toc

"Well, perhaps an opportunity will present itself for you to distinguish yourself from the pack. For instance, if the Queen were to develop an acute cardiac condition and there were no other surgeons available—you could volunteer to perform the procedure. And then *you* would be forever known as the doctor who saved Queen Lenora's life."

The Haddocks are distantly related by marriage to the Pembrooks. I've met Queen Lenora and her grandsons; Prince Nicholas and Henry are only a few years older than me. I like them all very much. They seem . . . warm, fun . . . at least when there aren't too many people around to see it.

It doesn't feel right to imagine an affliction befalling the Queen just so I could make a name for myself.

So I smile tightly and say, "Perhaps."

Tic-toc

Grandmother nods and closes her organizer, then she rings the silver bell beside her bread plate, summoning the butler.

"You may clear the table now, Grogg."

I stand and slip my textbook and laptop into my satchel.

"My new trial begins this Friday," Father says. "I'll be away for the next few weeks." Slowly, he gazes at each of us. "Be well, everyone."

"Be well, Father," I return softly, and we all wish him success.

Sterling, Athena and I don't live on the estate grounds with my grandmother and parents. My flat is in the city near the hospital. But there is one additional reason I enjoy coming to brunch at Bumblebridge. I look out the window, towards the rear of the house, and glimpse creamy Italian marble and sparkling aquamarine water.

As my grandmother walks past me towards the door to her private office, I tell her, "I'm going to swim a few laps to clear my head before heading to the hospital."

She pats my arm.

"Whatever may help, darling."

Tic-toc

———— ⚜ ————

The swimming pool is my happy place—my meditation altar and my yoga mat. I love the rhythm of the breaststroke, the coordination of the front crawl, the weightless, worriless repetition of each smooth, gliding movement.

Fifty good laps in the rectangular oasis later, I take off my goggles and float on my back into the middle, breathing slow and steady. My arms are out, eyes closed, muscles relaxed and my face tilted like a flower towards the warm summer sun.

After a few moments, I swim over to the ladder and climb out, pulling off my swim cap and shaking out my wavy auburn hair. Just as I'm about to slip on a robe and head into the house to dress, a familiar sound comes from behind.

Kersploosh

I turn and gaze down into the pool—where a fat little frog floats on his belly on top of the water. I kneel down to grab him, but the little bugger kicks away.

And I just can't leave him, not when I know he'll be bloated and drowned by morning. The small ones love to jump in, but they can never manage to find their way back out.

I move down the steps into the waist-deep water—and I'm able to scoop him into my hands. "Gotcha!"

Until he jumps right back out again.

Kersploosh

"Hey!" I trot after him. "Come back here, I'm trying to help you!"

After a few minutes of thrashing and splashing, I capture the little ingrate and tell him in no uncertain terms, "You can't swim in here. It's not good for you. Can you please not be stubborn about this?"

"I hope you're not expecting him to answer," a smooth, deep voice says from behind me.

I whirl around and come face-to-face with the man I've tried very hard not to think about for the past two years. For a moment, all the breath rushes from my lungs, because kissing Tommy Sullivan was the most reckless, thrilling thing I've ever done. A spontaneous, insane lapse in judgement.

And now he's here, looking even more handsome than he did then.

Broad-shouldered and tall, with careless hair, and full lips that I already know are strong yet soft—and very, very skilled.

And I'm standing in a pool . . . holding a frog.

Life is odd sometimes.

"Of course not. The frog larynx isn't sophisticated enough for speech. But I believe any living being can understand your intentions if you lay it out for them."

The corner of his mouth pulls up, like he's amused. Then he crouches down and gestures for me to hand the creature over. He holds him in his large hands and looks him sternly in the eyes.

"Stay out of the pool or I'll stick a firecracker up your arse and blow you into pieces, mate."

Then he tosses him on the grass.

"A bit violent, don't you think?" I ask.

"But effective."

As quick as I can, I get out of the pool and slip on my robe. The terry-cloth barrier makes me feel more confident, a shield against the grazing brown eyes watching my every move.

"I remember you," I inform him.

"Happy to hear it, I like to make an impression." He grins. "And I remember you—a woman who's good with her hands and her tongue is not one I'd soon forget."

Tommy Sullivan is over six feet tall, and every inch of him is wicked. It emanates from him—in the slouch of his stance, the curl of his lip, the mischievous sparkle in his eyes. He's the kind of man who could make a girl forget herself, without even trying.

"What in the world are you doing here?"

He jerks his thumb over his shoulder towards the main house.

"I just met with the Dowager Countess about the security position."

On occasion, when Father goes to trial against a particularly nasty adversary, temporary personal security is hired for the family as a precaution.

"Aren't you still on the Prince's team?"

He shakes his head. "After the fire at The Goat my partner, Logan, and I hung out our own shingle." He runs his tongue over his bottom lip, like he's tasting something there. "What about you, Apple Blossom? Are you still at Highgrove working to become a physician?"

"A surgeon," I correct. "Yes, I am."

"That's adorable."

"Adorable?" I don't like his tone—it's condescending. Cocky. I cross my arms and step towards him. "You think studying to become one of the best cardiovascular surgeons in the country is 'adorable'?"

He chuckles. "No, not actually, I just wanted to see you get riled up again. I figured that would do the trick."

"You like making women angry with you?"

"Not typically. But there's something about your ire that really does it for me." He leans in closer—all smooth, suave and seductive. "You have a beautiful frown, sweets. Has anyone ever told you that?"

His comment makes me frown harder. Which amuses him even further. Or maybe Tommy Sullivan just spends his whole life amused.

"Masochist," I counter.

"Never gave that one a go." His voice drops low. "But I'm game if you are—I'll try anything once—and then, again and again if it appeals."

With that, his tone shifts, reverts to casual, making me feel unbalanced. Off-kilter.

"Is your friend still there too? Henrietta? She seemed like a lively one."

I tilt my head towards him. "You remember that?"

He nods. "Sure."

"Most concussed patients can't recall details from the moments they first regain consciousness. That's fascinating."

He takes it as a compliment, and taps his temple.

"Big brain. You know what they say about men with big brains, don't you? We're big *everywhere*."

"Are you implying there's a correlation between the size of your brain and the size of your genitals?"

His brow furrows. "Well, I wouldn't have used those words—ever. But yeah, that's what I'm saying."

"Absurd. There's no scientific evidence to support that claim."

"I could be an anomaly. I think you should investigate it first-hand—just to be certain." He winks. "For science."

With the grace of an old screen movie star, he reaches into his suit pocket, takes out a pack of cigarettes and slips one into his mouth.

It's infuriating on so many levels.

Before he can light it, I pluck it from his lips. "For God's sake, man, it's the twenty-first century. Do you know what smoking does to a human body?"

I tick off the ailments on my fingers.

"Lung cancer, stroke, heart disease . . . Have you ever seen someone with emphysema, struggling for just one tiny gasp of breath?"

"Aren't you delightful?" He snaps the silver lighter closed and slides it back into his pocket. "I bet you're a real hit at parties."

Any calm and tranquility I found during my swim is gone now. I'm frazzled—like a live wire that's been cut and spliced and is sparking at its ends.

"I have to go. I'm not going to spend time chatting with someone who's hell-bent and determined to end up speaking through an electrolarynx. I have a surgery this afternoon."

"Are you free afterwards?" he asks. "Would you fancy grabbing some dinner with me?"

I pride myself on being a decisive person. An anticipator and a planner, clear and confident in my words and thoughts. I'm not a stammerer or stutterer. But Tommy Sullivan has a knack for turning me into both.

"I . . . I . . . don't have time for dinner."

He nods and moves in closer, so near I smell the warm, pleasant spice of his aftershave.

"I understand, I'm quite busy these days too. We can skip dinner and just go straight to fucking."

My mouth drops, but before I can craft a reply, his rough fingertips tenderly touch my cheek.

"It would be good between us. Can't you feel it, Abby?"

What I feel is a wobble in my joints and a knot of heat pulling tight and low in my stomach. It's my name I think—the way he says it—like a secret promise of dirty delights.

"I . . . don't have time for that either."

"Now that's a damn sin." He dips his chin mournfully and places his hand on his chest. "You're breaking my heart, lass."

I shake off whatever tempting spell he's weaving, and straighten up.

"Sounds like a medical condition. You should probably see someone about that."

I brush past him, walking up the path.

"Is that an offer to examine me?" he calls. "I accept, anytime."

And the echo of that deep chuckle chases me all the way back to the house.

Well, that was . . . interesting.

But now I can put Tommy Sullivan right out of my mind—it's not as if I'll have to see him again. The Dowager Countess of Bumblebridge would never employ someone so . . . improper. Incorrigible. *Incredibly good-looking,* a cheeky voice sighs inside my head.

But I ignore it.

Because it doesn't matter. Grandmother won't hire him.

I'm sure of it.

CHAPTER THREE

Tommy

THE DOWAGER COUNTESS HIRES US THE NEXT DAY.

It's her man who makes the call—that's usually how it works with the titled ones—assistants and secretaries do the legwork. Her insisting on personally interviewing me and Logan was unusual, but once we were in the library of the Bumblebridge estate, it made sense. She had control-freak micromanager written all over her. And her granddaughter is a chip off the old tiara.

Abby Haddock.

Technically, Lady Abigail. Technically-technically, Dr. Haddock—which is hot and inspires a plethora of naughty fantasies. But I like Abby best. It suits her.

Christ, just thinking her name has me grinning like an idiot. One of those fools that go on about butterflies flapping in their stomach and walking around on cloud sixty-nine.

There's just something so *enticing* about her. Fierce and fascinating and fuck-all arousing. On the outside, she's straitlaced, buttoned up and proper, but beneath the surface there's more. A sharp wit, a willfulness, a fire.

I remember the taste of it on my tongue—the taste of her.

And I could feel it yesterday reeling me in like a randy moth towards a slick, simmering flame. I can't wait to see her again, tease her again—make those pretty, pouty lips tighten in that kitten-fierce scowl again.

And if I play my cards right—I'll get to feel the scrape of her claws down my back, while I'm sliding deep inside, making her moan.

Abby'd be a scratcher—definitely.

That part will have to wait until *after* our job is finished, of course. I don't mess around with clients. It's a rule. While I've never put much stake in rules, in our line of work, messing around on the job is dangerous. If you're getting off with the woman you're supposed to be guarding, you're sure as shit not paying attention to possible threats.

At least not if you're doing it right—and I always do it right.

So, clients are off-limits. But former clients? They're fair game.

———◆———

"Keep your left up, Harry!"

The private protection racket is not a huge industry. The clientele pool is small and there are only a few companies who can meet their needs.

"Oh! Nice shot, Owen!"

Reputation, word of mouth, is everything.

Because those who require our services need to trust that we can keep them safe—and more importantly, that we'll do so discreetly. Old Winston, who first hired me to be on Prince Nicholas's team, used to say personal security is like a wireless fence that keeps the pups in the yard—impenetrable and invisible.

"Somebody call the priest—Harry's gonna need last rites!"

You've got your celebrities, entertainers—they can be particular about ridiculous things and get prickly if a bodyguard steps into their shot or bars the wrong person from sitting at their VIP table. But it's the politicians and dignitaries—bigwigs with pristine reputations—when things get really interesting.

"Sweep the leg, Johnny!"

I'm talking clandestine meetings, shady deals, bizarre compulsions, illnesses, secret lives and entire second fucking families. Once in a while, we'll get a disgruntled citizen gone mad or a run-of-the-mill assassin . . . but on an average day, the biggest threat to our clients is the press. They're usually chomping at the bit to sniff out any speck of dirt and splatter it across the front pages. Journalists are relentless, unmerciful and smart.

We need to be smarter. And that doesn't happen by accident.

"He's making a comeback! I told you he was a scrapper. Go, Harry, go!"

I left school after Year 10 and Lo didn't even get that far—but neither of us are stupid. Each round of new hires goes through seven weeks of training in defense, weapons and evasive driving. S&S Securities is housed in an abandoned warehouse that we refurbished into a reception area, offices and a full-sized gym with a shooting range and driving course out back.

"Aaand time!" I call from outside the ropes of the ring, where our newest crop of recruits is rotating through sparring sessions. I reset the stopwatch around my neck, while Logan claps Harry and Owen on their backs.

"Good match, boys."

Harry's a lanky fellow with shoulder-length dark hair and a careless, cocky attitude—nothing gets under his skin. Owen is stocky with fists like two bricks, but young. His ID says he's eighteen, but the baby fat of his cheeks and smooth, hairless chin make me think he's more likely two years shy of that age. They're East Amboy boys—a rough, poor neighborhood—but with the right guidance, they'll grow into outstanding guards.

Because when you come from nothing and belong to no one, you'll do anything to protect something worth having.

We only hire people with a raw skillset—they come to us like soggy, sad lumps of clay—and we mold them into polished, sleek, unbreakable shields. Also—we don't hire dicks. It's the Golden Rule. If a rotten apple will spoil the bunch, a full-blown wanker will make us all miserable.

I scan the clipboard in my hands. "Beatrice, Walter—you're up next."

Now this is going to be fun.

Bea is a tiny blond thing, but she's got mad skills. Her dad's American, former CIA—real covert operations shit that the general public will never hear about. Her brothers are Special Forces and from the time little Bea could walk, they taught her everything they knew.

"Are you joking?" Walter asks, gazing down at Beatrice like she's an insect we're asking him to swat with a sledgehammer.

"Threats don't just come in large and ugly," Logan explains. "You need to know how to take down the cute ones too."

Walter could be the twin brother of Lurch from *The Addams Family*. He's six foot five, in his fifties, and solid as a tank. He's a retired cop—too old to still be walking the beat but too young to waste away on his wife's couch drinking beer and watching television all day.

"Don't judge a book by its cover, Walter," I add, because I'm wise like that. "If you do, you're just asking to get your throat sliced by a paper cut."

He shrugs, giving me a don't-say-I-didn't-warn-you kind of look, and moves to the center of the ring.

Bea hops side to side, fists up, chin down, threatening. "If you go easy on me, old man, I'll rip your balls off and make them into earrings."

Creative shit-talking is always appreciated.

Logan swings his arm down, starting the match, and I click the stopwatch. Bea immediately scurries up Walter's back, wrapping her arm around his throat in a headlock, like a squirrel trying to take down a giant oak tree.

As Walter tries to shake her off, the door to the windowless back room of the shop—it's basically a broom closet—opens, and Stella walks towards me. She's thin and pale with straight black hair. The black lipstick on her lips matches her black clothes and she has several shiny piercings scattered across her body.

"The Haddock file," she says in that reliably flat tone, handing me a thick binder.

Stella and her twin brother, Amos, are our super-sleuth research team. They compile files on each client—quirks, kinks, debts, phobias, friends, enemies and routines—all the information we need to know, and some we wish we didn't.

I flip through the pages. "That was quick."

"I wanted to get it done right away. You know . . . since I might not make it to tomorrow."

Stella is a raging hypochondriac. But she's also Goth, so the idea of dropping dead at a moment's notice doesn't perturb her.

"Thanks, Stell."

She nods, turns around and walks straight towards the back room, closing the door behind her. I tuck the binder under my arm for some late-night reading—and when it comes to Abby's section, possibly some late-night tossing off.

Shame is for losers—which is why I have none.

In the ring, Walter manages to flip Bea off, and tries to pin her down with his foot, but she rolls away lickety-split, evading his stomping foot to the raucous cheers of the sweaty spectators.

"Tommy—a walk-in just came in. You're going to want to take this one."

Rounding out our band of misfit toys is Celia, our receptionist and bookkeeper. She's a brown-haired girl, with kitty-cat eyeglasses and a snug pencil-skirt vintage style that shows off her perfect hourglass figure. Celia's an upper-class lass who took the job to get out from under her father's thumb. She and I hooked up a whole lot when she first started—I think knowing her father would be ticked about her fucking a bloke like me offered her an extra level of thrill. But eventually, it ran its course for both of us.

Which brings me to our firm's non-fraternization policy. We don't have one.

Fighting, fucking, competition and ribbing are good for morale. Trying to one-up each other keeps our people sharp, alert. As long as it doesn't affect their professionalism in the field or infect the comradery of the team—Lo and I don't give a damn what or *who* they do, when they're off the clock.

"Show them to my office, Celia. I'll be right along."

I handle new client intakes. While Logan has a more cheerful disposition these days, he's not exactly chatty. And putting a stranger at ease, getting them to reveal the details of why they need our services, takes a certain amount of finesse. Charm.

I toss the stopwatch at Logan, who catches it one-handed without taking his eyes off the sparring pair. Incidentally, my money's on Bea for the win. Walter may have the stats on his side—but she wants it more. And in my experience, when it comes to fighting—and life—desire kicks logic's arse every single time.

———— ✧ ————

Every country has that one couple that epitomizes relationship goals. The impeccable partners, the passionate love story, the pair that all the regular Joes and Janes hope to grow up to be. William and Kate, Beyoncé and Jay-Z, David Beckham and Posh Spice, Brangelina and their gaggle of children before that went to shit.

In Wessco, Prince Nicholas and Olivia, the Duke and Duchess of Fairstone, are the reigning power couple of perfection. But for a while, it looked like Reid Frazier and Hartley Morrow would usurp them.

Reid was the bad-boy, hot-shot footballer who'd finally found the right girl, and Hartley was the celestially stunning American movie star who gave up her career to follow his. They saturated the internet and celebrity magazines that Fiona gobbles down like sweets. The courtship, the multimillion-dollar wedding, the Instagram polished pictures of the birth of their son—it was all a pretty fairy tale.

Until it wasn't.

Eventually it spiraled into tale-as-old-as-time tabloid fodder—infidelity, drugs, domestic disturbances and a nasty custody war over a smiling three-year-old boy.

And now Hartley Morrow is sitting in my office. Light blond and tragically beautiful in that fragile, ashen way sad women are.

"Hello, Miss Morrow—I'm Tommy Sullivan."

She stands, pushing her big round dark glasses to the top of her head and shaking my outstretched hand.

"Can I get you something to drink?" I ask. "Tea, water . . . whiskey?"

She lets out a jittery laugh. "A whiskey would be good."

At the minibar in the corner I pour myself a glass too, because no one likes drinking alone. Hartley's hand trembles when she takes the glass from me, sipping it as I sit behind my desk.

"What brings you here, miss? What can I do for you?"

She slips a ragged piece of paper from her purse and lays it on the desk like it's poisonous. "After I picked up Sammy from preschool today, I came home and found this. On my bed."

I read the lines scrawled across the paper—it's a fairly typical but nasty death threat. *Bitch, whore,* hurting her child while she's forced to watch, are big themes.

"There have been threats, as I'm sure you can imagine. Awful online messages, voicemails and emails to my lawyer's office . . . but this . . . whoever did this was *inside* my home, Mr. Sullivan. Where my son sleeps."

"Where's your son now?"

"At a hotel, with his nanny. I packed a bag and just left. I didn't know what else to do—we couldn't stay there."

"You did the right thing." I nod.

She breathes slow and takes another drink from the glass. "My friend—Penny Von—we did a film together years ago but we've stayed in touch. She recommended your firm."

Penny Von is the stage name of Penelope Von Titebottum, sister to Lady Sarah—Prince Henry's wife and the future Queen of Wessco.

"Reid's had a terrible season and the fans, his teammates, the whole club blames me for it. Even his teammates' wives . . . women who I thought were my friends . . . the ones who'll still

speak to me, just want the divorce finished so they can get back to focusing on winning games. My lawyer contacted the police about the threats, but they don't really seem interested in investigating who's doing it. They just add it to the file."

"Who do you think is doing it?"

People should trust their instincts more. Nine times out of ten their gut already knows the answer and their brain is just standing in the way.

"I think it was Reid. It's insane that I can say that about the father of my child—about a man I wanted to spend the rest of my life with—but I think it's him. He wants to scare me so I'll give in, sign the divorce papers, stop fighting."

She scrapes out a bitter laugh, shaking her head.

"And the joke is, I don't even want anything—he can have the houses, the cars—I don't even want child support. I just want Sammy. Full custody. Between practices and games, Reid is barely home most of the year. He hasn't seen Sammy in months. It's just about winning for him. He can't stand to lose—ever. And I think he's doing this now because it looks like I might actually win custody and that's just not acceptable to him."

Doing this job long enough turns you into an amateur philosopher on the human condition. Not so much when it comes to women—they're complicated, nuanced creatures. But men are simpler. There's only a few types to us.

Some are like my dad—kindhearted and gentle, but strong in their own way. In the way they provide, and the way they teach. Some are slick, underhanded—they get their jollies from pulling a fast one and getting away with shit they shouldn't. Some men are like me, like Logan—simple tastes and low maintenance. We don't care about much—but try to harm what we do care about? We'll rip your throat out without breaking a sweat or batting an eye.

And then there are men like Reid Frazier—possessive, with an undercurrent of anger and a desperate need to prove how big their cocks are. There's something ugly inside them, and no matter how much they try to keep it in, eventually it spills out over everything.

I really fucking hate men like Frazier.

And they definitely don't like men like me.

I pick up the phone on my desk and punch the button for Celia.

"Have Gordon come in, please. Tell him he's on the clock."

I replace the receiver and look into Miss Morrow's soft blue eyes.

"Gordon is one of my more experienced bodyguards—he's a

good man. He's going to go with you to collect Sammy and the nanny and then he'll get you settled in a new hotel so we can be sure you aren't followed. Then he'll stay there with you until we have a team in place."

Typically, teams of three are assigned to each client based on skills, personality and expectations. For example, old Walter's first go in the field will be with the Dowager Countess—lucky him— because the threat level is low and he's what a lady of her stature expects in a personal guard. If I sicced Harry on her, with his fresh mouth and fetish for pop music, it wouldn't go over well.

"We're not private investigators," I tell her, "so I can't promise to find out who's behind this, but I can refer you to some PIs who can."

Hartley seems surprised.

"Just like that?"

My tone grows gentler, becomes reassuring, because I think she needs that.

"Yeah. Just like that."

She sits up straighter, like she's just recalling something important.

"Mr. Sullivan, Reid has frozen all the accounts. My lawyer has been working pro bono and our nanny's been with Sammy since he was born. She's practically family. I won't be able to pay you until we sign—"

I hold up my hand.

"We'll get that part sorted when things are more settled. Don't worry about it now."

Her eyes go teary and she bites her lip as she whispers, "Thank you. I just . . . I just don't want to be afraid anymore."

In real life, the opportunity to be a hero doesn't usually come along, even if you've got the stuff for it. It's like that David Bowie song—*even just for one day* isn't attainable for most people.

But around here, we're not most people.

"You don't have to be afraid, Hartley. Not anymore. That, I can promise."

After Gordon comes in and he and Hartley head out, Lo walks into my office. "We're packing it in for the day. Was that Hartley Morrow?"

"Yeah, new client—I'll fill you in. We should call James, see if he's ready to come over full-time."

James Winchester was the third guard with me and Logan on Prince Nicholas's personal security team. He's top-notch and still works with the royal family—on Prince Henry & Co. Though he likes the job, he's been looking for something with less travel, that will let him stay home more consistently with his little boy, who he's raising on his own.

"I think this one is just what James has been looking for."

———— ✥ ————

Later that night, after the shop is locked up and our new brood of hires has been sent on their merry way, and the Morrow situation is being dealt with, I get comfy in my bed. I settle in, lay back shirtless between the cool sheets, with the Haddock file perched on my lap, as I prepare to discover all of Abby's filthy little secrets.

There's a formal picture of her—white coat, delicate chin raised, brow relaxed, her smart mouth settled in a slight, refined smile. It was taken just after she finished medical school and began her residency, around the time of our first unforgettable meeting.

I looked for her, in the days after our kiss and slap. I asked around, tried to see her again, to get her number before they discharged me from the hospital. When she remained elusive, I figured maybe she was involved with someone. Unavailable. For a moment, I considered maybe she wasn't even real—that she had been a seductive angel in my imagination, sent by God to bring me back from the pull of death. And then, after I'd fully recovered from my knock on the head, I got swept up in the rush of building the business, of starting something new that belonged to me and Lo alone, and the rough thrill of one dangerous job after the next.

I was a bloody fool not to have gone back for her, to have tried harder, looked more.

In my experience, second chances don't come around often and I have no intention of wasting this one.

I can't help but smile as I picture her in that swimming pool the other day—railing at an unruly frog, her wild mass of red hair glinting gold in the sun, and her wet, snug bathing suit highlighting those lissome limbs, the fine curve of her hips, and scintillating swell of her perfect breasts.

I get to guard that beautiful body for the next two weeks, up close and personal.

Fuck—I love my job.

CHAPTER FOUR

Abby

"WHO IS THIS PERSON?"

The surgical residency program at Highgrove Hospital encompasses rotations between several departments—general surgery, orthopedics, thoracic, plastics, pediatrics and oncology, to name a few. Each rotation lasts three to seven weeks, under the supervision of the department's attending physician.

"Who is this person and why is he on my rounds?"

Rounds commence at 6:00 a.m. and 6:00 p.m. sharp. They are teaching sessions—the observation and discussion of current patients between the attending surgeon and residents, interns and medical students. Rounds can make or break a career. It's the chance to show off, suck up—to demonstrate your knowledge and skill. Perform well and you'll be rewarded with scrubbing in for the most sought-after procedures—a hemispherectomy, a rotationplasty, or the unicorn, pot of gold at the end of the rainbow—an osteo-odonto-keratoprosthesis.

It's every bit as weird as it sounds and in surgery, weird is definitely what you want.

Perform poorly on rounds and you'll be banished to the tedious tundra of updating illegible charts and reinserting blown IVs.

I'm typically outstanding on rounds. I'm quick on my feet, confident in my knowledge, well-practiced in the ability to retrieve tiny tidbits of information we spent all of two minutes learning in medical school. I'm also a killer Trivial Pursuit player.

But this is not a typical situation.

"Anyone? Anyone!"

Dr. Dickmaster is the supervising attending on staff today and at the moment, he is not a happy man. He's never been a jolly fellow—not the sort who'd wear a silly clown nose or pull a coin out from behind a child's ear. But today, he's especially ticked.

Because today is the first day that Tommy Sullivan is guarding me.

Damn it all to hell.

When I met him outside the hospital early this morning, just before the start of my shift, he watched me approach with a cocky sort of air about him. Arrogance is a common trait among the aristocracy—I grew up surrounded by it, submerged in it—it's easy to sense. Tommy Sullivan's arrogance was the victorious variety, like a cat who already knows he's got the mouse right where he wants her.

I suspect he anticipated I was going to complain to the Dowager Countess about hiring him, and the fact that he was still on the job was a win in his column. There was a moment, when I *had* considered voicing my misgivings to Grandmother—but it was only for a moment.

Because Haddocks don't do drama. We don't complain or whine—and we never, ever nitpick. We persevere. Push on. It's one of the secrets to our success.

I ignored the weak-kneed, wobbly feeling that oozed up my limbs when Tommy Sullivan aimed that devilish smile at me and smoothly said, "Good morning, Abby."

And then I set out on ignoring *him*.

It shouldn't have been difficult—I've had personal security before, and disregarding them was as effortless as blinking. They blended into the background, like wallpaper in a room you've walked through a thousand times—you know it's there, but you don't actually see it anymore.

But Tommy Sullivan isn't the kind of man who can be ignored.

He was built to stand out, to be noticed, and I don't just mean his looks. He has a presence—the way he stands, the way he walks—with the confident swagger of a man who's capable of handling things. Handling *everything*.

Even now, as he leans innocuously against the corridor wall a few feet away—arms crossed, a dark suit molded to his impressive frame like he just stepped out of an Armani advertisement—the nurses can't take their eyes off him. Their heads turn and their gazes drag his way again and again.

He's a terrible, awful distraction. And I'm not the only one who thinks so.

"I have asked a question!"

Dr. Dickmaster's flabby cheeks and pointy nose begin to change color—going from its typical pale to dark pink and fast approaching crimson—like a chameleon on a hot brick. Because nothing, *nothing*, infuriates a doctor more than asking a question their underlings can't answer.

"Is someone going to answer me, or are you all just going to stand there looking like double-damned idiots?"

Professionalism is a valued trait in any field—mandatory in most. But no one cares if a king is unprofessional, or if they do, they rarely have the guts to point it out.

In the field of pediatric cardiac surgery, Dr. Wilhelm Dickmaster is not a king.

He's a bloody god.

And he knows it.

Pissing off a god is never a good idea.

I step through to the front of the group.

"He's with me."

But that doesn't sound right.

"I mean . . . I'm with him. But only for a few days."

And that sounds even worse.

I'm usually very good under pressure, but at the moment it's as though I'm having an anaphylactic reaction to the attention. My throat tightens and my tongue goes thick and sandpaper-dry.

Chad Templeton, our weasely chief resident, smirks over at me. The chief resident is the head tattletale—who reports to the attending about who's late or leaves early, who's slacking off on labs or charts. And I don't hold the weaseliness against him per se—sometimes weaseliness is necessary if you want to succeed.

Chad's just a real wanker about it.

"I . . . you see, Dr. Dickmaster, it's—well . . ."

Dear God, I'm fidgeting. Surgeons do *not* fidget. I'm sure that's written in stone on a wall somewhere.

But then suddenly, the air shifts and a sense of calm settles over me. Because he's there, standing behind my shoulder. I don't turn around to see him, I don't have to . . . I can feel him. The heat and bulk and presence of him.

"Tommy Sullivan, S&S Securities. I'll be shadowing Dr. Haddock for the next few weeks."

Dickmaster's gaze slices from me to him. "Why?"

"Not at liberty to say," Mr. Sullivan replies. "But it's nothing you need to concern yourself with. The hospital administration has given us all necessary clearances and permissions. They really ought to have informed you, Dr. Dick."

Oh noooo . . .

From somewhere in the back, a medical student with a death

wish snickers. But the rest of us don't move an inch—because that's what you do when you step on a land mine.

Nothing.

You wait—and hope to God it doesn't blow you to bits.

"Dickmaster," the doctor grits out, clenching his teeth furiously enough to crack them.

There's a story the nurses tell in hushed tones on slow nights in the hospital halls. The tale of the fourth-year resident who was complaining in the break room about Dickmaster's demands—and used the unfortunate nickname within earshot of the god himself. He wasn't fired or even reprimanded—that would've been too merciful. Instead, his life became a nightmare of overnight shifts, double shifts, bedpan duty, emergency department stitches, blown IVs galore and charts as far as the eye could see. He ended up quitting—forced out—taking a research position in a basement office at some subpar university whose name no one can remember.

But, they say sometimes when you're scrubbing in, if you listen very carefully, you can hear the mournful cry of the fourth-year resident's soul begging to be let in to a surgery.

I glance at Tommy Sullivan in time to see him lifting a careless eyebrow and cupping a hand around his ear.

"Pardon?"

"My name is Doctor Dickmaster."

"Ah, sorry about that." His face is unreadable, even innocent, but his eyes practically dance a jig—because he's not really sorry at all. "I'm hard of hearing on this side—old war injury."

Dickmaster exhales through his nose, like a bull who's been denied a spearing.

"Stay out of the way."

Mr. Sullivan salutes. "It'll be like I'm not even here."

I wish.

He's only been here an hour and he's already getting me into trouble.

"And as for you, Haddock . . ." Dr. Dickmaster glares down at me in warning. Because in some ways, medicine is the great class equalizer. It doesn't matter who your family is, your name, your title if you have one—it doesn't matter who you know.

It's *what* you know, what you can *do*, that counts. It's all that counts.

"Keep up."

———— ⚜ ————

"I think you're pretty."

It would be accurate to say the best surgeons in the world are arseholes.

Cold, clinical, egotistical bordering on narcissistic, emotionally impotent—practiced compartmentalizers. They have iron control over their thoughts, their focus, and are able to detach from any messy feelings that may seep in and trip them up. Like machines.

Arsehole machines.

All calculations and predictive outcomes and flawless performances.

Dickmaster is seen as a god around here, but the secret is . . . when he looks in the mirror, that's what he sees too. Utterly confident in his power over life and death, completely secure in his own infinite knowledge.

It takes a high level of arrogance and indifference to cut a human being apart and be certain you can put them together again. To slice skin, sever arteries and incise muscle—to crack bone. For some it comes naturally.

For me . . . I'm still working on it.

I straighten up, removing my stethoscope from the chest of the round-eyed, tiny, dark-haired five-year-old in the hospital bed. Her smile is precious and irresistible.

"I think you're pretty too," I whisper tenderly. "And very brave."

This is Maisy Adams's third surgery. I'm not required to know her name—it's her diagnosis that matters. Tricuspid atresia, a congenital defect in the atriums of the heart. Forty years ago she wouldn't have seen her first birthday . . . hell, twenty years ago she wouldn't have made it either.

But now she will. She'll have the chance to grow and dream and live. Because of grouchy men like Dr. Dickmaster. Because medicine is an ever-evolving miracle. It sets right and saves what it couldn't salvage before.

"That other doctor told Mummy that after this operation and then one more I'll be all done," she says.

Children like Maisy amaze me. So much resiliency and courage in such a small package. Enduring pain and procedures that would break most adults—and still retaining that innocent cheeriness the whole time.

"That's right. One more operation after this one and you'll be done."

"And my heart will be all better," she declares.

"Yes."

I run my hand down her soft hair, petting her, in the way I remember my mother did once when I'd won first place in the spelling bee at school.

"Do you promise?" she asks, her expression solemn.

I make an X with my fingertip over the left side of my chest.

"Cross my heart."

And the smile Maisy shines on me warms me from the top of my head to the very bottom of my toes.

But it shouldn't.

Her postoperative stats are what should warm me. The techniques used in her surgery should be what excites me.

This is why I'll never specialize in pediatrics. Because when you have a soft spot for patients, it makes everything else a little bit harder—treating them, operating on them . . . losing them.

Nothing shakes the confidence more than really wanting to fix someone—and failing. And a surgeon who doesn't have confidence . . . won't be a surgeon for long.

I turn away from little Maisy. I lift my chin and straighten my white coat and smooth my features into an expression of professional aloofness. It's as much a part of our uniform as our scrubs. And then I glance around to see if any of my colleagues have noticed my sweet exchange with the adorable patient.

They haven't.

But someone has.

Tommy Sullivan is supposed to have his eyes on the corridor, watching for breaches in security—but he's not.

He's watching me.

Intensely. Deeply.

His dark gaze is penetrating—and so very, very interested. I've seen that look on his face before. Right before he kissed me.

It's not something I let myself think of often, but my lips tingle now with the memory. The dominant slide of his mouth, the tantalizing stroke of his tongue, the sure, confident pull of his strong hands that told me he knew exactly what he was doing and wanted to do more.

I'm a grown woman. I've been kissed—I wouldn't say plenty of times, but I've had my share. A few were even nice kisses—wonderful kisses.

But none of them were like that one.

None of them came with a tidal wave of sensation. The kind of feeling that knocks you sideways and sends you spinning. And for that one perfect, carnal moment you forget who you are, where you are—or you simply don't care—because all that matters is him and you and the feel of him, the scent of him . . . and the craving, glorious desire that's fusing you together.

Once upon a time, Tommy Sullivan's kiss made me lose control.

And that makes him dangerous.

Discipline, control—they are the foundations of success. Without them, everything falls apart.

"Haddock!" Dr. Dickmaster shouts from halfway down the hall, where the group has moved on—his voice dousing my scorching memories with day-old bathwater. "Would you mind gracing us with your presence or are you going to dawdle there all damn day?"

I take a second to scowl at the security guard—because this is his fault.

Then I tear my gaze away and scurry down the hall to catch up.

"Why can't myyy daddy have a job that gets death threats?"

Henrietta Hindenburg has the whine of Veruca Salt, the heart of Mother Teresa and the constitution of Keith Richards—all wrapped in a Rebel Wilson-esque package. Her father's actual job is an American music producer instrumental in the success of boy bands like New Kids on the Block, Backstreet Boys, Hansen and NSYNC. Having been raised in the ways of boy band mania, the songs still frequently pour from the speakers of her custom baby-pink BMW convertible that her parents gave as a medical school graduation gift.

Henrietta looks out the glass door to the hall where Tommy

Sullivan stands sentry with his back to us. "I swear you are the luckiest duck."

Her mother purposely named her after Henry Pembrook, the now Crown Prince of Wessco, as a conversation starter—just in case they ever met. She'll be specializing in plastic surgery to save her father a boatload of cash on her mother's procedures. Her words, not mine. We met in our intern year and have been good friends ever since.

Even though we're like Felix and Oscar, Bert and Ernie, oil and vinegar that ends up making a very tasty salad dressing.

"I can't believe you get to bone him!"

"I'm not going to bone him, Etta."

I make a note of the time on Mrs. Lu's chart—the carotid endarterectomy patient we're moving from recovery.

Etta's eyes go wide and her head does a little shimmy—like she's having a seizure.

"Dear God, Abby, I will literally never speak to you again if you don't bone him."

"I don't even know him. He's my security guard for two weeks and that's all."

"Some of the best sex I've ever had was with people I didn't know! And two weeks is plenty of time—have you never seen the Kevin Costner *Bodyguard,* or the Richard Madden *Bodyguard,* or *The Protector?* Boning the bodyguard is a feature, not a bug."

She turns to the other third-year in the room, who's making sure the catheter tube won't catch on the wheel of the bed when it's moved.

"Tell her, Kevin! It would be blasphemy to pass up a prime piece like that."

Kevin Atkins is the sort of person who surprises you. He's quiet, calm, dependable—dull. Once you get to know him you learn that he's a former army medic, remarkably intelligent, with

51

the steadiest and most precise cutting hand I've ever seen. His reserved disposition shouldn't be mistaken for lack of interest or ambition—he's like the tortoise in *The Tortoise and the Hare*—consistent and confident he'll win the race but determined not to make a misstep along the way. It's a quality I admire.

Kevin isn't close with his family and is protective of the few friends he has. His dark brown eyes cut to the door then back again, and he shrugs. "He's not that good-looking. Sort of average if you ask me."

Etta waves her hand. "Don't listen to him. He's *American*—they drink lite beer and they can't even spell it right. No taste."

Eighty-nine-year-old Mrs. Lu lifts her head from the bed, aims her gaze at the hall and takes her time raking it over the backside of Tommy Sullivan. Then she nods.

"I vote for boning him. You only live once."

"Right on, Mrs. Lu," Etta cheers, lifting her palm. "Give me some. Hoo-rah!"

After Mrs. Lu gives a slow-motion high-five, Etta backs up towards the door, grabbing the knob with one hand and pointing at me with the other.

"And you—listen to the old lady, respect your elders. YOLO, bitch."

I roll my eyes. With friends like these . . . life would be so much easier if I just adopted a cat.

As we guide Mrs. Lu's bed out the door, Etta gives Tommy Sullivan a sly smile and says in a simpering tone, "Hiiii, Tommy."

He dips his chin and waves back.

Kevin seems to send a suspicious, unfriendly look the security guard's way, but his expression is so bland it's hard to be sure.

Mrs. Lu turns her head towards him as she passes—then she lifts her arm, giving me a mighty thumbs-up.

Once the lift's silver doors close with Henrietta, Kevin and Mrs. Lu inside, I take the stairwell, with my dark-suited shadow right on my heels. Though the chant of *don't ask, don't ask, don't ask, wallpaper, wallpaper, wallpaper* reverberates in my head, my mouth has a mind of its own.

"Do you really have reduced hearing capacity on that side?"

I know an excellent audiologist who could help him.

If he had any idea what I was talking about, which by his blank expression I realize immediately, he doesn't.

Feeling moronic, I gesture to his ear as we move up the steps.

"Your old war injury?"

"Aye, right."

"What war was that again?"

"The Great Sullivan Pudding Conflict," he says with a perfectly straight face. "I remember it like it was yesterday. There was only one trifle left on the table—me and my sister Janey went for it at the same time, so we ended up tussling for it. I had the upper hand, until she landed a vicious kick to the side of my head. The ear hasn't been the same since—a fact I've used to guilt her out of her pudding ever since."

"That's awful. Is your sister frequently given to fits of violence?" I ask as we reach the landing outside the door to the sixth floor.

He laughs. "Yeah—but not really. I mean, it's all in good fun, you know?"

I don't, actually. I can't imagine my siblings and me "tussling" at all, let alone with each other.

Mr. Sullivan breathes in slowly and his eyes drift over my face in a savoring sort of way. And I suddenly realize how quiet the stairwell is, how alone we are, how close we're standing to each other. Close enough that I can count each strand of rough stubble on his chin.

"There you go with that sweet frown again, Apple Blossom. You keep looking at me like that, I'm going to have to break my vow and kiss you again."

I ignore his compliment on my frown, and the silly nickname, and the sweeping, swirly feeling in my stomach at the mention of kissing.

"You've taken a vow?"

"That's right. I don't mess around with clients." He makes the sign of the cross. "So for as long as you are one I will be a complete professional. It's probably for the best that we're discussing it, so you don't mistake me not trying to get in your pants as me not wanting to get in your pants." His eyes slide downward, and his voice dips to a whisper. "I *definitely* want in."

My mind goes blank and I have no idea what to say. Because I'm not used to being pursued so directly, honestly—naughtily. And while the logical part of my brain knows it's a very bad idea, there's a less used, curious side that thinks being pursued by Tommy Sullivan feels very, very nice.

The shrill clang of a door closing below us echoes through the stairwell. He takes a step back, clearing his throat. "I also meant to ask, you and that bloke from downstairs—is anything going on between you?"

"Do you mean Kevin?" I ask. "No, he's a friend."

"You get he wants to fuck you, right?"

I gape at him.

"This is your idea of being professional?"

He lifts one shoulder, shrugging.

"You're mistaken. Kevin's just a good friend—it's not like that."

"Is he married?"

"No."

"Into guys?"

"No."

"Then it's exactly like that." He shakes his head, grinning. "Sweet Abby—you're so smart in so many ways, but so clueless in others."

He doesn't say it in an insulting way, more . . . like I'm a riddle to be figured out.

"But it's all right. I'm here now—I've got you covered, lass."

His smile is easy and shameless. And not for the first time, it makes me almost want to smile with him.

Almost.

CHAPTER
FIVE

Tommy

ON ONE HAND, THE REPORT STELLA AND AMOS compiled on Abigail Haddock was disappointing. It contained no filthy little secrets, no tales of wild naked exploits—or even better, photos—no clandestine memberships to BDSM clubs, or seedy nightclubs . . . or even a bloody knitting club. Abby's as good as she appears—an ambitious, focused, studious girl—straitlaced to the point of strangulation.

On the other hand, her lack of illicit adventures just makes her even more tantalizing. Because nothing is more exciting than discovering sexy black lace hidden beneath bland, plain cotton. And Abby may not be the sort of girl who wears lace or leather now . . . but somewhere inside her, there's a woman who wants to.

I wouldn't know that if I hadn't kissed her—but I did. So, lucky bastard that I am—I do. I sensed it in her that day, the rowdiness buried deep, just waiting to swim to the surface. And I saw it again at the hospital today—in how she bucked her superiors in tiny ways and gave small kindness to her patients when she wasn't supposed to.

She's a tightly shut door, who just needs the right key to pop her lock. In more ways than one.

And that key is me.

But slipping into snug locks is for another time.

At this moment, I'm standing in the front room of Abby's third-floor flat after her shift at the hospital. I already know the layout of the place from the floor plan that was included in Amos and Stella's report. The guard in me automatically scans for anything off or out of place—any sign of attempted entry. Her door is solid with a shiny steel deadbolt that hasn't been tampered with, and the two large windows that face the street are locked up tight and undisturbed.

The human being in me looks around the room and thinks something else entirely.

"It's so . . . beige."

That wasn't in the report.

But the walls, drapes, sofa, throw pillows are beige as far as the eye can see. Even the floor-to-ceiling bookshelves that line one wall and are filled with neat rows of thick textbooks are a painted taupe.

Abby turns towards the room, as if she's just noticing it for the first time.

"Neutral tones are calming—clean." She crosses her arms defensively. "I suppose you're going to say that's dull."

"No, not dull."

And then I grin.

"Lifeless. That's the word I'd go with."

Not that I was expecting a décor in a rainbow of fruit flavors, but something besides the color of condensed milk would be nice. And Abby herself is so vibrant—deep red hair, eyes the color of stormy seas, creamy skin, a hot pink flush and lips the shade of a rose in full bloom.

Her pretty frown makes an appearance.

"My flat is not lifeless."

I glance around, confirming another detail Amos and Stella dug up.

"You don't own a television."

Abby shrugs. "Television is junk food for the brain."

"What do you do for fun? When you want to kick back and relax?"

"I read."

My sister Bridget reads. Romance novels covered with bare-chested blokes and sultry-eyed, shapely women. I flipped through one once—and if that's the type of literature Abby enjoys, I whole-heartedly approve.

I wonder if she's into role-play? It's not like we'd have to play very far—I already have the profession for it, the accent . . . and the handcuffs. It practically writes itself.

"What do you read?"

"Medical journals. Articles about new procedures and surgical techniques."

And it's a swing and a miss for the dirty role-play hopes.

I scratch my forehead. "Your idea of a good time is reading about cutting people open?"

She thinks it over, toddling her head to and fro.

"I guess you could put it like that, yes."

I take one large, deliberate step back from her, raising my hands in mock submission.

"All right then, Jackie the Ripper—I'm going to do a sweep of the rest of your place. You can wait here . . . and don't make any sudden moves."

That gets me a quick snort of a laugh and an effervescent smile.

And I feel like the king of the world.

————— ✛ —————

After I sweep her flat, Abby goes into the bedroom and emerges a few minutes later wearing velvet gray lounge trousers and a snug navy tank top that I imagine peeling off her with my teeth.

Over her arm she carries a massive poof of fuzzy white fleece that at first look seems to be a blanket. But when she slips her arms through it, I see it's actually a robe. An immense, gigantic robe three times her size, tied tight in the front, that makes her look like a stuffed, redheaded teddy bear.

I wonder if she's wearing it for my benefit or if she just likes walking around in a cocoon.

Abby sets herself a rather formal place setting at the dining table—fabric napkin, sterling silver forks and knives—all carefully placed in the proper order. In the kitchen, she heats a premade plate of bland fish and vegetables, with a dry salad on the side. And to wash it all down, after a long, hard day . . . water.

With no ice.

Christ, this girl needs to loosen up. It's fucking heartbreaking.

She's in the prime of her life—beautiful, obviously brilliant—and she spends her nights alone, eating food like a granny who needs to mind her dentures, without even background noise for company.

I was raised a strict Catholic, but more than that, I believe in God—those two are not always mutually exclusive. I believe God has a plan for all of us, a purpose. And now, more than ever, standing in this dreary flat, watching this stunning girl eat her sad, lonely little meal—I believe God wants me to screw some joy into Abby Haddock's life.

Lucky for me, the Almighty's desires coincide with my own.

And I'm more than up to the task.

A gentle quiet settles over the room as Abby eats her dinner, save for the occasional hushed scrape of her flatware. Some clients struggle with personal security—it makes them uncomfortable having someone present who's all up in their business all the time. But I don't sense any awkwardness now. Because Abby was raised amongst servants—and because I think she's accustomed to the quiet. To being alone.

"Are you hungry, Mr. Sullivan?" she asks shyly—like she was debating if she should pose the question. "My personal chef, Miles, prepares my meals several times a week. There's plenty to eat if you'd like some."

She's being polite. Because she's stuffy in every sense of the word . . . but not rude. There's a natural friendliness to her that, for some reason I haven't figured out yet, she tries so very hard to suppress.

"It's nice of you to ask. But I'm good."

I'd like to share a pint with her—or a bottle of anything—wine, whiskey, champagne. I bet piss-drunk Abby would be hilariously adorable. I'd love to see her take a swig straight from the bottle—loose and laughing and lovely. And I make a promise to myself that I'll make that happen . . . but it won't be tonight.

I hear Bea's approaching footsteps out in the hall before she knocks on the door. Abby follows behind me as I move to answer it, and Bea walks in wearing the standard uniform—dark trousers, dark blue blouse and her own personal touch—black combat boots.

I make the introductions and Abby holds out her hand. "It's a pleasure to make your acquaintance, Bea."

"Why is she a pleasure?" I complain. "I'm so much more of a pleasure than she is." I give her a wink. "I'll have to work harder at making our time together more pleasurable for you—I have a few ideas."

Abby shakes her head. "And there you go being professional again."

Bea jerks her thumb in my direction, telling Abby, "Professional bodyguard *and* a professional charmer, this one—don't take anything he says seriously."

Abby's glittering green eyes meet mine—almost playfully, and her lips tease the hint of a smile.

"That makes so much sense."

Then Bea amends her statement.

"Unless he tells you to get down or run or don't move—that sort of thing. Then you should definitely listen to him."

I don't take my eyes from Abby's because . . . well . . . she's just damn nice to look at. And it's even nicer when she's looking back at me.

"Much appreciated, Bea."

"Always trying to help, Tommy."

Abby squares her shoulders and straightens her robe, even though it didn't need straightening. "Well, good night then, Mr. Sullivan."

I dip my chin and soften my voice. "Sweet dreams, Abby."

———— ⚹ ————

"You've got to be joking."

Abby Haddock rides a bicycle.

"Not in the least."

A ridiculous bicycle—bright yellow with a light and a wicker basket in front and a silver bell attached to one handlebar—that she wants to ride to the hospital.

"It doesn't seem very sensible."

I discover this the next morning when I relieve Bea of duty outside Abby's building.

"It's perfectly sensible. We each need to do our part to help the environment—too many cars will be the death of us all. Also, surgical residency involves insanely long hours; I have to squeeze in rigorous physical activity where I can."

She completely set herself up for that one—I just can't resist.

"I know some rigorous physical activities that are a hell of a lot more fun than riding a bike."

When that doesn't get a reaction, I lean forward, whispering. "I'm talking about fucking. The really good, sweaty kind."

It's all good—long, hard, sweet or sweaty—any which way will do.

Flirting is fun. Teasing is foreplay. And playing with Abby like this—making her laugh and blush and frown—is all part of warming her up and breaking her down. How I'll enchant her and charm her and show her what an irresistible man I am.

So when the night comes that she's not a client and I'm no longer on the clock—we're locked and loaded and rearing to go.

The corners of Abby's mouth quirk and I even get an eye roll. *Nice.*

"I'm aware of that, yes, thank you."

I lean back. "Just making sure."

"But we really must leave now if we're going to be punctual," Abby insists.

I tilt my head up to the still-dark sky, squinting into the misty drizzle and coming back with a face full of wet.

"It's raining."

Without a word, but still defiantly, Abby reaches back and pulls the hood of her perfectly practical brown poncho over her head. Then she tugs on the ties, knotting it tightly under her chin.

And a chuckle rolls up my throat.

Because she looks damn adorable—in her scrubs and rubber rain boots, with the snug hood highlighting her lovely face and lush lips, and the feisty challenge in her eyes.

I want to kiss the daylights out of her.

Right here on the wet pavement. I want to kiss her mouth while she moans into mine, and bite her neck, and whisper hot, dirty nothings in her ear until she's soft and pliant and clinging to me.

But no matter how stupendous of an idea that is and no

matter how much I want to . . . now's not the time. Sometimes vows are a real pain in the arse—and the balls.

"You realize, it'd be more sensible to ride your bicycle when your family isn't potentially under a threat of harm?"

"But that's what I have you for. Unless you don't feel you're up to the task? I thought you'd jog along beside me the whole way, but maybe you don't have the stamina?"

I lift an eyebrow.

"Attacking my manhood? Cheeky."

She shrugs one shoulder.

"Whatever works."

I nod. "I respect that."

I mentally go through the route from here to the hospital.

"All right. But we stay away from the populated areas along the way. Follow me."

Abby holds up her hand, shaking her head.

"Out of the question. I ride the exact same route each time."

"Why?"

She gazes up into my face. "I know every pothole on the way, every bump in the road. There are no mishaps, because I know to avoid them. I know exactly what time we'll arrive at the hospital. Riding the same route helps to begin my day on the right foot."

"So it's like a superstitious thing?" I wonder.

"It's a repetition thing. Consistency. Routine breeds excellence."

I sigh, rubbing the back of my neck.

"All right, we'll take your route." I jab a finger in her direction. "But . . . if we do get ambushed, *after* I heroically save your life . . . I'm definitely telling you I told you so."

Abby swings one leg over her bike, looking extremely pleased with herself.

"Noted."

CHAPTER SIX

Abby

"Y ou really weren't joking when you said you didn't have time for dinner ... or screwing, were you?"

For the last week that Tommy Sullivan has been guarding me, he's had a front-row seat to the demanding, one-day-runs-straight-into-the-next existence of a surgical resident.

Ding

His mobile pings with an incoming message.

"No, I wasn't."

I've felt his eyes on me, following me, as I attended rounds, treated patients, spoke with supervisors, viewed surgeries in the observation suite and scrubbed in. He watched me run a jugular venous catheter in the emergency room, and later as I assisted in the delicate removal of a pipe impaled through a man's chest that somehow missed any internal organs or arteries—a fascinating case.

His mobile pings again.

And he's watching me now. His eyes heated with interest, at my flat, as I'm hunched over my dining table, beneath a bright spot lamp, snipping and suturing.

"What the hell are you doing again?" he asks.

I look up, momentarily distracted by the rich warmth of his voice.

"Practicing."

His expression turns distasteful.

"On chicken's feet?"

"Yes. The tendons in chicken's feet are challenging to get to, but once you do, their consistency is very similar to humans."

He snorts. "If my mum were here, she'd make soup out of that. What else do you practice on?"

"Oh, let's see—grapes, oranges, drumsticks, hogs—cadavers are best, but they don't let us take them home."

He grins. "But I bet you would if you could."

I glance towards my kitchen, perfectly serious. "If I had freezer space for it, absolutely."

He laughs then—full throated and amused.

"You are an odd bird, Abigail Haddock."

"So I've been told."

Ding goes his mobile once more.

"It doesn't seem like you were joking either—when you said you were quite busy. I imagine running your own business and still working in the field yourself is time consuming."

"It is." He nods, glancing with a furrowed brow at his mobile screen.

Ding

"Is everything all right?" I ask.

"Yeah—sorry—it's the Realtor for a flat I've been interested in. She says if I want to take a look at it, it's now or never." He slips his mobile in his trouser pocket. "But it'll have to be never."

Bea isn't scheduled for her shift for another few hours.

I take a deep breath and rub the back of my aching neck. And for reasons I couldn't articulate if I had to, I offer, "We could go look at it now, if you like? I mean . . . I could go with you."

He narrows his eyes. "It's not your concern—and you're practicing—I wouldn't want to get between you and your chicken's feet."

"No, it's fine—truly." I switch off the lamp. "I can do with some fresh air—and a break."

The smile he gives me is warm and grateful. "All right, then. Let's go."

And though it's just a small thing—the change in my routine, the newness of going to a different place, with this man beside me—it feels like an adventure.

—————⚓—————

Tommy Sullivan's prospective flat is located on the other side of town, near the river, a few miles from my building. I wouldn't consider it a "bad" part of town, but it's noticeably older, slightly more run-down than my area. We take his car and though there's no odor, I scowl fiercely at the pack of cigarettes and lighter nestled in the center console.

When we pull up to the building, I want to grab them and toss them in the bin—but I don't think I can manage it without him catching me in the act.

The Realtor is a bristly, brusque woman with dark hair pulled up into an overly tightened bun. She unlocks the door to the fourth-floor flat, ushering us in and rattling off the amenities.

"Just a block from the tube station, oak floors throughout, new kitchen appliances, two bedrooms, two full baths. Plenty of space for a couple . . ." she glances at me ". . . or a growing family."

A moment later, she excuses herself to take a call in the hallway, closing the door behind her.

Leaving just the two of us. Alone.

The front room is bare, lampless, and the newly polished floors give off a pleasant, earthy wood-oil scent. The moonlight coming from the large windows that line the rear wall casts everything in soft shadows and gray hues. The streets below are unusually quiet, and it feels isolated, but not in an uncomfortable way. More . . . intimate.

Secluded. Like Tommy Sullivan and I could be the only two people in the whole world.

Silently, we walk through the rooms, passing the kitchen with an overhead light above the stainless-steel sink. Until we end up in the back room—the master bedroom.

Sarcasm isn't my forte, but I give it a go now, gesturing to the painted walls. "Would you look at that . . . beige. Must be a popular color."

"Your favorite," he concedes.

"It's a very nice place," I say.

"It is." He nods, then leans back against the wall beside the bedroom door, crossing his arms, watching me.

My shoes click on the floor as I drift around, seeing what it could be in my mind.

"You could put a standing mirror in the corner, here. And there's room for a bureau there. And a television here on the wall, if you're into that sort of thing."

He chuckles and the sound strikes the strangest chord in me. I'm not a naturally jovial person and I don't make people laugh—but I seem to amuse him often and without even trying.

"Such a planner you are."

I move to the wall opposite the windows, closer to the corner where he stands.

"The bed would go here, I think."

He hums in agreement. And I'm close enough to see his eyes now—trained on me—golden brown and heated. Like he's imagining it all in the most vivid detail—the bureau, the bed . . .

"It would be a large bed," he says in that soft, decadent tone. "I like room . . . to move."

There's nothing overtly inappropriate about the words, but the way he says them—the tone of his voice, the shape of his mouth— makes the skin of my chest go warm and flushed.

Because now I'm doing it too—imagining how Tommy Sullivan would move in his very large bed. What he would look like with the moonlight caressing the ripples and ridges of his arms, his back—and lower. How it would feel to move with him.

My voice has a breathy, hazy air to it. "That sounds about right."

I swallow, pulling my gaze from his to the window.

"Oh, look! You can see the hospital from here."

I move across the room, bracing my hands on the light wood windowsill, gazing at the tall rectangular building dotted with bright, white-lit windows.

"That's the surgical floor," I say, pointing, "the fifth one down from the top. That corner window there is just outside Operating Room C—the largest operating room. It's used for procedures that require multiple teams like transplants or especially risky procedures. They separated conjoined twins there two years back."

"You really love it, don't you?"

He's next to me now, his arm just a breath away from mine.

"Surgery?" I smile without even thinking. "Oh yes. The human body is a miraculous thing. Infinitely fascinating."

His gaze drags slowly down over me.

"Some bodies are more fascinating than others."

I allow myself to do some looking of my own. Letting my eyes graze along the swell of his biceps prominent beneath his dark gray suit jacket, the broad expanse of his chest, the tapering of his waist and hips that lead down to sturdy, powerful legs—and everything in between.

I know anatomy well—and from what I can tell, Tommy Sullivan's is first-rate.

"That's true," I agree softly.

Movement on the windowsill catches my eye—it's a small gray spider, scurrying frantically across the wood. He sees it too and lifts his hand to swat it.

"Wait, don't kill him."

I scoop the spider up with one hand and open the window with the other. Then I reach out towards the tree branch beside the building, pursing my lips and blowing at him to get him moving.

I feel the warmth of Tommy Sullivan's body beside me, his head dipped toward me, his eyes caressing my face. Once the arachnid has safely creeped out onto the branch, we straighten up and I close the window.

"You don't make any sense," he tells me.

"I make it a point to make perfect sense all the time," I reply.

"You can slice someone's jugular open and jam a tube down their neck—"

"Artery," I correct.

"I've seen you do it. But you can't bring yourself to kill a spider?"

I shrug and explain, "I don't slice into people to harm them. It may hurt for a time—but the pain will be worth it because they'll be better off in the end. And as for the spider—he was just doing what spiders do; it wasn't his fault he ended up in here. I don't like it when things die—not when I can prevent it—especially small, helpless things."

"Did you always want to be a surgeon?" His eyes glint now— teasing again. "Did little Abby dream of scalpels and scrubs, sutures and chicken's feet?"

I laugh, pushing my hair back behind my ear, thinking it over.

"It's funny, but I can't recall now ever wanting to be anything else. But—I don't just want to be *a* surgeon, it's important that I become an extraordinary surgeon. The best in the world."

"Why is that important?"

"My family," I explain. "They're very, very talented. They have high expectations."

He nods in the dim light. And it's so easy talking with him like this. Effortless and right somehow. Natural.

"Their sort usually does."

"And you? Does your family have expectations of you, Mr. Sullivan?"

He rubs his bottom lip in a way that makes my knees go floppy—because it's impossible to forget the hot, hard press of that lip.

"I suppose they did with Bridget and Arthur, but by the time they got down to me it was simpler. Stay out of jail, go to school if you're good at it, get a job if you're not."

"By the time they got down to you? How many of you are there?"

"Eight at last count."

"Eight! My goodness, your parents must really like each other."

He laughs again. "They do. They're good together. Partners, you know? They . . . even each other out. Fill in each other's gaps."

I like that . . . partners. The word rings through me with a familiar yearning reverberation. Lots of little girls dream of growing up to be princesses—especially in this country. Of becoming polished wives and pretty mothers.

And it's not that I don't want a family for myself, I do. But in my dreams, that part—a handsome husband and drooly tots—always comes after.

After my name has been engraved on a diploma and doctor's license, and perhaps a plaque or a hospital wing. After I've done the work, proven I can stand on my own two feet. After I've built something all by myself.

I never before considered doing the building bit with someone, but I do now. A partner. That having someone to lean on and support in return would make the striving for success not just easier and smoother, but better in every way.

And I don't know why I ask him—it doesn't matter—in another week, Tommy Sullivan will be nothing to me but a memory. But I want to know and here in this quiet, shadowed space I can ask.

"Do you love it?"

That wicked grin slides across his mouth. "I love lots of things. Drinking, fucking, joking, dancing . . . conversing with stunning redheads. You'll have to be more specific."

I realize how true those words ring—the things he loves—how well they fit him. Tommy Sullivan is all about fluid, shifting sensation. About satisfaction and spontaneity. Not breaking the rules—but making his own.

I find that as fascinating as medicine. It's almost mysterious—so different than anything I've ever known. So . . . lively.

I mean, Henrietta's always up for a good time, but she's still a doctor—still like me when she needs to be. Ruled by facts and knowledge and structure—dosages and practiced techniques and treatments.

Tommy Sullivan is nothing like that. If he were a doctor, he'd probably shock himself with a defibrillator just to see what it feels like.

"Being a bodyguard—do you enjoy it?"

His grin broadens. "Yeah, sure I do."

"Why?"

"It's a challenge for myself—like a contest. It's keeps me sharp, quick . . ." he wiggles his eyebrows ". . . hard. The work is interesting—sometimes dangerous, always an adrenaline rush—the money's good. But in a way, it's not so different from you. God gave me a very special set of skills—I like using them to keep small, helpless things alive too. To protect them, when they can't protect themselves."

The thud of the door closing and the steps of the Realtor echo off the bare walls and break the solitude of the moment.

He lifts his gaze from mine and scans it around the room.

"I'm gonna take it."

"Just like that? You don't want to take time to consider it? Speak with your accountant, weigh the pros and cons?"

"No. I like the view, I like the feel of the place—my gut says take it."

I tilt my head, still mystified by him.

"Do you always do that? Just . . . go with your gut?"

He shrugs one shoulder. "Hasn't steered me wrong yet."

"What about you?" He lifts his chin in my direction. "Are you always so logical? Always waiting to sort everything out in your head before you make a move?"

I smile wistfully. "Hasn't steered me wrong yet."

--------⚬--------

I remember the day I graduated medical school—the mixture of accomplishment that I'd done it and disappointment that I hadn't placed higher in my class. I remember it as clear as if it were yesterday—even though it was over three years ago.

Time speeds up when you're busy. Focused. Hours go by like minutes, days like hours, months like just a few days. And so I'm shocked when Tommy Sullivan's last day of guarding me arrives so quickly.

As we had anticipated, the threats against my family never materialized. I've gone about my life as I would have if they hadn't happened. Nothing of significance has changed.

And yet . . . it feels like something has.

"Can I ask you a question?"

Tommy Sullivan and I are in my kitchen. Did he follow me here when I came in for a glass of water or when I was washing up from dinner? I can't remember and it doesn't matter.

It's late, dark outside the window, but I'm not sleeping—not even tired. I'm in my bedclothes—a satin, long-sleeved violet top with matching trousers.

"Of course."

"If I try to kiss you at midnight, when I'm off shift and you're officially not a client anymore . . . would you let me?"

My breath whooshes from my lungs. Because I remember his kiss—it was like a roller coaster—the swooping upside-down invigorating sensation that you want to feel again, and again, and again.

"Is this why you gave Bea the night off?"

He moves closer.

"It is."

"This was your plan all along?"

And closer.

"It really was."

My eyes dart to the clock above the stove—11:59. So soon.

"It wouldn't be proper—"

"That's not what I asked."

His face is so near to mine, my eyes slide closed on instinct.

And it's even better—because my other senses come alive—and there's the scent of him, the teasing brush of his nose against mine, the sensation that his stubbled jaw is *right there* and if I move a millimeter, I'll be able to revel in its tantalizing scrape.

"I want to kiss you, Abby. More than I can remember wanting anything, in a long time. I want this. You. And I think, deep down you want it too."

I can almost taste him. It. The kiss. I know how good it will be. Perfect.

And a very bad decision. The kind that opens up all the boxes—of Pandora and all those other Greek gods, whose names I can't remember right now.

By most measures, parachuting out of a plane is also a very

bad decision. But people do it all the time. Because they love the fall. The flight. The feeling of soaring air and whipping winds.

I've never been the jumping sort.

But with him—a reaching, yearning, desperate part of me wants to give it try.

"Open your eyes, Abby."

When I do, I'm met with warm honey-brown eyes—like they're lit from within.

"Three . . . two . . . one . . ."

I'm going to say yes.

The word is there on my lips, the tingling, thrilling taste of it on the very tip of my tongue. Because I want this—the brush of his lips, the feel of his hot skin and firm muscle beneath my palm. The feel of him everywhere.

It's been so long since I wanted anything just for me.

But before I can say the words, his head turns away, snaps around in the direction of the front room. His shoulders are tense and the tendons of his neck are pulled taut.

"Are you expecting someone?" he asks very quietly.

Instinctively, the volume of my voice matches his.

"No."

That's when I hear it. The jostle of the front doorknob. The sharp whine of the hinge as it opens. And then . . . footsteps, slow but distinct.

Someone is here. Someone is inside my flat.

Oh my.

Oh my, oh my, oh my, oh my . . .

Without a sound, Tommy Sullivan pulls a gun from the inside of his suit jacket—and my panicked thoughts come to a record-scratching halt.

It's the first time I've ever seen a handgun up close. It's black and weighted and looks right at home in his grip.

"You didn't tell me you were armed!" I whisper-yell.

"Shh."

"Do you have a permit for that? Do you know the statistics on—"

His large hand covers my entire mouth.

"Shush." He looks down at me with an expression I've never seen on his face before—hard, harsh and deadly serious. The kind of look that says he could kill a man with his bare hands, and walk away whistling a merry tune afterwards.

Goosebumps prickle on my skin . . . but they're not the bad kind. Because maybe it's wrong, but deadly Tommy Sullivan is sexy as all get-out.

"Stay."

And without a sound, he slips out the kitchen door.

But I don't stay. Because I'm not a dog.

But mostly because . . . what if something happens? What if there's more than one of them? What if they manage to get the upper hand?

What if he needs me?

I pull the drawer open, careful not to make any noise, and grab the thick, hefty wooden rolling pin that I've never actually used to roll anything. It's just one of those things you get when you move into your own place.

I give it one practice swing, then tiptoe out the kitchen door.

There are sounds of a tussle from down the hall, grunting and struggling. There's a scrape of wood, a thud that vibrates the wall and the crash of my corner lamp when it smashes to the floor, and the light that had been spilling out from the living room goes out.

I flick on the hall light, to give the room some illumination, and then I lift the rolling pin over my head—and charge to the rescue.

But when I get there, it's apparent the only person who needs rescuing . . . is my brother. Who's pinned to the floor on his stomach, with his arm wrenched behind his back and Mr. Sullivan's boot pressed to the back of his neck.

"Luke?"

He angles his pain-filled, floor-squished face my way, as much as he can.

"Hello, Abby. Sorry to drop in without ringing first. Thought I'd surprise you." He chokes out a laugh and lifts his eyebrows. "Surprise."

Mr. Sullivan replaces the bulb in the lamp and cleans up the glass while I make Luke a cup of tea and get him settled on the sofa, hovering about him the way I always do when he comes home.

His color is good, his cheeks ruddy. His thick blond hair longer than the last time I saw him. And he's put on a bit of weight—always a good sign, especially with the active, adventurer lifestyle he's adopted for himself.

I introduce him to Tommy Sullivan and in spite of their unfortunate first interaction, there don't seem to be any hard feelings.

"Sorry about putting you down like that," Mr. Sullivan says.

"Not a problem." My brother nods. "Completely understandable."

I fluff the pillows behind his back, making him spill his tea.

"Abby—you're fussing."

"Sorry." I force-fold my hands in my lap. "It's just so good to see you. Are you staying home for long?"

"A few weeks."

"And you're going to schedule your physicals? I can help with that if you'd like."

He grins, indulging me as he always does. "No need for help,

Dr. Sister. And yes, I'll be a good little patient and see to all my checkups."

I exhale a sigh of relief. Because even though he's a grown man and four years older than me, I worry about him. It's a constant thrum in the back of my mind—like tinnitus—that I've learned to live with. I worry that something will happen to him and we won't even know, or if we do, he'll be too far away for us to help him—for me to get to him in time. But seeing him here in the flesh, solid and strong and healthy, is a sweet salve for my anxiety.

"And you've been well?" I ask. "Any recent infections? Shortness of breath or fatigue? Have you been tolerating your medications?"

Luke pats my head and doesn't answer any of my questions.

"Do you have sisters, Mr. Sullivan?" he asks.

"A few—yeah," Tommy says, snorting.

"Any of them physicians?"

"No, but two are mothers, so ... I can sympathize."

A look passes between them, like they're sharing a joke.

"Sympathize with what?" I ask.

My brother chuckles, shaking his head. "Nothing, Abby. Never mind."

Before I can push the issue, Tommy Sullivan smacks his hands together, rubbing his palms. "Well, everything looks good here, and I'm officially off the clock—so I'll leave you to your reunion and head out."

The first thought that pops into my head is *already?* Because while it's been two full weeks, it seems so soon for him to be leaving.

So ... unfinished.

I look up at him from the couch, meeting his eyes. "I'll walk you out."

---◆---

Tommy Sullivan and I walk side by side down the stairs to the main floor of my building.

"You two seem close," he comments.

"We are. He travels mostly now, only visits a few times a year. But Luke and I have always understood each other in a way that no one else in my family ever did."

Based on the way he's spoken of his sisters, I know he gets just what I mean.

"Is he sick?" he asks. "You were asking him about medications?"

"No, he's not sick—not anymore. He was ill when he was a boy—I was eight when he collapsed in the middle of a chess tournament."

There are moments in life that change us. That change what we want, how we see the world.

When Luke fell out of his chair that day—limp as a ragdoll, his lips and the thin skin beneath his eyes tinted a bruisy blue— that was one of those moments for me. I remember how the chessboard was knocked over and emergency services rushed to him, and how the white king rolled across the marble floor. And I remember the wrenching fear burrowing in my stomach—but worse—the helplessness. Because I had no idea what was happening, what was wrong with him, and no ability to fix it.

I never, ever wanted to feel like that again. I still don't.

"Chess, huh? Aristocrats must play a rougher version than I'm aware of."

I let out a little laugh. "He didn't collapse because the match was too strenuous—he had a heart condition. Completely undetected until then. We almost lost him." I take a deep breath. "But, he was put on the transplant list and there was a match and a brilliant surgeon gave him a chance to grow up—to still be my brother."

Tommy Sullivan nods, meeting my eyes.

"And that's why you want to be a cardiac surgeon."

I nod back.

"And that's why I want to be a cardiac surgeon."

We stand on the stoop for a few quiet moments, and he shakes his head, murmuring, "This isn't how I thought tonight would go." He turns toward me. "But I'm glad you get to visit with your brother."

Then he pushes a hand through his hair, and his words rush out—a little tense, a little desperate. "I can come back, Abby. Tomorrow or the next day or the next after that. You're busy, I'm busy—we can make it simple. It doesn't have to be complicated—but it'll be hot, and so bloody good. You know it will be. I know you know. I see it when your pretty eyes look at me—I feel it every time I touch you."

He touches me now. His hand slides up my arm and my heart pounds in the back of my throat.

And he's right. It is good. Amazing, exciting . . . reckless.

But no matter how good a fling with him would be, how thrilling it would feel . . . I can't be distracted. Not now—not when I've worked so hard to become all my family expects me to be. To become all I expect of myself.

I need to stay focused. To stay on my path.

Tommy Sullivan is a beautiful whirlwind that I can't let myself get caught up in.

My words come out soft—regretful.

"I can't."

He nods slowly, disappointed but not surprised—as if he already knew what I was going to say.

"Another time, perhaps."

And then he leans in, running his nose against my cheek, inhaling . . . before pressing a gentle kiss right beside my mouth.

"Goodbye, lass."

And I watch him walk away. Descending the front steps, out onto the pavement, retreating down the street.

And it's as if there's an invisible rope, hooked around my rib cage, that's tugging me toward him, dragging me after him.

"Mr. Sullivan!"

He stops beneath the streetlamp, hands in his pockets, his handsome features lit with surprise. I rush down the steps, standing a few feet away.

"You . . . you were the best bodyguard I ever had."

His lips slide into a grateful, wicked grin. And then he winks.

"I could've been the best you ever had, full stop."

I laugh—because he's funny. And because with him, laughing is easy.

He curls his shoulders and cups his hands, and there's a flash of flame and then the glow of an orange ember between his fingertips as he lights a cigarette.

"If you change your mind, Abby, look me up. Don't be shy—I'm certainly not."

And then Tommy Sullivan turns around and strolls down the street, fading into the shadows . . . and walking out of my life.

CHAPTER
SEVEN

Abby

AUTUMN ARRIVES EARLY AND COMES QUICKLY. Almost overnight the sweet scent of summer fades away, and I wake up to the crisp bite of cool air and blustery wind that swirls the leaves into funnels in the street. Puffy coats and boots and fuzzy hats come out, and the decorations in the children's ward morph into the browns and yellows of the Autumn Pass holiday and even some occasional Christmas reds and greens.

It's been three weeks since Tommy Sullivan stopped guarding me. It's strange that I think of it that way—that I mentally mark time based on his presence or lack thereof—but I can't make myself stop.

Tommy Sullivan was a distraction when he was here—but, strangely, he's an even bigger distraction to me now that he's not.

Sometimes I find myself picturing him in my mind. The curl of his smile, the rich rumble of his laugh, the shape of his large hands. Sometimes I lie in bed and picture him then too. I wonder if he's settled into his flat—if he's sleeping in that very big bed he mentioned—or perhaps he's in that bed but *not* sleeping at all.

And sometimes, late at night, I indulge in the deliciously dirty thoughts of what it would have been like, the scintillating sensations of what it would've felt like . . . if I'd taken him up on his offer.

"Did you hear me, Abby?"

Right. So, those thoughts don't come *just* at night.

"Yes, Dr. Whitewater. You were saying . . . about my performance review."

Dr. Caledonia Whitewater is the Chief Surgical Administrator at Highgrove. She's the head honcho, the big kahuna—all the bucks stop with her. If Dr. Dickmaster is a living, breathing god in these halls, she's whatever entity is above that. She has the final word on which surgical residents are accepted into their specialty programs, who qualifies for fellowships, or other specialized training opportunities. She's also the one who conducts the biannual performance reviews with every surgeon in the building.

Dr. Whitewater smiles at me from across her desk, glancing at the paperwork in front of her.

"As I was saying—your breadth of knowledge and grasp of procedures is outstanding."

I smile in return—because this was exactly the evaluation I was expecting.

"Your surgical techniques are impeccable."

I mentally pat my own back—because they are. Thank you, chicken's feet.

"Your attendance, diligence, focus and manner are beyond reproach."

There's an American phrase Kevin is fond of: *I love it when a plan comes together.* But when years of discipline and hard work come together . . . that's pretty grand too.

"However, there is one consistent thread of feedback that gives me a slight cause for concern."

My head tilts. Like a dog who's watching its master give a command—but can't decipher what the bloody hell they're going on about.

"Concern? Really?"

"Yes. While your ambition and assiduousness are to be commended, your supervising physicians worry you may be a bit too single-minded."

"Single-minded?" I squint.

"Overly tenacious."

"Overly tenacious?" My voice goes a pitch higher against my will.

"High-strung," Dr. Whitewater declares firmly.

I digest the words, lifting my chin—trying to take the criticism in stride. Even though it feels like I'm dying inside.

"I see."

Dr. Whitewater nods.

"Good."

And then I opt for honesty. "No—that isn't true—I don't see. Isn't single-minded tenacity a beneficial quality in a surgeon?"

Her expression softens.

"Abigail, you are very young and I'm aware you have a very illustrious name to live up to. I have every reason to believe that you have a long, bright career ahead of you. But the surgery suite is an extremely high-stress environment. Without a consistent way to relieve that stress, you could falter under the pressure. Break—burn out—we've all seen it happen before. In my experience the most successful surgeons find outside activities to relieve stress and incorporate them into their daily lives. Some take up yoga, or hiking, or photography—Dr. Dickmaster writes poetry."

I choke on my own saliva. Because—*dear God.*

"Don't look at this as a censure. But as someone who has been in this field a long time, I know finding a physical outlet to channel tension will make you a better surgeon."

I stand up on stiff legs, the wheels in my mind already turning.

"Thank you for your advisement, Dr. Whitewater. I'll certainly take it under consideration."

"A physical outlet to channel my tension . . ."

I crunch down on a baby carrot as I relay my conversation with Dr. Whitewater.

Crunch, crunch, crunch.

". . . What do you think she meant by that?"

"She means you need to get laid," Henrietta says not so helpfully.

We're in the hospital cafeteria, on an unusually coordinated lunch break, because the surgical department is uncommonly slow. Henrietta sits across from me, between Kevin and my brother Luke, who's come down from the Bumblebridge estate where he's been staying to join us.

I roll my eyes. "I'm certain that's not what she meant."

"I'm certain it is," Etta replies, resting her head on my brother's biceps, curled against his side, sliding her hand up and down his arm like she's petting a mink stole.

Henrietta idolizes my brother.

Though "idolizes" is probably too platonic a word. She worships him. The only person she worships more is that NSYNC chap who had that freakishly curly hair when he was in his prime.

Luke doesn't return the worship, but he adores her enough to let her accost him as much as she likes whenever he's in town.

"I love you, Abby, but you're as uptight as all get-out. Especially recently—you've been all clenchy and sour-faced. It makes me tense just looking at you."

Luke nods. "I have to agree with Henrietta. About your sour-puss . . . and that Dr. Whitewater was saying she thinks you need to get your rocks off."

I frown at him. "Traveling has made you vulgar."

"It's made me honest," he says, chuckling.

Like a hive mind, Henrietta elaborates.

"Dr. Whitewater wants you to have some regularly scheduled freaky-freaky between the sheets. You need to get boffed, a little rumpy-pumpy, ride the stone pony, spend a little time impaled on a hot rod of steel." She wiggles her eyebrows. "Vroom, vroom."

"You're both impossible." I scoff. "And, for the record, I engage in self-administered rumpy-pumpy every Tuesday and Saturday. That's all the stress relief I need."

I can't believe I actually just told them that. I can't believe we're even discussing this.

Etta slaps her forehead. "You have scheduled days for masturbation? That's just sad. And a self-administered orgasm is like performing the Heimlich on yourself—really not as effective as having someone else do it for you."

I roll my eyes. "An orgasm is an orgasm."

"Spoken like a woman who hasn't popped off with the participation of another actual human being in far too long," she counters, her expression infuriatingly sure. "It's not the same."

"It's really not," my brother agrees, shaking his head like a traitorous traitor.

Even dependable Kevin piles on, shaking his head as well. "It's not the same."

Then he leans forward, his brown eyes bold and brave. "But I'd be willing to help you out."

And I am . . . confused.

"Help me how?"

"I'm free on Tuesdays and Saturdays. I'll be your hot rod of steel. You can use me—I volunteer as tribute."

My stomach roils at the suggestion. Kevin is handsome and sweet, but I've never once thought of him as more than a friend. Certainly never a "hot rod" of anything.

Henrietta breaks the news to him gently.

"Settle down there, Katniss. Your role in this scenario is best mate, not bedmate. Firmly in the friend zone, dearie."

His face falls with disappointment. It seems Tommy Sullivan was correct about Kevin wanting to "fuck" me.

And maybe he was right about me being clueless as well.

"I do appreciate the offer, Kevin, but Henrietta's right. Sleeping with you would be like sleeping with . . ." I point at my brother ". . . him."

My tongue reflexively juts out and I gag an honest-to-God gag.

"Bleck!"

"Besides," Henrietta goes on, swirling the spoon in her bowl of chowder contemplatively, "Abby is used to being large and in charge—if she's going to loosen up, she needs a man who can boss it out of her. A man who's bossier than she is—and that's not your way, Kevin."

Kevin nods, conceding the point. And Henrietta turns to me, her eyes glowing with sneaky, suggestive satisfaction. "Do you know who is man enough for the job? A bloke who's the opposite of *bleck* in every way?"

My eyes roll closed and I feel a headache coming on.

"Don't say it."

She says it.

"The bodyguard."

After a moment, my brother rubs his chin thoughtfully.

"He did seem fond of you, Abby."

"Like I said," Henrietta prods, "a feature, not a bug."

I sigh, because I don't want to talk about this. I don't want to be thinking about it. Or *him*. Not when he already takes up so much time in my thoughts.

"I can't just take up with a bodyguard."

"Whoa," Kevin says, holding up his hands. "Snob alert."

"I'm not being a snob, I'm being realistic. My grandmother would have a conniption. Have you ever seen a dowager countess pitch a fit? It's not pretty."

"Why do you give a rat's arse what Grandmother would say?" Luke asks.

"You were raised in the same household I was—how can you not?"

"Because I've gotten out. Broken free of the Haddock bubble of influence. If you weren't still firmly entrenched inside, you'd be able to see our family for what they are: The Umbrella Academy, but more dysfunctional. Our parents, Sterling, Athena and especially dear Grandmother have no business judging anyone. Ever."

"Do you want to know what I think?" Henrietta asks.

I rub my temples. "I really don't."

"I think you liked him. I think, deep down, you know you could like him a whole lot more." Henrietta's voice gentles, and she's not teasing me now—she's speaking as a friend. My best friend. "And all those feelings you work so hard to pretend you don't have might make things messy—and I think messy scares you, Abby."

I shake my head—deny, deny, deny.

"Messy doesn't scare me, I just don't have time for it. I'm trying to accomplish something here—become something, not just for the family, but for myself as well. What's wrong with that?"

"There's nothing wrong with it," Luke says softly. "I just hate to see you close yourself off . . . from life. From joy. You have to give yourself a break once in a while, Abby, or you won't be able to become all you want to be. That's what Dr. Whitewater was really saying."

"It doesn't have to be messy," Kevin adds. "I mean, you don't want him to be your boyfriend—you want him to be your . . . professional banging buddy. There could be rules to keep it simple.

If he wants you bad enough—and he'd be an idiot not to—he'll agree."

I take a moment to consider it—because Kevin's plan sounds promising . . . and familiar.

"He said something to that effect," I admit quietly.

"You didn't tell me that!" Henrietta gasps. "What did he say?"

The image of Tommy Sullivan comes unbidden again. His heated, teasing gaze—his wicked, whispered words.

"That it could be simple with us. Uncomplicated."

And good. Don't forget so very, very good.

My skin starts to tingle—across my neck, up my thighs. The thought of Tommy Sullivan—of this—makes me tingle everywhere.

"It's Saturday night," Henrietta says. "I bet he'll be at Paddy's or Katy's Pub. That's where all the rowdy boys go."

Henrietta knows her pubs, and beer . . . and boys.

"We could go there and you could lay it all out for him. See what he says. Come to a mutually beneficial agreement."

This does put a different light on things.

I wouldn't be sleeping with Tommy Sullivan because he's handsome as sin and probably has moves that could make my head explode. I'd be doing it to further my career. In pursuit of my goals. To become a better surgeon.

It sounds plausible. Permissible. Sensible.

And in that moment, I give myself permission to give it a go. To try. To step into the seductive whirlwind that is Tommy Sullivan . . . come what may.

The tingles are at full charge now and a thrilling, intense excitement pulses in my veins.

But then . . . a different, unfamiliar sensation swamps me. My palms go clammy and my heart rate picks up, and my face is suffused with uncomfortable heat.

"What's the matter?" Luke asks.

I swallow past the constriction in my throat. "I'm nervous. I've never propositioned anyone before."

Henrietta looks at me like I've said the silliest statement that's ever been said.

"You have tits, Abby. They'll do all the propositioning for you."

CHAPTER
EIGHT

Tommy

DON'T BELIEVE IN REGRET. IT ALWAYS SEEMED pointless to me—a waste of time and energy. There've been mornings when I've woken up half-dead and sick as a dog, and wished I'd thought twice about the drinking I did the night before. When I was nine, I let it slip to my mum that I'd seen Arthur and Annie Donaldson humping out behind the shed—and afterward, while Arthur was giving me the beating of my life, I wanted to go back in time and keep my trap shut.

But when it comes to women, I find it easy to let go, move on, part amicably and not look back. No regrets. Like the great Dr. Seuss once said: *Don't cry because you're not in balls-deep any-more—smile because you were.* Or something to that effect.

It's different with Abby Haddock.

The thought of her . . . sticks.

Hangs on.

Accompanied by a cold side serving of, not regret exactly, but disappointment at a missed opportunity. That feeling that one—a really fucking good one—got away.

And it's not that I read her wrong or that she wasn't interested—I'm still sure she was. What niggles at me is that she wasn't ready to be interested. At least not that night. And that keeps me hoping. It keeps me thinking of her. Imagining in filthy, illicit, high-definition detail how damn hot it would've been between us.

Could still be.

When she's ready.

"Turn your shoulders," I instruct Owen from behind the bag, in the gym of the shop where I'm giving him pointers. "Don't just hit with your fist. Put all your weight behind it."

Owen jabs at the bag again.

"Better."

He does a dozen more repetitions before we call it a night, lock up and head out.

Lo and I alternate driving days to save on gas and today was my day to drive. We pull up to the front of his house—a two-story, brick home that he built himself. As we get out of the car Ellie comes skipping out the door in a fuzzy sweater and leggings, her blond hair bouncing as she meets us halfway up the front walk.

Well—she meets Logan there—jumping up into his arms and wrapping her legs around his waist, gazing at him with baby-blue eyes like he's the only man in the whole world.

"You're home! I love it when you come home—I missed you today."

Logan holds her tight, searching her face.

"You're feeling better?"

Ellie's pregnant again. It's early still so they're not sharing the news wide, but Logan mentioned the sickness has been especially tough on her this time around.

Ellie nods. "Much better. I put Finn down late for his nap, so he should sleep for about another hour. I think we should enjoy every minute of me feeling better while we can."

That's all Lo needs to hear. He kisses Ellie sweet and desperate and starts walking toward the house with her still clasped around him. He moves his mouth to her earlobe, making her giggle—and that's when she notices me.

"Oh, hey, Tommy."

"Hey, Ellie."

Logan doesn't stop walking towards the steps—or sucking on his wife's neck like a starving vampire.

Ellie taps his shoulder.

"Logan, Tommy's here."

"He's leaving."

"We're being rude," she whispers like I can't hear.

"He doesn't care," Lo insists.

They make it up the steps to the porch.

"We should at least invite him in for tea."

"He doesn't want fuckin' tea, Elle."

"Well, now that you mention it," I say cheerfully, "a spot of tea would really . . ."

Logan turns back over his shoulder, glaring hard enough to punch me in the face with the force of his eyes alone.

I laugh—and stop fucking with him.

"On second thought, I'm going to swing by Katy's for a pint—the rest of the lads are probably already there."

A group of us meets up at Katy's weekly to let loose and get stupid. Before Finn came along, Ellie and Logan were included in that group, but these days they prefer to hibernate in the comfort of their own home.

"You two kids have fun."

Just before they disappear into the house, Ellie waves over Logan's shoulder. "Bye, Tommy."

I wave back. "Bye, Ellie."

And the door slams shut behind them.

Katy's Pub is a rough-and-tumble gem of a place, situated smack dab in the middle of a bad part of town. It's not dangerous exactly—at least not for me—but they get a special discount on the wooden tables and chairs from the local supplier to replace the ones that tend to get smashed when a brawl springs up.

Tonight, the place is packed and I'm greeted like a returning hero when I walk through the door. Most of the boys and Bea are already in the back at a table full of half-empty beer mugs. A few hours later, when those mugs have been drained and refilled a few times over, the good time—and the stupidity—are full steam ahead.

Harry is messing around with the karaoke machine, Walter is arm wrestling with some tatted-up bloke a few tables over, and behind me Gordon's rapidly getting indecent with some girl up against the wall. I lean back in my chair, twirling the toothpick in my mouth—watching Gus and Owen alternate standing in front of the dartboard, flinging darts at each other's heads. They're not wagering money—it's just about balls, bravery and bragging rights.

In my opinion, mixing men, alcohol and pointy objects is asking for trouble. And like the Bible says—ask and you shall receive.

"All right, let's piss off with the darts, that's schoolyard stuff," I tell them, setting my chair down on all four legs. "Time to separate the men from the boys."

Then I slip an eight-inch, double-blade knife from my ankle-strap and lay it on the table.

Gus nods, and Owen grins. "Wicked."

Across the table, Bea swallows a mouthful of beer.

"This isn't going to end well."

"It's important to be responsible," I explain. "Start with your hand on the board first—then work your way up to your heads."

As the boys move to set up, I give Bea a wink. "Don't worry—they keep a first aid kit up behind the bar for just such occasions."

"Why do you I have the feeling you know that from personal experience?" she asks.

Before I can answer, a path clears in the crowd from our table to the door.

And the toothpick falls out of my mouth.

Because Abby Haddock just walked into Katy's Pub.

And she looks fucking fantastic.

Her flaming hair has a tousled, bed-mussed wave to it, a dark green dress with a teasing slit at the cleavage hugs her in all the right places and a camel wool coat, open in front, is draped across her shoulders. On her feet—stilettos—high-heeled and shiny, accentuating the sculpted shape of her endless legs.

She's all polished perfection and sexy class—good enough to eat from top to bottom and back again. And of all the things I've fantasized doing to her, eating her is at the very top of the list.

Abby's head swivels—searching—until her eyes land on me as I approach. And I don't think she even realizes how she's looking at me—avidly, openly needy—soaking me in like a randy little sponge. Her gaze grazes my arms, pausing at the center of my chest beneath my cream, cable-knit sweater, then coasting downward, lingering at my waist before settling in for an unmistakably long stare in the direction of my cock.

I like her looking at me. I've missed it these past weeks.

Standing before her, I lift one brow. "Fancy meeting you here."

"Hello, Mr. Sullivan." She smiles. "It's good to see you again. You look . . . well."

My voice comes out rough and raspy.

"You look beautiful."

For a moment, we stand there, and it's like one of those

fanciful moments in a movie or a book when the rest of the world fades away into the meaningless background—and it's just the two of us, drinking each other in.

Until Henrietta appears at our elbows—a pint of cold beer already in her hand—looking between us, grinning wolfishly.

"Me and Kevin will be in the back, Abby, if you need us." She pats Abby's arm. "Though I'm sure Tommy's capable of giving you everything you need."

I glance at the two of them as they walk away. Henrietta fits in more with the general atmosphere, wearing a short denim skirt and low-cut white top with her blond hair teased high. While the bloke—*Kevin*—looks like he just walked out of a Nirvana music video in a sloppy flannel and jeans.

"Can I take your coat?" I ask Abby, because I'm a gentleman—and because I want to see more of her.

She hands it over to me, exposing the ivory skin of her arms that would look so bloody good around my shoulders, my waist, clasped tight and frantic across my back.

"You want a drink?"

She seems like she could use one. She's fidgety—flustered. It's very cute.

"A gin and Dubonnet with lemon, please," she tells Hubert the bartender.

And he looks at me like she's spoken alien and he wants me to translate.

"Give her a gin and soda."

The moment Hubert sets the glass on the bar, Abby swipes it up—and downs it fast—exhaling a long breath afterwards.

"Another, please."

I watch as Hubert sets a second glass in front of her and she drinks half of it in one gulp, squeezing her eyes and clearing her throat after she swallows.

"Is everything all right?" I ask. "I mean, are you in some sort of trouble?"

"No trouble." She shakes her head. "Henrietta finally convinced me to come out with her for a drink after our shift."

"And you ended up at this place?"

"Yes." She nods vigorously.

Too vigorously to be telling the truth.

"Well—no—that's not precisely accurate. I was hoping I'd see you here. There's a . . . matter I'd like to discuss."

Before I can unpack that, Harry taps the microphone on the karaoke stage, sending a screech of feedback straight into the eardrums of every patron in the place.

"This one is for my mates at S&S Securities," he announces, like the pop star he imagines himself to be.

The song begins—a soft string of acoustic guitar notes. Harry's wavy dark hair sways in time, and then he sings the opening lines of "I Want It That Way" by the Backstreet Boys.

I sigh—embarrassed for him—and a little for myself.

"He's not really with us," I tell Abby.

From the corner of the bar Henrietta lets out an ear-splitting scream and rushes the stage like . . . well . . . like a girl at a Backstreet Boys concert.

"Same," Abby says.

And we're both laughing.

I dip my head closer to hers. "Now about this 'matter'?"

She looks up into my eyes. "Yes. It's been brought to my attention—"

A drunken lout bumps into Abby from behind, sending her crashing into me. I shove him back and wrap my arm around her, eyeing the door. Because between the music and the crowd I can barely hear her voice. And I'm keen on her voice—as well as hearing clearly what's brought her here looking for me.

With my hand on her lower back, I guide her to the door and out into the brisk night air. I lay her coat over her shoulders and move us a few steps down from the door—to a quieter, shadowed space on the pavement. Then I lean back against the outer brick wall of the bar.

Abby stands in front of me, chin raised, her delicate hands clenched at her sides.

"Were you serious?" she asks.

"I'm rarely serious, love—you'll have to be more specific."

She swallows, the hollow of her throat rippling.

"About wanting me. About it being simple. About us . . ."

"*Fucking?*"

Yes, I'm purposely being crass. Playing with her. Toying with her.

Goading her.

Because I enjoy it. I enjoy the tiny gasp that escapes from her lips. I enjoy the stain of color that flushes on her smooth cheek. And more than anything—I enjoy the flash of fire that sparks in those big, brilliant eyes.

"Yes. About us fucking."

And, Christ, I enjoy that too—hearing the crude word in Abby's elegant, refined tone. It makes me feel like I'm marking her, dirtying her up. It makes me want to show her just how fun filthy can be.

"As serious as a hard-on," I answer her.

"That's not an expression."

"It is to me. I take my hard-ons very seriously." I cross my arms and watch her for a moment—reading her. "Why are you asking?"

She looks away down the street. "It's been brought to my attention that I'm a bit high-strung."

"High-strung?"

"Stuffy," she confirms.

"Yeah, that's true—but I'm still not getting what that has to do with us fucking?"

"I'm in need of relaxation," she explains. "Stress relief on a regular basis."

Suddenly it all becomes clear. What she's asking. Offering. And every drop of blood in my body heads south—tightening my trousers in anticipation.

"And you're thinking I could be your personal stress reliever?"

She gives a little shrug.

"You did say you were interested. And I admit, there's an attraction between us. You're the best-looking man I've ever seen . . ."

My ego is a lot like my cock—large and fully capable. But if it ever needed a boost, that compliment from this particular woman would certainly do the job.

". . . and our kiss, in your hospital room, it was—"

"Hot," I finish for her.

Abby's voice goes low and husky.

"Yes, it was hot."

Because she's remembering that kiss the same way I am—the addictive feel of it, the sensuous taste. But then she remembers herself. She steps back and shakes her head, like she's trying to clear the lusty sheen that's fallen over us both.

"But, there would be rules to our arrangement. Parameters."

And she's back to prim and proper and dignified. Like she's flipped a switch. But it's still sexy as fuck.

"What sort of parameters?"

"Well, as you know, I have a very demanding schedule. We would have to coordinate our time together in advance. I have the most flexibility on Tuesdays and Saturdays—I could pencil you in if those days work for you."

I laugh out loud.

Because my sex drive is more the free-range, voracious type.

It's not the kind you pencil in. Although this flexibility she speaks of is intriguing . . . I'd like to hear more about that.

"Also, I have no time for emotional entanglements. It will have to be purely physical. When it's run its course, for either of us, we tell each other. Simply, honestly—no dramatics, no regrets."

Now I think she's messing with me.

I actually glance around to see if one of the boys is hiding behind a bush or something. If they put her up to this to prank me. Because talk about too good to be true.

It's like all the falling stars and fairy godmothers got together to grant one perfect, massive wish—and this is it. It's like a fucking miracle.

Without thinking, I reach into my pocket for my smokes. But before I can even tap one out of the pack, Abby holds up a scolding finger.

"And no smoking—that's one of the parameters too. For as long as our arrangement is in effect, you have to promise me you won't smoke. Whether you're with me or not."

"Why does it matter if I'm not with you?"

"Because it's bad for you." Her brow furrows sweetly, "It's harmful and I don't like the thought of you being harmed."

I tilt my head back, thinking on it.

"So it's an ultimatum. You're saying I can put my lips on this"—I wiggle the pack of cigarettes—"or I can put them all over that." I gesture up and down her beautiful body.

"I suppose that is what I'm saying," Abby agrees.

I click my tongue.

"No contest."

I crush the pack into a ball in my hand—and toss it, in a perfect arch, into the trash bin on the corner.

Abby smiles then, laughing a bit.

"So, you agree?"

It's the look on her face that gets me—that tightens my chest and hits me in the gut—and tells me she could become so much more addictive than any tobacco.

Her expression is hopeful. Open with uninhibited yearning.

Stress relief or not—Abby wants this. She wants me to say yes. This talented, smart, stunning woman wants *me*, period.

"Give me your fuckin' cash!"

That snarl comes from a wild-eyed, tweaky bastard—who's now standing about two feet away on my left. Holding a jagged-edged buck knife in Abby's direction.

I'm typically better about being aware of my surroundings, but Abby—and our topic of conversation—was an epic distraction.

"This isn't a good time, mate," I tell him lightly. "We're in the middle of something here."

He waggles the knife around. "I said your cash—and make it fast or I'll cut you!"

Now I'm annoyed. And the terror on Abby's pretty face makes me think dark, merciless, creative thoughts.

But it's better if I resolve this quickly. Cleanly.

So, I take my wallet out and hand the twat a twenty.

"This is all you're getting. Walk away. And stop looking at her like that or I'll remove your eyeballs from your fucking skull."

He leers at Abby harder, baring rotten teeth.

"Maybe I'll do something more than look. You talk a big game, *mate*—but I'm the one holding the knife."

Three moves.

That's all it takes for the knife that was in his hand to be gripped in mine. I could've done it in two, but I slapped him for good measure. I press the blade under his chin, against his throat, hard enough for him to feel the sting.

"You were saying?" I ask him softly.

While it would be poetic justice to slice and dice the arsehole with his own knife, Abby's beside me and that isn't a memory of me I want her to have.

Plus, blood is a real bitch to wash out, and this is one of my favorite sweaters.

But, he can't go without retribution. Life doesn't work that way.

I don't work that way.

"My girl here, she's quick as a whip—brilliant actually. Do you want me to demonstrate?"

He's not so snarly now.

"No."

"Too fucking bad."

Still holding the knife, I brace one hand against his shoulder joint in front and grip his bicep with the other. Then I push and pull up and back at the same time. And pop goes the weasel.

He screams, but I hold him still.

"What's the diagnosis, sweetheart?" I ask Abby without taking my eyes off him.

"You . . . you just dislocated his shoulder," she replies quietly.

"Right-o." I smile, taunting the aspiring assailant. "Should we go again, for old time's sake?"

"No," he whimpers, "wait!"

Too late.

Another howl, and his other shoulder bites the dust. And he stands there, groaning, both useless arms dangling at his sides.

"Well, my job here is done." I give him a small shove in the right direction. "The hospital's that way. Make better choices."

After I'm sure he's gone, I toss the knife in the bin and wipe my hands off on the front of my trousers.

Then I chance a look at Abby.

And she's not fearful anymore. Or disgusted, as some might be.

She's turned on. Staring at me with a mixture of shocked awe and spiked desire.

Her green eyes are dark and round and her nipples are two hard, beckoning points beneath her dress and her soft pink lips are parted and panting in a way that goes straight to my dick.

Fucking Christ, I want her. And she's right here, for me, for the taking.

"So . . . your place or mine?"

CHAPTER NINE

Tommy

THE WALK TO MY APARTMENT ISN'T FAR, BUT IT SEEMS to take forever—the way the best Christmases always seemed to take too long to arrive when you're a child.

And also because of Abby's shoes.

They're a work of hard-on art, but they aren't made for high-speed walking—or walking at all. The urge to manhandle her, to just toss her over my shoulder and carry her like a caveman, is strong. Pure, primal adrenaline is pounding in my veins. Having the gorgeous girl you've been lusting after for ages tell you she wants you to put your cock inside her will do that to a man.

But I tamp it down and settle for holding Abby's hand instead.

I unlock the door to my flat and lead her in, tossing my keys on the table near the door. I don't turn on the lights—the silver sheen of moonlight coming through the windows gives just enough illumination to see and sets the mood I'm looking for—shadowed and secluded and shrouded enough to let loose.

Abby slips out of her coat and I hang it on the hook while she moves to the center of the room. "I like what you've done with the place."

She's being polite again—because except for the epically large-screen television, black recliner and sofa, and dark gray crocheted blanket, courtesy of my mum, folded across the back, I haven't done much.

"Moved in?" I ask.

"Yes," she says with a smile, "it's obviously a bachelor pad, but it's warm—laid back. It feels like you."

I wander closer to her. "Do you want something to drink?"

Now I'm being polite too.

Abby shakes her head, her eyes drifting down to her shoes.

And she suddenly looks fragile to me—unsure and out of her depth. Because despite the fierceness I've glimpsed from her—her brilliance and ambition—I'm hit with the certainty that Abby doesn't have a lot of experience with men. That a one-night stand or fucking without commitments is unchartered territory. That knowledge makes me feel privileged, honored—and ferociously protective.

"Are sure you want to do this, Abby? It's all right if you change your mind. I can take you back to your friends at the pub."

She lifts her chin, looking into my eyes. "I don't want to change my mind." Abby inhales a deep, slow breath—the kind that you take right before you dive straight into deep water. "I'm sure that I want this. That I want you."

She puts her hand on my chest, her fingers pressing into the thick roped fabric of my sweater.

"Come on, Tommy. You can't back out on me now."

And there's something about my name on her lips that captures me—holds on and doesn't let go.

Because when it comes to women I'm used to doing the chasing. I *like* the chase and I'm good at it. And the pinnacle of the best seductive pursuits is that singular moment when you know in your bones that you've won . . . and all that you've been craving is right there at your fingertips.

But this moment with Abby is different, better, infinitely sweeter.

Because it isn't just that I've won her or wooed her—she's turned it around. Against her nature and better judgement, outside her comfort zone—she's chasing me. Enticing me, reeling me in to her. And for the first time in my life being wanted that way doesn't make it feel too easy or uninteresting.

Because of her—because I know this isn't her way—that she's doing it just for me, only for me. It's hard-won and worthy. Important.

It makes what's happening here and now precious to me.

I slide my hand up her bare arm—her skin is warm and soft as satin. I cup the side of her face in my palm and wrap the other hand around her waist, drawing her forward.

"Say that again."

"What?"

I stare at her mouth.

"Say my name again."

A smile teases at her mouth as she reaches up, grazing the tip of her nose against mine—as soft as the brush of a butterfly's wing. And her lips are *right fucking there*.

"Tommy . . ."

I was hard before, but the whispery plea in her tone turns me to granite. And I curl over her, covering her mouth with mine— thrusting my tongue in deep and demanding, desperate to devour every inch of her.

She gasps at first, stiffening for just a second.

But then . . . then she melts.

Yeah, that's the way.

She presses her breasts against my chest, her stomach to mine, twining her arms around my neck like she can't get close enough. And it all comes rushing back—the feel of her in my hands, the taste of her tongue. It's wild and consuming and more perfect than anything my pitiful memory allowed me to recall.

I sink my hands into the soft silk of her hair, gripping a bit, and she rewards me with a throaty little moan. I angle her head, slowing down the kiss, so I can suck at her lips and slide slowly against her tongue—savoring the velvet feel of her mouth the way we both deserve.

And Abby isn't idle. Her hands roam and clutch, before gripping the bottom of my sweater and pushing it up my rib cage. I stop kissing her long enough to tug it over my head and drop it on the floor. But I don't go back for her mouth straightaway.

Because she's staring at me—at my bare torso—eyes wide and dark with naked hungry want. With wonder.

And then she touches me.

Pressing her palm against my hot skin, following it with her gaze as she skims the swells of muscles across my chest, over my arms, then down my abdomen.

"There's so much to you," she breathes out. "I've imagined so many times what you would look like."

Abby brings her other hand into play, nails scratching lightly across my stomach, caressing the indents where my jeans hang low on my hips. Making me groan—driving me mad.

"But this is more—better—than I envisioned."

I yank her back into my arms, kissing her roughly so she'll stop saying things that make me want to rip her clothes off and fuck here on the hard oak floor.

It would be fast and filthy—and she would let me do it.

But I don't want to rush this. I want to relish every sensation and delight in every gorgeous moan I pull from her.

I drag the zipper down the back of her dress and Abby slips it off to a pool of dark green around her feet.

And I think this woman may actually be trying to kill me.

Because she's not wearing a bra.

How the hell did I not notice this before?

Her breasts are high and pale and perfect—her nipples two tight rose points, begging to be worshiped and sucked. Abby stands before me in nothing but her sky-high heels and a scrap of sheer black lace that can be called knickers in only the barest sense of the word.

My cock is so hard it throbs in time to the beat of my heart, like it's trying to pound its way through the zipper of my jeans.

She shifts her arms, but before she can cover herself—because that just won't fucking do—I sink to my knees in front of her like the sinner I am. I cup her tits in my hands, squeezing gently, rubbing the full mounds and dragging my thumbs achingly slowly across her nipples.

Abby's head rolls back as she hisses my name.

"Tommy."

I bring my mouth to her breast, wrap my lips around one needy little peak and suckle. She tastes sweet here too—soft and smooth and fragrant. I move to her other breast, flicking with my tongue before drawing her nipple into my mouth with long, suctioning pulls.

"Oh yes." Abby clasps my head, leaning forward, giving me more of her flesh.

And it's all so good. My blood simmers with fire and flames lick at the surface of my skin.

Because she likes it, loves it, is desperate for it—my touch, my mouth, my cock.

And nothing in the world is more of a turn-on than that.

I nibble a wet trail down the center of her flat, taut stomach. I bite the waist of her lace knickers with my teeth and tug, pulling them down her legs—leaving her bare.

She watches me stare—her chest rising and falling in quick pants—as I take in the loveliness of her smooth, sweet pussy and tiny trimmed strip of auburn hair. I rest my hands on her hips and press a delicate kiss to her hip bone, her pelvis. The scent of her, the wetness already glistening on her lips, weakens my grip on sanity.

"I want to taste you, Abby. I want to lick you and love you here until you can't think straight. I want to make you come just like this."

I look up and meet her eyes.

"You on board with that?"

She can't seem to catch her breath.

"I . . . if you . . . I mean—" She swallows hard. "Yes—most definitely."

Thank Christ.

"Fantastic answer, sweets."

Then I pull her against my mouth. I lap and lave at her with the flat of my tongue—slow and deep—getting off on how soaked she is for me, on how good she smells and *fuck*, how delicious she tastes. Like spiced sweet luscious apples.

"Oh God," she moans.

I use my fingers to open her up so I can lick circles on her swollen bud of her clit and thrust my tongue inside where she's hot and tight.

Abby's body calls to me like a siren's song. And I have a complete understanding of the sailors, back in the olden days, who let themselves crash against the rocks—just to try and get closer to the sound.

Because I would let myself get crushed for this. Risk being obliterated. As long as it meant I could keep tasting and licking and fucking her with my tongue. As long as I could keep hearing the whimpering moans that sing so sweetly from Abby's throat—almost as sweet as her pussy—but not quite.

"Oh God, oh God," she gasps above me.

I grip her arse, and her fingers tighten and tug at my hair as her hips rotate, jerking against my mouth. I lash and lick at her relentlessly . . . until she's there. Until I feel her coming—taste the wet, hot, writhing pleasure of it. Her muscles go stiff and clenching, her knees buckle and her choked, gasping moan echoes off the walls.

With a final kiss to her pelvis, I stand and scoop Abby up. Her limbs are relaxed and weighted as I move us to the sofa, slipping off her shoes so she'll be more comfortable. With my heart jackhammering in my chest, I sit down and arrange her so she's straddling me—her knees bracketing my thighs. And then we're kissing again—chests rubbing, hands roaming.

"I've got condoms in my bedside drawer," I say against her mouth.

If there was a patron saint of sex and passion and orgasms to come, she'd look just like Abby does now—with her breasts high and her red hair wild and her skin flushed the perfect shade of warm pink.

"I have condoms out here—in the pocket of my dress."

I chuckle. "Dresses with pockets are awesome."

Abby slips off my lap and moves over to her dress. I kick off my shoes and socks and unbutton my jeans, pushing them off in record time. When she comes back to the sofa, I've got my cock in my hand, stroking it slow and good.

And she watches, with dark eyes and parted lips—enjoying the view. She holds out the condom to me, but I shake my head.

"Put it on me."

Because if we're really doing this—and I plan on doing this a lot—shyness has no place. She's going to need to be nice and familiar with every inch of me.

"Bossy," she teases.

"I like telling you what to do. There's a twisted thrill in it."

"Is that so?"

"Yeah." I crook my finger at her. "And you're gonna like it too—I'll make sure of it."

She lowers herself down beside the sofa—looking oh-so-pretty on her knees. She replaces my hand with hers, gliding up and down my shaft, jerking me off, and I sink back into the pleasure.

And then she's rolling the condom down my thick length. And I'm guiding her over me, legs spread, lining us up, pressing the head of my cock against her heat. My hand clenches harshly at her hip as she sinks down slowly—so fucking slow—taking me in until our pelvises are flush and Abby's arse is against my thighs and my cock is cradled inside her.

She's wet and tight and everything.

She molds around me—every bit as blissful as I knew she would be.

"Fuck, that's good. It's so good."

We kiss and grind, and I cup her tits and suck on her neck.

Abby puts her hands over mine at her hips.

"Show me," she pants. "Show me how you like it."

I'm all for taking control, but in this particular juncture, with Abby's perfect pussy squeezing around me—I'm in the mood for something else.

"Get yourself off on me. Ride me until you come. I want to see it, Abby." I kiss her hard. "I want to feel it."

Every woman has that pace, that one way of fucking and being fucked that they absolutely love. That's guaranteed to get them off every time. Some are too timid to ask for it and some men are too damn dumb to notice when they do—but that's what I want now.

I want Abby to show me—and I want to watch her fall apart as she does.

She moans low and long at my words, her eyes sliding closed and her hips shifting—her muscles instinctively clamping. I skim my hands from her arse to her waist and up to her breasts—cupping and teasing them—and leaning forward to suck and lick on the sweet berry of her nipple.

And then she starts to move, to find that rhythm that will make her gasp and whimper and scream.

Abby likes it deep, and slow. She doesn't rush or bounce up and down frantically.

She glides.

My cock is rigid and hot and buried inside her the whole time, as she grinds back and forth and then in circles—rubbing her clit against my pelvis with a steady, intensifying pressure.

I lie back against the sofa cushion, tilting my head up, watching her.

And for a second my breath catches in my lungs.

Because she's beautiful like this. Open and bare and chasing her pleasure—and brave enough to let me watch. Her eyes are closed, her lashes fanning, her pretty brow scrunched in slight concentration and her plump lower lip captured between her teeth.

Her hips slide faster, and she widens her legs, pressing me inside deeper. I feel her pussy tightening around me, getting wetter . . . getting close.

I grip the back of her neck, pulling her down to me so I can whisper against her lips. "It's so good, love. It's so fucking good like this. Give it to me—let me feel you come."

Abby opens her eyes and presses her forehead against mine and her pussy presses down on me and her hips jerk and her mouth opens in a broken, grasping groan.

And her muscles squeeze around my cock so good, she almost makes me come with her.

But I tamp it down, breathing harsh, and pull it back from the edge.

After she comes down from her orgasm, I grip Abby's arse and stand up from the sofa. We kiss roughly on the way to the bedroom. She licks at my neck, my jaw, chanting God's name and mine in my ear. I pause halfway down the hall, press her back against the wall and thrust inside her—'cause it feels too good not to.

And then we're in the bedroom. I lay Abby on her back and pull out, resting on my knees so I can look her over, touch her. So I can spread her legs wide in the middle of my brilliant bed.

I start at her mouth, rubbing her lip with my thumb, down her chin, drawing a slow line to her breasts, then down the center of her stomach and between her legs.

"Tell me to fuck you."

She's extra warm and slippery now. I pump two fingers inside her and use her own wetness to rub her clit slick. Rubbing soft and teasing—not to get her off, but to keep her hot.

"Say it sweets."

Her voice is small and for the first time since we walked in my door—unsure.

"I don't know if I can do that."

I wedge my hips between her thighs, bracing over her on one hand and holding my cock with the other—sliding the head up and down her slit.

"But I want to hear you say it, Abby. It'll feel so good to hear." I lean down and kiss her gently. "You want to make me feel good, don't you?"

I already know she does, but her chin jerks up and down in confirmation.

"Then give me the words, beautiful girl."

Up and down I slide my dick—pressing close but not pushing in. Abby braces her feet against the bed, knees bent, raising her hips up, trying to take me inside.

"Tell me what you want, Abby. What we both want." I suck at her lips. " Let me hear you say it."

She looks right in my eyes and in her perfect, refined voice—she begs.

"I . . . I want you inside me, Tommy."

"You want me to fuck you?"

"Oh God—yes. Please . . ." Her hips rise again—searching—and my dick is right there at her tight opening. "Please fuck me, Tommy. Fuck me now."

And it's so good and I'm so pleased with her—I don't make her wait a second longer.

I drive into her. Full and flush. When I can't get any deeper, I rotate my hips, rubbing back and forth just how she likes it.

Then I pull back and thrust back in. Hard and again, and over and over. I look down, watching how she takes me in—and the view is beautiful.

"Take it," I rasp, mindless now. "Take it all."

Abby's tits bounce with every thrust. Her chin is raised and her brow is damp as she chants and moans. "Yes, oh yes . . . yes . . ."

My hips speed up—thrusting faster. Thick heat gathers low in my gut—building and rising and so, so good.

I press Abby's hands above her head—our fingers twining.

And then she gasps, chin rising, her pussy squeezing around me in clenching spasms.

"Tommy."

And she takes me with her.

I drive into her one last time, buried deep as I come and come inside her in thick, exquisite pulses that rip the pleasure through me.

Moments later, I'm still twitching with aftershocks. But I lift my head from Abby's neck, and brush her hair back from her face.

I dip my head and kiss her lips softly, and I eat up the sweet smile she gives me in return.

———⟡———

After about ten minutes of lying in bed, when our skin has cooled and our pulses don't beat like we're having matching heart attacks, Abby stretches beside me. Her spine curves beautifully, her succulent breasts lifting, her long arms reaching back and her hands pressing against the headboard.

Which gets me thinking about tying them there. That'd be all kinds of fun.

"That was amazing," she says on a dreamy, languid sigh. "I feel outstanding."

It's a tone I'm familiar with . . . but it's always nice to hear.

"I have that effect on women." I smirk.

She glances at the bedside clock and frowns. "I have to get home. I have an early shift tomorrow. Well . . . today."

I roll to my side, bracing my head on my hand, tracing her collarbone with the tip of my finger. "You could stay the night. A first-thing-in-the-morning fuck is the best way to start the day."

She's tempted, hesitating, but then shakes it off—sitting up and taking the sheet with her—back to sexy Miss Proper.

"I don't think that would be a good idea."

I shrug. "Suit yourself."

I swing my legs off the bed and head out to the parlor to collect our clothes. But when I walk back in, Abby's gaze follows my every move, like her eyeballs are long-distance superglued to my flesh.

And I'm hard again—my dick jutting out thick and long and ready to go. 'Cause I'm talented like that.

Abby's mouth hangs open a bit—the perfect width for me to walk over and slide my cock between those pouty lips. That would also be fun.

"You sure you don't want to stay?" I tempt her—'cause I really think she does.

"No." She drags her eyes off me by sheer force of will. "Too personal."

"I fucked you with my tongue until you came, love. I don't think 'too personal' exists any longer."

Abby shuffles her sweet little arse across the bed, slipping on her dress quickly—and hiding as much of herself from my eyes as she can in the process.

Rude.

"Too intimate, then. This is an arrangement, remember? No entanglements—which means no sleepovers."

I blow out a breath and rub my hand down my face.

"All right. I'll take you home, then."

"You don't have to do that."

"I really do."

"Tommy, we agreed—"

"It's the middle of the fucking night, Abby. Any man who would let a woman see herself home in the middle of the night is a first-class tool—and I'm a lot of things, but I'm not a tool."

I walk around the bed, stepping behind her and zipping up her dress.

"And it's not about entanglements." I brush her hair off her shoulder, and scrape her earlobe slowly with my teeth, breathing against her neck. "I just want to make sure you get home safe and sound . . . so I can fuck you again."

She shivers at my words—the good kind of shiver. And then she nods, seemingly convinced.

And I almost have myself convinced as well.

CHAPTER
TEN

Abby

E TTA AND LUKE AND KEVIN WERE RIGHT. SELF-administered orgasms are most definitely *not* the same as orgasms delivered by someone else. And ones delivered by a sex-god bodyguard are a whole new definition of better.

Tommy was—*Tommy and I*—were nothing short of magnificent. I didn't know sex could be like that—wild and reckless, yet safe at the same time. And that's how it felt when I was in his arms, above him and beneath him—safe.

Wanted and protected.

Secure enough to say anything, do anything. Everything.

It was mind-blowing. Eye-opening. Perspective-shattering.

And though a voice in my head warns me to stick to the plan—to not allow myself to be distracted—another bolder, braver voice says I can't wait to do it again.

To feel all Tommy made me feel, over and over, and as soon as humanly possible.

When he dropped me back at my flat last night, I kicked off my shoes, fell face-first into my beloved bed and slept like the dead for four blissful hours. The bottomless, dreamless sort of sleep that pulls you down deep and wraps you in darkness and sends you back into wakefulness refreshed and energized—like fizzy soda has been injected into your veins.

Medically speaking, I know that's not feasible. That in reality I'm experiencing a cocktail mix of hormones and endorphins and dopamine—but it's how it *feels*.

Wonderful.

I should've slept with Tommy weeks ago, or hell, years ago—he was right about that too. I've never felt so fantastic to have been wrong. The intensity of it, the release and joy that surged through me, was breathtakingly exquisite. And those sensations stayed with me—had me humming my way through my morning shower, and I'm still humming when I step out of the lift onto the surgical floor.

It's possible, at some point, I may break into song. A bawdy ditty about a dark-haired lad with a shameless smile, muscles to spare, and an absolutely brilliant cock.

Dear God—only one night and I'm already talking dirty in my own head. And I don't even mind.

Though I'd suspected I appear as good on the outside as I feel on the inside, it's confirmed when Etta spots me near the nurses' station before rounds. And she shakes her head, smiling in a secret, silly sort of way that says she knows precisely what I did last night.

"The magic peen is a hell of a drug."

I laugh. "The magic peen?"

"You're practically floating on air. Like he jizzed pixie dust all over you."

I giggle out a groan and cover my eyes with my hands. "Etta. Too much."

She wiggles her eyebrows.

"And yet not nearly enough. I want the details, you dirty girl—don't even think about holding out on me."

Before I can begin to answer, the lift pings open behind us and Kevin strolls out of it. His hair is sticking up at odd angles, as if it was tugged so forcefully the style is now permanent. Dark sunglasses cover his eyes, even though he's inside. Familiar-looking sunglasses . . . bodyguard-looking sunglasses.

And he's whistling "Zip-a-Dee-Doo-Dah."

"Top of the morning, ladies."

"Well, well—it seems like Abby's not the only one who got lucky last night," Etta says.

Kevin takes off the sunglasses and folds them reverently in his front coat pocket.

"Lucky is the understatement of the year."

"He went home with Bea last night," Etta tells me.

I didn't spend a tremendous amount of time with Bea on the nights that she was guarding me, but what I know of her, I like. She's forthright, spirited, a little rough around the edges but a good egg all around. A potentially excellent yang to Kevin's ying.

Etta concurs.

"If my medical career doesn't pan out, I think I'll become a professional matchmaker. I told Bea she'd be a fool not to give Kevin a go—and that she shouldn't be put off because he's quiet."

Kevin grins like the cat who ate all the canaries.

"I can officially say she likes the quiet ones. A lot."

Then he leans toward us, wondering, "But do you think it's weird that all three of us hooked up with bodyguards last night?"

Looking completely sincere, Etta says, "I didn't hook up with Harry."

"Harry?" I inquire, trying to keep up. "The lanky Backstreet Boy–singing karaoke chap?"

Kevin nods. "They were practically welded together at the hip." He turns to Etta. "You left together."

The way she blew her top when he was on the stage, I'm shocked Etta didn't hook up with him right there at the bar.

"He does seem like your type."

"He is," Etta confirms with a sigh, and her tone goes dreamy. "We went for ice cream and walked around the city talking the whole night. Then he walked me to my front door and kissed me on the cheek. We're soul mates. I want to take things slow with a soul mate."

"Right." Kevin nods. "So you're going to rock his world on the second night?"

"Absolutely. He's coming over for dinner tomorrow. I'm going to bang him so hard I'll probably sprain something."

There's the Etta I know.

Our conversation cuts off there when Dr. Paulson appears across the other side of the nursing station.

"Haddock—you're scheduled to assist me on my transplant this week."

She's tall and statuesque with short silver hair, a gracious, deliberate demeanor and a long, flawless career. Dr. Paulson is the surgeon all other surgeons want to be when they grow up.

"Yes, ma'am."

"I'm going to push you. You'd best be prepared."

My nod is sure and steady.

"I'm ready. You can count on me."

Though I've said the words before—because no one wants to admit to the worry that they're not up to snuff—this is the very first time that deep in the center of myself, I genuinely believe they're true.

Dr. Paulson narrows her gaze, analyzing and assessing me.

"There's something different about you this morning. Did you have something new for breakfast?"

"No, ma'am."

Behind me, low enough that only I can hear, Etta snickers, "But she had dick for dinner."

I slide my foot back and kick her in the shin.

"Well, whatever it is," Dr. Paulson tells me as she picks up a chart and moves towards the lift, "keep it up."

I nod, smiling. "I will."

Once she's gone, I glare at my terrible, awful best friend.

"The next time you're napping in the break room, I'm going to smother you with a surgical mask."

Etta sticks out her tongue at me and drags Kevin by the arm towards the group congregating at the end of the hall to begin rounds. I'm a step behind them when my mobile vibrates in my coat pocket.

It's a text from Tommy—as he programmed himself into my contacts last night.

Godly Orgasm Giver: Free tonight?

A bolt of heat strikes low in my stomach at the sight of the simple two-word question. But before it can burn me up, I type a reply.

Me: It's Sunday.

Godly Orgasm Giver: I know. The day of rest. I rest best after fucking. I bet you do too.

The man knows how to make an argument. But still I stick to my guns, shaking my head even though he can't see.

Me: I have reading to do to prepare for a surgery this week.

Godly Orgasm Giver: You can read while you're riding me. I'll give it to you nice and slow so you don't lose your place. Win-win.

My breath whistles out of me. Because that's how it was last night, on his sofa. Slow and deep. There's a slick throbbing between my legs at the remembered feel of him inside me. Hard and thick and amazing. I felt so exquisitely filled up—tight and helplessly clenching around him.

But still . . . I try to keep things in perspective.

Me: We agreed to Tuesdays and Saturdays.

Godly Orgasm Giver: I actually didn't agree to that part at all. I don't particularly like schedules.

There's a pause, the three dots taunting me. Then he adds a reply.

Godly Orgasm Giver: And I want you again.

My chest balloons with the sweetest thrill of sensation. And my lips slip into a giddy smile, without conscious intent or awareness.

Because he wants me.

And everything about Tommy Sullivan wanting me makes me feel alight and alive—more sure of myself, more powerful, than I can ever remember feeling before.

Godly Orgasm Giver: This time I want it in your bed. Been thinking about it all morning. Your red hair splayed over those pink silk sheets you have—on your back, your breasts high and pointed and begging for my mouth. And your legs spread wide for me—aching for my mouth there too.

A moan slides up the back of my throat—because I can almost hear him saying the words. Whispering them roughly against my ear. Sure in the sensual knowledge that all the things he wants to do with me, to me . . . I want as well.

I send a reply, trying to tease.

Me: You're a very persuasive fellow.

But Tommy's done teasing now.

Godly Orgasm Giver: Say yes, Abby.

My hand trembles a little as I grasp my mobile. Because this is bad. Dangerous. I'm already breaking all my rules. But there's a frenzied, frantic desire pulling inside me. Twisting me up and twirling me around. I'm caught in it, captured by it, completely at its mercy.

At *his* mercy.

So my fingers slide quickly over the screen, typing the only reply that's possible.

Me: Yes.

CHAPTER
ELEVEN

Tommy

FROM THAT FIRST NIGHT ON, ABBY TAKES TO OUR arrangement like a kitten to warm milk. We hook up at her place and at mine, for long, slow, sweaty hours and hard, hot stolen minutes. Sometimes it's planned days in advance—other times there's just a moment's notice. It's consistently spontaneous, regularly impulsive . . . and there's not a single thing about any of it that isn't bloody fucking grand.

Take where we are at the moment, for example. On Abby's bed with her on all fours and me on my knees behind her. I like the way my hands look on her pale skin—gripping her waist as I pull her back and forth on my cock. I like the way her arse quivers each time my pelvis slaps against her. And I love the way she feels—the heaven of her slick, snug heat squeezing all around me.

It doesn't get better than this.

"Tommy . . ." Her perfect moan floats through the room.

Until it does.

Abby's head falls forward, her shiny hair swaying in time with the push of my hips.

"You close?" I ask—but only to hear her say it out loud.

Even through the condom, I can feel how close she is. How she gets wetter and her muscles begin that telltale tightening flutter.

"So close," she pants. "Please, Tommy. Please, please, please . . ."

Abby Haddock begging to come is the sweetest sound I will ever hear.

I run my palm up her spine, digging my fingers into the hair at the nape of her neck and pulling her up. Because I want to be closer, need to feel her deeper.

My arm is a band across her stomach, holding her still as the pace of my hips quickens. Abby's back presses against my chest and she turns her head, silently reaching for my mouth. I kiss her roughly and slide my hand between her legs, pressing two fingers to her clit. And then she's stiffening in my arms and moaning down my throat as the bliss takes her. Her pussy clenches me, making my balls draw up and electricity race down my spine. I come hard, surging hot inside her as a string of curses falls from my lips.

For a bit, neither of us moves. We stay there still on our knees, pressed together and panting, with the same pulsing pleasure throbbing through our veins.

Then Abby opens those pretty green eyes and laughs.

"I swear it gets better every time."

And she's not even a little wrong.

A few minutes later, I'm buttoning my trousers getting ready to head for home and Abby's in her gargantuan fluffy robe, heading for the bath.

"What's your schedule tomorrow?" she asks, her hungry eyes on my abs as I pull my shirt over my head.

"I've got training with the new hires and a logistics review with a client's security team. You?"

"Rounds, clinic, and an observation of a frontal craniotomy that will run late."

"A brain surgery?" I lift an eyebrow. "I bet that turns you on."

"It's very exciting, yes."

I nod. "Text me when you're home no matter the time. I'll come by and go down on you before you go to sleep."

Even after what we just finished doing, and what we did before that—which involved a whole lot of her mouth and my dick—Abby blushes.

And it's too damn adorable. I take her face in my hands and kiss her slow and soft. Then I reach around and slap her arse, just to keep her on her toes.

And that's how it is with us. No tiresome talk about feelings or the future, no hard-on-deflating debates about where we stand or where this is going, or even worse, where it's not, no annoying arguments about priorities or divided attention.

It's just this simple. And easy.

Just this fantastically good.

———⚓———

Speaking of priorities—mine are obviously in full working order, as evidenced a few days later when I get an incoming text from Abby first thing in the morning. I'm at the S&S offices bright and early, and right in the middle of a tutorial from Stella and Amos on our new computer software that reports on the arrest and release records of local police departments around our security system clients' homes.

Apple Blossom: My morning surgery's been delayed. Can you come here?

Like the best sort of magic trick, my smirk—and my erection—appear instantaneously. Because while it might not seem like she means it in a dirty way, I know better.

Me: There, here, on your tits, your arse, against your lips—I can come lots of places.

I practically see her rolling her eyes on the other end of the phone. And it's hot—my fondness for Abby's eye-rolling is almost as perverse as my rabid fetish for her frown.

Apple Blossom: Meet me in 20?

Me: I'll be there in 15.

Apple Blossom: Even better. 6ᵗʰ floor, end of the hall closet. Knock twice. I'll be inside waiting.

I'd knew she'd be like this. Reckless and wild. Bordering on dangerous with the right man. No—fuck that—with *me*.

Me: Don't start without me.

My cock twitches at the mental images of just what Abby starting without me would look like. And I rethink that statement.

Me: On second thought—do start without me. But only if you take photos.

I don't think she's ready for sexy selfies just yet . . . but it never hurts to try.

I slide my phone in my pocket and jerk my thumb over my shoulder, looking at Logan.

"Duty calls. I have to head out—something suddenly came up."

And here's where Lo's serious side rears up to try and ruin all my fucking fun.

"We're right in the middle of this. It's important."

I move backwards, holding up my hands like a lad sneaking out on chores to go and play. "You're on top of it. You're doing great. I have complete faith in you, mate."

"Tommy—"

I make the sign of the cross in the air, blessing him—and then I'm jogging out the door, over to the Tube, because morning traffic is a mess and I don't plan on wasting a minute.

Fifteen minutes later I stand outside the hall closet door at the hospital. No one gave me a second glance on my way up, because here's a bodyguard trick: if you look like you know where you're going and act like you belong there, rarely does anyone have the balls to question you about it.

I rap twice on the door and a moment later it cracks slowly open on its own. Like a horror movie . . . only with stupendous sex waiting on the other side instead of an ax murderer. I step in and close the door behind me and an endless black engulfs me before my eyes can adjust.

"Abby?" I whisper.

I can't see her but, Christ, I can smell her. I inhale deep, devouring the scent that makes my mouth water—not for apples, but for her.

There's a rustle of fabric behind me, and I feel soft lips pressing slow kisses to the back of my neck. When I find her in the dark and pull her against me, my palms are met with heated, smooth, perfect skin.

And nothing else.

Because Abby is naked for me. She slipped her clothes off when I stepped inside the closet.

Fuck me, this girl.

She's like a sex-toy shop—full of the best surprises.

I groan out a laugh as my dick aches to get out of my trousers and inside Abby.

"You're going to be the death of me, lass."

And I'd go out smiling, that's damn certain.

After we hump fast and fantastically against the wall and our joints are languid from the kind of orgasm that just sucks all the tension clean out of you, I help Abby dress in the darkness. We kiss and nibble and accidentally bump heads one time in between slipping on articles of clothing. Then we step out of the closet and walk casually down the hall.

I even whistle.

Abby's friends are at the other end, outside the lift. Henrietta leans her elbow on the nurse's station, resting her head on her hand, bleary-eyed from an overnight shift, I'd guess. An extra-extra-large breakfast tea is beside her.

Over the past few weeks, screwing Abby has begun to feel like an addiction. Insatiable and unrelenting. The more I do her, the more I crave her.

And if her pussy is my heroin, my cock must be her crystal meth. After she takes it she's always more energetic than she was before.

"Who's ready for a great surgery?" she asks her friends cheerfully. "It's going to be a good one, I can feel it!" She raises her palm. "Come on, Etta, give it up high."

Kevin laughs and Henrietta stares at Abby through grumpy, heavy-lidded eyes. "I think I've changed my mind about this. I hate you right now. I honestly hate you."

———— ❦ ————

In my line of work, ice can be an extremely helpful entity. A balm for bruised knuckles and overtaxed muscles. But it's a delicate dance between pleasure and pain. Ice awakens the nerve endings, shocks the surface of the skin, making everything it first touches oversensitive and ultra-responsive.

I love ice. When it's melting on my tongue, floating in my scotch—and especially when a smooth, glossy cube is between my fingers, like it is right now, slowly circling the delicious peaked pebble of Abby's bare nipple.

A reedy gasp leaks from her throat and melts into a whimpering moan when I replace the cold ice with my hot mouth. I worship her with my mouth—twirling my tongue and sucking gently, soothing her chilly flesh.

She's never done this before—experimented with the sensations of hot and cold—and I love that too. That I get to show her, teach her all the dark, dirty delights my deviant mind can conjure.

We're in my office at the S&S shop long after everyone else

has gone home. I was working late and Abby got off late from the hospital, so she took a cab here so we could get off together. And now my clothes lay in a ragged heap on the floor beside the dark blue scrubs she arrived in.

Those scrubs—they're sexier than any lace or leather lingerie to me now. Because to the outside observer they're shapeless and bland, but I know . . . fuck, how well I know . . . the paradise of curves and sweet flesh that hides beneath.

Abby's on my desk, leaning back on her hands, arching her back so her breasts push out towards me. Her knees spread wider, making room for my hips, pleading for my touch.

And what kind of bastard would I be to deny her?

I lift my head from her breast so I can watch the glistening trail of the ice cube as I slide it between the valley of her breasts, down her contracting stomach. I follow it with my tongue, lapping at the liquid, swallowing the taste of her.

And despite the demanding spike of my cock straining for relief, Abby's too delicious for me not to kneel down and pull her to the edge of my desk, and drag the ice cube between her legs. Along her slick folds and around and around her plump pink clit, not touching directly—that would be too much—but near enough to make her hips lift and incoherent needy whimpers sing from her throat.

When the ice is almost melted and neither of us can stand a moment more, I envelop her with my mouth. Giving in, giving what she needs, and taking for myself. Her pussy is cold against my tongue, so I lick and lap at her lips to warm them. But inside— inside she's hot as honey and tastes twice as sweet.

Abby writhes above me and my own hips rotate, fucking air in the same tempo as my tongue. And then she's mindlessly gripping my hair and shamelessly pressing against my mouth, all stiff and tight and too lost to the sensations to make a single sound.

When she shivers one last time and her fingers loosen and her limbs go boneless, I stand, running the back of my hand across my mouth and cradling her in my arms. She pecks grateful, worshiping kisses across my chest, and I reach into the glass of scotch beside her on my desk and scoop out another ice cube. I tilt Abby's head back and trace her lips with it.

"Open for me, love." My voice is ragged and rough, and every muscle in my body is strung tight with wanting her.

When her lips part, I slip the cube inside.

"Suck on it."

Does she know what I'm thinking? Does she know what's coming next?

Her eyes are adoring and come-drunk, and her lips are puffy from my kisses. She holds on to my hips with the soundless plea for more—because by now I know Abby relishes my pleasure every bit as much as her own.

I lift her chin. "Now give it back."

She holds the ice cube between her lips like a good girl, and I pluck it with my fingers and slip it into my own mouth, so I can taste her again.

Because I can't kiss her—not yet.

Then I turn Abby around and lower her gently, so her back is flat on the desk and her neck rests along the very edge, and her head is angled just off the end.

And her mouth is right there—perfect and waiting.

She can't stay in this position long and she won't have to—just seeing her laid out like this for me has me close to bursting.

And then Abby looks up into my eyes . . . and she opens her mouth.

Because she's brilliant and beautiful and for the moment—all fucking mine.

I grip my cock and press it between her lips, just the head at first. I hiss out a groan and my eyes roll closed as the cool cavern of her mouth closes around me. And it's like my blood is on fire—the need and want to take her and ride her, fuck her and come for her is this scorching, monstrous, miraculous thing.

Abby sucks as I push in deeper, her tongue still cool but the back of her mouth and throat warmer, hotter against my cock.

And Christ Almighty the feel of it—that she's letting me have her this way is more stark white bliss than I ever dreamed or deserved in my life.

I'm stripped bare and helpless . . . utterly mad for her.

With harsh breaths and a pounding heart, I brace my hands on the desk and pull out slowly . . . then steadily slide back in. I glide back and forth, fucking her perfect mouth—the raw, carnal gratification ratcheting higher with every thrust.

Abby moans rapturously around me and my vision goes hazy and it's as if ecstasy detonates in my cells. I pump into her mouth and groan her name as I come hard and long down her throat.

———⚓———

Later, we need food. Abby slips into my dress shirt and I step into my boxers, and like two starving savage animals we raid the break room. The pickings are slim—a carton of juice, two apples and a bag of nuts—but they'll do. Out in the workout area, I lean against the wall and pop a handful of almonds in my mouth, watching Abby drift curiously around the room.

I can't take my eyes off her.

She stops beside the sparring ring and takes a bite of her apple.

"So this is where you work? This is where the magic happens?"

I tilt my head towards my office door.

"The magic happened in there. This is where we train."

Abby wanders to one of the weighted bags and I walk over to join her.

"And that's how you relieve your stress?" she asks. "Sparring? Fighting?"

"One of the ways, yeah."

I lift my fists and lay a hard punch to the bag, rocking it back on its base. Showing off for her just because I can.

Abby smiles. "Could you teach me to fight?"

She lifts her small fist and moves to punch the bag—but I catch her wrist before she can make contact and wrap my arm around her waist, lifting her up and turning her against me.

"No." I shake my head. "Not ever."

She seems indignant.

"Why not?"

I take her hand in mine, grinning. And I kiss the back of it, then her palm, then each of her pretty knuckles—punctuating my words with the press of my lips.

"Because these hands—these talented, beautiful hands—are too important for fighting. Too precious. They must be protected at all costs."

"By you?" she asks, like a dare.

And she looks good enough to eat right now.

All over again.

"Absolutely. And besides—we already have a way to relieve your stress that's so much better than fighting." I brace my hands against the bag behind her, caging her in with my arms. "Want to work on that some more in the middle of the sparring ring?"

My desk is already ruined—I'll never be able to sit at it again without getting hard. Might as well go all in with the rest of the place.

A bolt of heat flares in Abby's eyes. She lifts up on her toes and scrapes my chin with her teeth.

"Yeah, Tommy. I really do."

———— ✦ ————

And that's how it goes—smooth as silk and piercingly pleasurable and effortless in its simplicity. We meet up, we fuck, we dress, we leave.

Rinse and repeat.

Abby's heart isn't invested, but her pussy certainly is—and that keeps things interesting. Keeps the challenge and the chase invigorating.

Though she's eased up on the scheduling aspect, she sticks firm to the other walls and parameters she proposed the first night of our arrangement—no emotions allowed. And that suits me fine.

At least . . . I thought it did.

Because while Abby and I spent all that time fucking each other blind, I'd forgotten that stunning, secret gardens have walls too. And only magnificent treasures get locked away behind brick and steel. And the greatest prizes are never easily won—they require seeking and searching and the scaling of obstacles. But Christ, it's worth it in the end.

These are the truths that punch me in the face a week later . . . on the night sweet Abby's walls come tumbling down.

CHAPTER
TWELVE

Tommy

I WALK THROUGH THE DOOR OF MY FLAT AFTER HAVING dinner at my parents' house. Since I moved out, I try and get over there once a week to keep from being buried beneath the weight of the mother-guilt my mum rains down if I don't. And because my family is a hell of a lot more entertaining now that I can take them in small doses.

I'm only just through the door when my mobile pings with a text.

Apple Blossom: I need to see you.

I smile—it's like she read my mind.

Me: I'm at my place. I can come to you.

Apple Blossom: No. Stay there. I'll take a cab.

Hmm . . . Abby's feeling a mite bossy tonight. This will be fun.

In no time at all, there's a rapid knock on my door. But when I open it, there's no time to flirt or tease—no time to even say hello—before Abby has her mouth fused to mine.

Her hands are on my shoulders, tugging me down, and she's up on her toes and her tongue strokes mine in a demanding, tantalizing rhythm.

It's rough and unexpected and glorious.

I kick the door shut behind her and she's clawing her coat off and tearing the top of her scrubs off like it burns. And then her mouth is back to mine and she's knocking me back against the wall like she wants to suck out my soul.

I drag my lips to her ear, her neck.

"Easy, sweets. Slow down."

I feel her shake her head, but she doesn't say a word.

Abby takes my hand and presses it to her breast, squeezing her hand over mine, digging my fingers into her tender flesh harder than I ever would. She shoves my other hand into her hair, tangling it there and pulling—yanking. Her mouth presses harder, her lips against my teeth . . . until I'm tasting the copper tang of blood that's not my own.

Abby wants it rough and hard—and while I'm always up for that, this doesn't feel right. *She* doesn't feel right.

There's a desperation all about her. A frantic urgency that doesn't come from passion.

It comes from someplace else.

I slip my hands from the death grip of hers and rest them on her shoulders, lifting my head.

"Hey." I brush back her hair. "Are you all right, Abby?"

I want to see her eyes, but they're closed. Her nod is quick, jerky, and her face is so pale it practically glows in the dim light. Then she's climbing me, scratching at me, shoving my hand into her bra, scraping my fingernails across that soft, tender skin.

"I want you to fuck me, Tommy," she whispers in my ear. "Hard. Make me feel it. All of it."

She cups my cock over my jeans, rubbing and stroking with the perfect amount of pressure. And I want to go with it. My dick *really* wants to go with it—spin her around and tear at her clothes and fuck her rough against the wall just like she's begging for.

But her voice is raw. And choked. Like invisible hands are strangling her.

And I won't pretend not to hear it.

I break her kiss, but I don't push her away. This time, I pull Abby in, wrapping my arms tight around her and holding her still.

"What's going on with you, Abby?"

Her head thrashes side to side. "Nothing. I just need you. Please, please just do it."

Wetness glistens on her closed lashes, liquid silver in the moonlight from the window. And she shakes harder in my arms. And my ribs tighten and compress—a heavy, squeezing pressure around my heart.

Because she's hurting. Badly.

I pet her hair and press my lips to the soft strands at her temple.

"If you want me to fuck you, Abby, I will. I'll happily fuck you so hard you won't be able to walk tomorrow. But first I need you to talk to me . . . tell me what this is about."

Abby opens her eyes and they're swimming with tears, drowning in pain. Her lips tremble and she shakes her head, and I hold her tighter because her voice is broken.

"We lost her."

"Lost who?"

"Maisy Adams. Today was her final surgery. She was done. And I promised . . . I promised her she'd be all better."

Abby's breath shudders in her chest and she steps back from me, moves away into the center of my front parlor. She looks down, her eyes darting between her empty hands, staring horrified at things I can't see.

"She coded on the table and we tried . . . we tried for so long . . . but we couldn't get her back. I've gone over it in my head—every dosage, ever step—we did everything right . . ."

Abby looks up into my eyes—begging for forgiveness. For absolution. For a reprieve from the pain that's crushing her.

And it's a shock to realize I'd cut off my fucking arm to be able to give her that.

To take this from her if I could. To make it all better.

"But we lost her."

Her shoulders shake and she slips down to the floor. And I go down with her, holding her close and rubbing her arms and letting her get it all out.

"I'm a surgeon," she sobs. "This is why I do what I do. I'm supposed to be able to save them . . . but I couldn't."

"You do, Abby. But you can't save them all."

Her mouth twists angrily at that and her eyes go sharp.

"You don't understand. I have to—I need to know that I can. Because if I can't, what the fuck am I doing this for?"

I brush her hair back from her face, forcing her to look at me.

"You're doing this because no one will give them a better chance than you. They're in the best hands, because they're your hands. But sometimes . . . death is going to win. And it's not because you did anything wrong, and it's not because you're not capable—it's because that's how it works, Abby. It's part of the package. And you have to be able to know that and keep going in spite of it."

She shakes her head. "But what am I supposed to do with this? I don't know what to do with all this . . . hurt. It's so hard."

I nod and kiss her forehead. Then I stand.

"Do you have to go in to the hospital tomorrow?"

She swipes at her cheeks, even while her tears continue to trickle down.

"No. Dr. Dickmaster said I'm not allowed near the hospital for forty-eight hours."

"Smart man."

I walk over to my cabinet and take out the bottle of good scotch. Then I uncork it and come back and sink down beside her on the floor.

"Then we're going to sit here and talk, and you're going to let yourself feel it. If you don't, if you block it all up, it'll just build and build and one day it'll shatter you. So you're going to feel it and we're going to get fucking drunk because it's going to hurt like a bitch . . . and I'm going to be here with you the whole time."

I take a swig from the bottle and pass it to her. She gazes at it for just a moment, and then she relents—putting it to her lips and pressing the back of her hand to her mouth as she chokes the amber liquid down.

She turns to me and her face crumples, pitiful and pleading.

"She was just a little girl, Tommy. A tiny, beautiful little girl. It's not fair."

I draw her into my arms, rocking her gently.

"I know, sweetheart. I know. I'm so sorry."

Abby clasps herself to me, soaking my shirt with her sobs. And eventually, we finish that bottle together. And she stays the night. There in my bed—in my arms—her head on my chest, her hair loose and lovely, her soft breaths tickling my neck.

We don't have sex. Because Abby doesn't need me to fuck her.

Tonight, she just needs me.

In the weeks after Abby cried in my arms for little Maisy Adams, things change. Slow and steady and undeniable—the way winter drifts each day into spring. Abby and I still fuck like beastly bunnies every chance we can, but after that night—it's not *all* we do.

There's talk in between the moaning. Actual conversations about everything and nothing, small things and big, embarrassing moments and silly memories. It brings a closeness to our time together—something more intimate than fucking.

And a tenderness.

I've always felt protective of Abby, but this is something different—something sweet that feels like cherishing.

We don't just enjoy each other's bodies—we enjoy each other.

Like right now, we're lounging in Abby's gigantic porcelain tub—it's late, sometime around two in the morning—a few hours after she finished an eighteen-hour shift at the hospital. I'm not typically a bubble-bath man, but the heated chest-deep water—and the slick, slippery company—might turn me into one. The tub is big enough for us both to stretch out our legs, facing each other, with Abby's foot clasped in my hands as I massage her poor, aching arch.

I'm preoccupied by the glistening bubbles clinging to her peaked pink nipples. It's like a tantalizing peep show—as each bubble pops, a little more flesh is revealed. I want to pop them all, clean them off the tight-tipped buds with my tongue, and suck until she begs for mercy.

Later, when I think back about it, I won't be able to recall how it came up or who posed the question—but we're talking about our first times.

"Mrs. Sassafras," I tell Abby, "my mother's best friend."

"Your mother's friend?" Her face scrunches. "That's wrong, Tommy."

"Yeah, sort of—but the wrongness only made it better." I wink.

She covers her face, laughing.

"How old were you?"

"Just shy of sixteen. She was a young widow and my mum would send me over to help her in the garden. She was beautiful, outspoken—an excellent teacher."

I can tell by her expression that Abby's still not convinced of Mrs. Sassafras's redeeming qualities.

"Did your mother every find out?" she asks.

"Christ, no. My mum would've ripped her head off her shoulders, and last I heard Mrs. Sassafras was still in fine health."

"Mrs. Sassafras . . ." Abby shakes her head, chuckling.

I switch to Abby's other foot, pressing my thumbs into the soft tissue in deep, slow, penetrating circles. Abby's eyes slide closed and her head tilts, exposing the pretty hollow of her throat. I've yet to find a single part of her that's not scrumptiously pretty.

"Ooooh, that's nice," she moans.

And my cock does a spot-on impression of an up-periscope on a submarine.

"Keep moaning like that and I'll be rubbing a whole lot more than your foot."

A grin tugs at the corner of her mouth, but her eyes stay gently closed.

"Later. Right now this is everything." A long, breathy sigh slips from her lips.

We lay quietly for a few moments just like that—cut off from the world, with the fragrant, still steam enclosed around us and warm water droplets sliding on our skin. Abby's loveliness is one I don't imagine I'll ever get tired of looking at—it just grows more intense, more enrapturing, the longer I'm near her.

"What about you?" I wonder softly. "Who had the honor of popping your cherry?"

Some men have issues with a woman's past—with jealousy—but I'm not one of them. Whoever came before had their moment in the sun—and between her legs—but now they're gone. History. A memory. No more a threat to me or my place there than a ghost.

What interests me more is Abby—the pieces and parts that make her who she is.

She's fascinating in her contradictions. A brilliant surgeon with a kind heart for tiny things. A beautiful girl who's deeply suspicious of anything remotely fun. A confident woman who doesn't give herself nearly enough credit. A lass who rides a bike with a bell and a basket . . . but only on the very same path each time.

"I bet it was your first serious boyfriend, wasn't it? Candles and flowers and satin sheets?"

Abby's grin slowly fades away.

"Not exactly."

She sits up straighter, slipping her foot from my hand and drawing her knees towards her chest—wrapping her arms around her legs. "Do you know the Liptons? You must've heard Nicholas railing about Sir Aloysius in Parliament. He's frequently on the opposite side of the Queen's agenda."

I shake my head. "I make it a point to ignore aristocrats' conversations—breach of privacy and painfully boring."

Abby snorts. "Well, Sir Aloysius Lipton is a member of the House of Lords and my father's law partner. They're old friends of the family. Their eldest son, Alistair—I had the biggest crush on him forever. He was a few years older than me, all handsome and charming. And I was decidedly . . . not. I was fifteen and awkward and convinced I was incapable of doing anything well."

She laughs at herself a little, shaking her head—but there's something off about it. Something sad.

"They were at our estate for a dinner party. Alistair asked me to go for a walk around the property, and you could've knocked me over with a feather I was so shocked. And delighted. It was the very first time I didn't feel painfully ordinary."

I don't know if it's her tone or the look in her eyes—but I find myself bracing. Like just before taking a punch to the gut.

"He kissed me behind the gazebo in the garden. And it was nice. And then he kept kissing me . . . but it became not nice. When I told him to stop, I remember thinking he must not have heard me, because he just kept right on like I hadn't said a thing."

I taste sour in the back of my throat and my stomach twists.

Abby's voice drifts away, going airy and thin. Not her lovely voice at all—but the memory of it. A ghost voice.

"So I said it louder. I looked him right in the face. But he . . ."

"He what?" I bite out, harsher than I should.

Abby lifts her shoulder, shrugging in a way that breaks my heart into pieces. As if her next words aren't going to cost her.

"Well . . . he insisted."

The meaning of what she's saying stabs deep. Touching a lethal, primal part of me that's capable of terrible things—that wants retribution.

Because emotion doesn't give a shit about reason. And caring about someone has nothing to do with logic. And I want to slash and burn and destroy, because once upon a time someone hurt her . . . and I wasn't there to protect her from it.

Abby sniffs, staring at the bubbles floating on the bathwater.

"Afterwards, he stood me up and straightened my clothes and plucked the twigs from my hair. And we went back into the house."

"What happened then?" I ask, softer now.

She looks at me from big, dark, bottomless eyes. Her face is pale as marble and her voice is flat as stone.

"We had dinner."

And I want to kill someone. I want to kill *everyone*—and lay their corpses at Abby's feet like an ancient offering. Alistair Lipton and his father and her parents and every cunt who was at that dinner party and didn't see. Couldn't tell. How the fuck did they not see her?

I swallow down the gravel in my throat.

"Did you ever tell anyone?"

"Yes . . ." She nods. "I just told you."

It's like my lungs have been hit with a sledgehammer, forcing out all the air, making it impossible to breathe.

"Abby—"

"Don't. Don't look at me like that."

"Like what?"

"Devastated." She tucks her knees under her, moving to me. "Don't look devastated. It was a long time ago. It doesn't matter. I'm fine now."

Now.

She's fine *now*.

My hands clench into fists beneath the water and I yearn to make the Red Wedding look like a fucking garden party. Because Abby should've been more than fine—she should've been safe and happy and sublime—for *always*.

But I force my features to relax and my muscles to release, and I nod for her, just for her—giving her what she wants.

Because there isn't anything I wouldn't give her.

"All right, love."

The water sloshes over the side as she shifts, curling onto my lap. I wrap my arms around her, holding her close—but not too tight. Just enough that she feels me, that she knows I'm here, that she knows she's safe.

Abby's cheek rests against my chest.

"I've had relationships, Tommy," she insists.

"I'm aware," I answer softly.

"I've been with men—I've been with you."

"Very, very aware."

"It doesn't change anything. There's nothing wrong with me."

My head snaps to look at her.

"Of course there's nothing wrong with you. You're perfect, Abby." I cup her cheek in my palm, stroking. "Extraordinary."

Something about the word tugs at her, captures her, makes her eyes go liquid and shiny. I don't know why . . . but I know I want to find out.

Because this is more than an arrangement. More than convenience or fun or stress relief. More than fantastic, filthy fucking. It's all of that—but it's not *just* that. Not anymore.

I don't think it was ever just that for me. I think that's what I told myself, what I agreed to, so I could have her.

This brilliant, beautiful girl.

But now . . . I want to keep her. And fuck me sideways, I hope she wants that too.

"Do you really think so?" she asks.

I press a light kiss to her forehead, to the apple of each cheek, and to the very tip of her nose.

"Absolutely."

My hands stroke up and down her spine.

"I knew it the first time I saw you."

"When you had a concussion?" she reminds me cheekily.

"Yeah, when I had a concussion."

"I'm not sure that's the compliment you think it is."

I chuckle, squeezing her waist and pulling her just a bit closer

"Was this when you thought you were in heaven?" Abby asks.

"Just after that part. I looked at you and said to my myself . . . *Self, that girl there is something special. Something extraordinary. You're going to want to hold on to her.*"

She snorts against me, giggling, and I press my lips to her damp hair.

And I do want to hold on to Abby. Any which way I can.

ℭHAPTER THIRTEEN

Abby

*T*IC-TOC

It's not just the sex.

It's not just the plethora of pleasure-wracking orgasms Tommy can conjure like a magician with a flick of his hand. It's not just the fanny fun-times, the randy rides on the John Thomas Express, or any other ridiculous euphemism Etta would use.

It's more than that. *God help me.*

That realization didn't seep in gradually, the way you sink into sleep and slowly submerge into dreaming. It slammed in—like the steel grate of a lorry that unexpectedly rams into you from behind.

And it happened the night Maisy Adams died.

When I stepped out of the operating room broken and bleeding from the sharp shards of defeat and sorrow. And I stood there beside Dr. Dickmaster, cemented to the floor as he told Maisy's parents she was gone. That they had lost their daughter.

That *we* had lost her.

As I watched those poor people fall apart in front of me, the ache in my chest was so crushing I couldn't breathe—I didn't know if I would ever be able to breathe again.

And in that moment . . . all I wanted was him.

Tic-toc

That wonderful, infuriating rascal of a man.

I wanted to run to Tommy, throw myself against him, because he would make it better. I wanted to feel his arms around me and know through and through that he would keep all the bad away—he wouldn't even let it get close. I yearned for the soothing rumble of his voice, the warm sandalwood of his skin, the solace of that irresistible smile.

After I told him and we got absolutely sozzled and he held me all through the night, I awoke in the morning still feeling dreadful and yet . . . comforted. More in control, slightly less shattered by it all.

That's when I knew Tommy had become my refuge. Not just the impressive appendage between his legs—but him, the man.

Tic-toc

At first, I was not pleased.

I didn't have time for an attachment. For complications. To be mooning over him like some silly schoolgirl. I didn't have time to *need* him—to need anyone.

But the horror lasted only a moment.

Because I'm a surgeon.

And if I'm deep inside a patient's heart and the unforeseen happens—an unexpected bleed or complication—I can't run away or throw up my hands and say, "This wasn't supposed to happen. This isn't part of the deal." I have to address it, reevaluate and adapt to it.

I've decided to treat my own heart the same way.

By all accounts, the prognosis is good. I've been sharper, more sure of myself, more balanced and capable in the past few months than I can ever remember being in all the years before.

I've been . . . happy.

Tic-toc

I picture Tommy's smirk if he heard me make that admission.

Of course you're happy, lass—that's how my cock works. It makes everywhere it goes a very happy place.

Tic-toc

Telling him about Alistair Lipton was unplanned.

It's not something I think about anymore. It happened—the way Luke's heart condition happened—I don't dwell on how it might have altered me or changed the outcome of my life. I've moved past it.

But there was a comfort in telling Tommy, a sense of relief. Not because of the ravaged, murderous look that sprung up in his eyes—though that was nice to see—but because for so long I was all alone with it. Holding it close and tight, all by myself.

It felt freeing to share it with him, to know that I could. That I had truly put it behind me—like removing a scar from an already closed wound.

Tic-toc

And Tommy may be cocksure and teasing, but he's wanted me from the moment we met—he couldn't have been more upfront about that. And more than any part of who he is, Tommy Sullivan is a protector. A shield. A guarder of bodies and minds. I've seen that—I've felt it.

So I have to believe that whatever these feelings are and wherever they may lead . . . he'll be careful with me.

And for now, that's enough.

Tic-toc

"Did you hear me, Abigail?" My grandmother's voice cuts through my wandering thoughts.

Glancing up from my brunch plate at the Bumblebridge dining table, I find her looking at me expectantly. The rest of the collective is also here—my parents, Sterling and his wife and their wonder twins, and Athena and Jasper. Luke left for South America several weeks ago, but we text almost every day.

"No, I'm sorry, Grandmother. What were you saying?"

"I asked about your residency."

"It's going exceptionally well." I nod. "My confidence and skills are growing every day and I'm developing a very solid reputation with the supervising surgeons."

My mother's face softens behind her teacup. "That's wonderful to hear, darling."

Grandmother frowns. "Does that mean you'll be completing the program ahead of schedule?"

"No, but I've come to realize that's not really the most important thing. It's the experience that matters. Getting the most out of the program so I can become the best surgeon I know how to be."

I catch Father smiling as he reads the paper. "Well said, Abby."

Grandmother opens her mouth to reply, but my phone vibrates on the table and I hold up my finger. "Excuse me, this may be the hospital."

When I glance at the incoming message, I have to smother an immediate, giddy smile. I shield the screen with my palm to protect it from any prying eyes that may try to sneak a peek—and would end up thoroughly scandalized. Tommy is delightfully talented with dirty texts.

Godly Orgasm Giver: Are you still at your Granny's?

Me: Yes, we're just finishing up.

Then Tommy's next message comes through—and my smile dissolves.

Like a severed limb immersed in a vat of battery acid.

Godly Orgasm Giver: Good. I'll be there soon.

Panic punches into my veins in a frenzied rush, making my pulse sprint and my palms sweat.

Me: What do you mean?? You can't come here!

I've accepted the fact that I have an attachment to Tommy Sullivan that goes beyond the *boisterous boffing*. I'm even enjoying it. Telling my family, on the other hand?

That's a whole other kettle of stinky fish.

To be dealt with later—much, much later.

Godly Orgasm Giver: Are you ashamed of me?

Tommy's a man—every delicious inch of him. Rough and rugged, charming and demanding—and *proud*.

It's the pride part that I get stuck on. That makes my mouth go parched as I think of a way to reply that won't wound him.

But then he beats me to it.

Godly Orgasm Giver: I'm just messing with you. You can be ashamed all you like—I'm not offended.

Wanker.

Me: You can't pick me up here.

Godly Orgasm Giver: I'm nearly there already. Meet me out front. There's something I want to show you—you're going to like it.

Like one of Pavlov's randy dogs, sensual heat curls and coils low in my stomach. Because there has yet to be a single thing that Tommy has shown me that I don't like very much.

In the biblical sense.

But then a completely different thought occurs to me. And that heated desire immediately shifts to simmering frustration.

Me: Are you texting while you're driving??

Apparently, Tommy and his bodyguard brethren are trained to text without actually having to look at their phones, so they can communicate covertly with the device in their pocket.

But I've explained to him—*at length*—that that doesn't matter worth a damn.

I've informed him of the overwhelming statistics on the dangers of texting while operating a vehicle *and* I've disclosed my firsthand experiences of seeing the deadly carnage of such behavior during my emergency room rotations.

And still, after a weighted pause, he replies:

Godly Orgasm Giver: Maybe.

Me: Well, STOP IT!!

For a moment, the screen remains quiet . . . and then those sneaky little dots appear again.

Godly Orgasm Giver: I like it when you get all shouty caps at me—have I ever told you that? Very hot.

I'm going to revisit the idea of Tommy teaching me how to throw a punch. It would come in handy at moments just like this.

"Is everything all right, Abby?" my mother asks. "You're all flushed."

She examines me above her glasses like I'm an exhibit at a science fair or a bug under a microscope.

"I . . ."

Grogg, the butler, bends down and dips his large, square head towards my grandmother.

"A gentleman is out front, Lady Agatha . . ."

Oh no.

"On a motorbike."

OH NOOOO.

"Well, send him away." The Dowager Countess shoos her hand in the air, as countesses do. "We don't accept solicitations."

I scramble to my feet. "Actually, he's here for me."

I throw my tablet and phone and books into my satchel, to hasten my not-so-great escape.

"Pardon?" my father inquires.

"He?" my grandmother prods.

I swallow hard, rushing out the words. "Yes. He's a friend. I have to be going, so I messaged him for a lift."

My brother Sterling's eggs-Benedict-laden fork pauses midair on its way to his mouth.

"I didn't know you had the sort of friends who rode motorbikes."

"I didn't know you had friends," my sister Athena comments, not in a cruel way, but with sincere surprise.

I shrug, looping the strap of my satchel over my shoulder.

"Yes, well . . . you know . . ."

With that brilliant retort, I turn and walk out of the room.

I head towards the foyer, the heels of my knee-high boots clicking rapidly on the marble floor like a ticking time bomb. I yank open the giant front door and . . . come to an immediate stop on the veranda outside of it.

Because Tommy's there, down the long gray steps on the front drive, sitting easily astride a shiny contraption of chrome and steel like it was made for him, wearing work boots, snug blue jeans and a black leather jacket—looking so sinfully good it might actually be illegal.

A hazard to others. A moving violation. A beautiful disaster just waiting to happen.

I have to remind myself that I'm cross with him, and when I do, I march straight down the steps. His eyes alight on my boots, skirt and light gray sweater—the ensemble gives off an unintended "naughty schoolteacher" feel—and the corner of Tommy's wicked mouth hooks up accordingly.

"Hello, sweetheart."

"Are you mad?!"

He takes a moment to think it over.

"Not the last time I checked."

"What are you doing here?" I hold out my hands. "And what is this?"

"It's a motorbike."

"It's death on wheels."

He chuckles. "My mate James loaned it to me for the day. The hills are beautiful this time of year—I thought we'd take a ride together. You wanted stress relief, didn't you?" Tommy taps the shiny handlebar. "A ride on this is as stress-relieving as it gets—better than normal-bloke sex."

I peer at him. Do I want to know?

Apparently I do, because I hear myself asking, "Normal-bloke sex?"

"Yeah." He winks. "I mean it's not better than how I do it—obviously. But the way an average bloke has sex—this is definitely better."

I shake my head, folding my arms. "Do you have any idea how dangerous these things are? The statistics on motorbike fatalities are—"

Tommy covers my mouth with his hand.

His palm is warm, and so is his voice—a thick, sweet, honeyed tone.

"Do you trust me, Abby?"

After a moment, he takes his hand away and I gaze into those deep, dark eyes, falling into them so easily it should be frightening.

My answer is simple. True ones always are.

"I do."

Tommy smiles fully, and my stomach flutters with that lovely swirling sensation.

"Then climb on."

He places a helmet on my head, buckling the strap under my chin.

"And you might want to do it fast—your granny's coming."

I glance over my shoulder to see the whole family gathered outside the front of the door, a spectrum of curious and gobsmacked expressions plastered on their typically reserved faces. And my grandmother is indeed headed this way, her jeweled necklace jingling as she quickly descends the long slope of stone steps.

"Abigail!"

Her voice is high-pitched and harried—a tone I've never heard her use before, and one I'm not keen on exploring now.

"Right, then—have to be going!" I lift my hand and give them a thumbs-up. "Talk soon!"

Like a teenager running off with the town bad boy, I hike up my skirt and climb onto the motorbike behind Tommy. He clasps my hands together securely over his stomach.

"Hold on tight, lass."

I do just that—squeezing my arms around his solid frame and resting my cheek against the warm leather on his back as he revs the engine to life and we pull away with a roar that vibrates in my bones.

And as strange as it is—or maybe it's not strange at all—I've never felt safer.

———— ✿ ————

Tommy was right—the hills were beautiful, and the motorbike ride was exhilarating—though it's not something I'd want to do regularly. After riding for a few hours, we stopped to rest at a pretty glen in the middle of nowhere. Tommy brought a flannel blanket, wine, fruit and cheese, and we had a little picnic under a tree.

And then we were kissing and touching and the next thing I knew . . . all our clothes were gone. It was chilly, but Tommy kept me perfectly warm.

And that was beautiful too.

Three days later, I'm in my flat on my sofa, reviewing literature on the latest laparoscopic technology. Tommy's coming over in a few hours—with takeout dinner and his computer, because he's insisting I watch some American show from a few years back about a science teacher who goes into the methamphetamine business. Tommy swears that once I start watching, I won't be able to stop.

There's a knock on the door and I assume he's arrived early. But when I open it, it's not him standing on the other side.

"Grandmother." This is the first time she's been to my flat. It may be the first time she's been to this side of town, ever. "This is a surprise."

She strides in purposefully—that's how she is—every move predetermined and planned and for a specific reason. Her chin is up, her nose high as she stands in the middle of the room, glancing at the décor with dispassionate eyes.

I close the door and face her.

"What are you doing with that boy, Abby?"

For as long as I can remember, I've craved her approval. She's been my idol, my example—her control, her poise, her self-possession—everything I've always wanted to be.

"His name is Tommy Sullivan. He's the owner of S&S Securities, the bodyguard firm we hired a few—"

"I know *who* he is. That's not what I asked."

I straddle the truth, trying to call forth my mind-set from back when it all began.

"He's . . . we have an arrangement. It's not personal."

"When you were riding off with him on the back of that motorbike, it looked very personal to me." The disappointment in her tone vibrates through me, as powerfully as the motorbike's engine.

Then she straightens up, her expression hardening to a cold, commanding mask, like a sniper taking aim.

"You are to stop seeing him straightaway," she orders. "You have an unblemished family name to uphold—I'm not going to watch you sully it by running around with the help."

My eyes dart to hers. And a grade-A steel, the same kind used to make scalpels, fills my spine.

"I'm not a child—don't speak to me like one." I'm a doctor, a bloody surgeon, a fully grown woman. I have my own accomplishments, my own plans . . . my own life. "This conversation is inappropriate. I'm not discussing this with you."

She stays right where she is, like a mountain that can't be moved and knows it.

"I'll cut you off. You won't receive a penny from the family trust from this day forward."

Mettle, pluck and moxie are funny things. Sometimes they hide themselves so thoroughly you don't even know they're there.

Until they rise up—just when you need them most.

"Keep it. I don't need the family trust. I can support myself with my salary at the hospital just fine."

She's not surprised, her expression doesn't change; it's as if I've said what she already knew I would.

"And what about Tommy Sullivan? Can he support himself just fine as well?"

A dawning awfulness slithers through me, because a threat conveyed in an elegant, refined tone is still a threat.

"What do you mean?"

"From what I understand, this personal protection business of his is still just starting out. Among his caliber of clients, rampant and poisonous gossip is the best kind. A few well-placed words from me to the right people will kill his firm in its infancy. It won't be difficult."

"Words like what?"

"About his guards being untrustworthy, incompetent, drunk on the job."

My hands go numb and the color drains from my face.

"Why would you do that?"

"Because it is what's best for you, best for the family—and there is nothing I won't do for this family. You may not see that now, but when the day comes that you are a distinguished surgeon you will."

"You have it all wrong. He makes me better."

"Better at what?"

"Everything!"

"The fact that you actually believe that shows he's already done more damage than I suspected. You're becoming dependent on him."

"No." I shake my head. "That's not true."

Her green eyes glitter as she looks down on me, and her smile is pulled tight with an aged bitterness.

"You remind me so much of myself, Abby—you always have. When I was a bit younger than you are now, I was studying advanced archeology—did you know that?"

I shake my head, because our family doesn't talk about such things. We don't talk at all.

"I was brilliant at it; I had so many plans. Places I would go, papers I would publish, discoveries I would make. And then . . . I met your grandfather and everything changed. We were very different people, opposites really, but that just made falling in love with him all the more thrilling. When we first married, I tried to carry on with my studies and career, but it's impossible to walk down diverging paths at the same time. Choices must be made. Sacrifices. And for women and wives and mothers—the sacrifices will always fall on us. I won't let you make the same mistakes I did."

"But it's not your decision to make!" I shout. I clasp my hands together beseechingly. "Please, Grandmother, don't—"

"Stop." Her voice strikes out like a whip. "I have neither the time nor the stomach for dramatics. Your singular talent has always been your practicality. Your ability to see your shortcomings clearly. Don't let that fail you now."

Lash, lash, lash.

For a moment breath escapes me, taking my words with

it. And I don't know what I would say even if I could, but the Dowager Countess doesn't give me the opportunity.

"If you care for this boy—even just a little—you will end your relationship with him immediately. I'll know if you don't. And when I ruin his business prospects, I'll be sure he is informed that your stubbornness was the cause. Which I suspect will resolve the situation to my satisfaction anyway."

It hurts to hate someone that you love—but right now, in this moment, it's not hard.

She moves towards the door, sparing me a stiffly benevolent look before she goes.

"Chin up, Abby. You'll thank me for this one day, I promise."

———❖———

I compartmentalize at first—the way good surgeons are able to do. It still doesn't come naturally to me, but I'm getting better at it. I push it away, lock it down, bury it deep until I barely sense that it's there.

Then, clinically, coldly—like I'm running through the pros and cons of treatment options—I consider my choices.

A) I could tell the Dowager Countess to stuff it and let the chips fall where they may. The only problem with that is I care about Tommy—he's so easy to care about. And he's been good to me—caring and passionate and so sweet my heart aches. And she'll do what she said, I'm certain of that. And he'll be harmed, he'll pay the price—because of me. And I think about my own career, all the hours and years of work I've put in and I know how devastating it would feel if that was all taken away on a whim.

B) I could tell Tommy what my grandmother is threatening. I probably *should* tell him—I already trust him more than I've ever trusted anyone, and he deserves to know. And what will a man like

Tommy Sullivan do in face of her threats? He'll tell her to fuck off—and to keep fucking off, and after she's done fucking off she should fuck off a bit more. I can practically hear him already. And then again—he'll be harmed, he'll pay the price—because of *me*.

C) I could do as she told me. It will hurt, badly . . . but this was never supposed to be anything. It's not his fault I've come to depend on him, want him, need him. It was an arrangement; that's what we said. It was always going to end at some point—wasn't it? And this way, if I just do it, choke it down and get it over with, Tommy is *not* harmed, he *doesn't* pay any price—he walks away unscathed and free of me.

When he strolls through the door a few hours later with his laptop and a brown paper bag of food in his hands, I take extra time to look at him. His smooth grace as he slips out of his coat, the stunning lines and proportions of his body, the strong angles of his cheekbones and jaw.

I stand up from the sofa and go to him, resting my hands on his corded shoulders and reaching up on my toes to kiss him. It's not desperate or frantic like the night we lost Maisy.

It's slow and deep and savoring—a kiss I'll remember.

Tommy sucks on my upper lip, stroking it wonderfully with his tongue. Then he pulls back, gazing down at me with a slight tilt of his head.

"Are you all right?"

"Yes," I lie.

He tucks a strand of my hair gently behind my ear.

"Did something happen at the hospital?"

"No." I stare at his sternum, running my palm back and forth across his chest, committing the warm, solid feel of him to memory. "I just want you."

His eyes go heated and hungry at my words. Tommy pulls me to him and we're kissing and tugging at the annoying barrier of our clothes. And I let myself drown in him—slowly dragging my lips and tongue across his collarbone, his chest, down his bunching abdominals . . . and lower. I delight in the taste of his skin, in the way his hot, silken thickness fills my mouth, in the feel of his fingers clenching desperately in my hair.

And though I want to relish each moment, I'm swept up in him, in the blissful blur of sensations and want and piercing pleasure so deep it's almost painful.

We end up in my bed, a writhing mass of moans and lips and clasping limbs. Tommy's breath is a sharp rasp against my ear—whispering beautiful, filthy words that make my skin tingle and my head light. And I kiss him and kiss him, pouring all my feelings—all the words I can't say—into the wet dance of our mouths. I don't want it to end, but it does—in a perfect swirling rush of pleasure and groans, thundering heartbeats and pulsing, contracting muscles.

After, we lie next to each other, and I look at him some more—soaking up the image of him in the bed beside me.

Perhaps in a bid to stave off the inevitable, I ask, "How's work?"

He glances over at me and smiles.

"Things are good. The crop of new hires has potential and we've got a nice stable of recurring clients."

"You're building a reputation," I say flatly.

"Yeah."

"And that's important in your field, isn't it?"

"Sure." Tommy nods. "Clients need to know they can trust us, count on us—that's everything."

Gangrene is a potentially fatal condition that results from a lack of blood and oxygen to an extremity, causing the tissue to die. It can be treated with antibiotics, but if the affliction is too far gone the only way to effectively cure it is amputation.

You lose the limb to save the life.

Right now, I'm gangrenous to Tommy. And the surest way to save him . . . is to cut myself off.

I sit up straight, and it's a miracle that I'm able to, with the heavy weight of remorse that presses on my chest like a boulder.

"I can't do this anymore. We can't do this anymore."

I don't look at him, but I hear his voice behind me as I rise and wrap myself in my robe, tying the belt tightly.

"What?"

"Our arrangement. It's over. I'd . . . I'd like you to leave now."

I head out of the room—moving swiftly, like I'm in triage. It's all movement and training and instincts. No thoughts or feelings allowed.

Slice.

Suction.

Clamp.

"Abby! Where the fuck are you going?"

Tommy follows me to the parlor, watches as I gather his clothes from the floor—pushing them at him.

"It's been wonderful, truly. Exactly what I needed." I stare at the floor and I sound like a robot—an idiotic fucking robot. "But it's run its course."

"No, it hasn't. It's just getting started," he says stubbornly. "Just . . . just slow down a fucking minute."

Tommy grips my shoulders, holding me in place, and dips down to try and catch my eyes.

"Why are you doing this?"

Separate the limb.

Cauterize the veins.

Clean.

"I'm starting my fourth year. It's going to be very demanding. I need to focus."

"Then we'll see each other a bit less. We can do that. I won't tempt you as much with dirty texts, I swear."

He's trying to tease me, to cajole me back—and it's so hard. Every cell in my body is screaming to hug him and hold him and say yes to anything he offers.

"No." I shake my head. "That's not going to work for me."

Stitch.

Stitch.

"I'm done, Tommy. I need this to be done. Please go."

Close.

Wrap.

Tommy puts on his clothes and his shoes but doesn't move towards the door.

"Abby, listen to me. If you would just—"

I close my eyes, even though I wasn't looking at him.

"We said there wouldn't be any drama—no hard feelings. That's what we agreed—you agreed." I point at him. "You promised."

Yes, I'm using his integrity against him and, yes, it's unfair—but necessary. Because I need him to leave. I won't be able to go through with it if I have to look at him, smell him, feel him close to me for much longer.

I pick up his computer from the table and his coat by the door and press them into his hands.

"Abby—"

I look up into his eyes one final time.

"Goodbye, Tommy. Thank you . . . but goodbye."

His brow is furrowed with so much worry, but he doesn't push me.

Because I've asked him to leave and he's honorable enough to do that for me, even if he doesn't understand. His gaze drifts over my face, like he's memorizing it, and he touches my hair, leans

DIRTY CHARMER

down and presses a single soft kiss against my lips that almost breaks me.

Then he's walking to the door and stepping over the threshold into the hall. At the last moment, Tommy turns back, his mouth opening to say something that I won't be strong enough to hear.

So I slam the door in his face.

Classy.

And I lock the bolt.

I rest my forehead on the door, my breaths coming quick and harsh. And I can feel him standing on the other side in that strange way human beings can sense the presence of another person even when you can't see them. As a cacophony of opposing wishes echoes in my head. *Just go, stay, leave, please don't go . . .*

Then, after an interminable moment—he's gone.

Tommy

What in the holy fuck just happened?

That's the question beating like a drum in my head after I leave Abby's. I head home, but I don't stay there. Because I can see the hospital from my bedroom and my sheets still smell like her.

I go to the shop instead.

And proceed to get completely sloshed.

I drink vodka straight from the bottle until it's empty and I can't see straight. So I don't do something really stupid—like go back to Abby's door and ask for another chance. Another night.

I tell myself it's the unexpectedness of it that makes it hard. The sudden end that's making me feel like a hollowed-out husk. That I didn't know the last time was the last time . . . and that's why I miss her already.

161

At some point I pass out on the sofa in my office, on my back, my arm slung over my face and a pitiful playlist I won't remember compiling playing on repeat from my phone.

In the morning, that's how the lads find me.

"Is he breathing?" I hear Owen ask beyond my still closed eyes.

"Breathing? He's snoring loud enough to wake the dead," Walter replies. "Are you deaf?"

"Is that a Milli Vanilli song playing on his phone?" Gus wonders.

It is. "Girl I'm Gonna Miss You." A classic.

"Maybe he's trying to tell us something."

"Yeah," Harry agrees, disgustedly. "Like he wants us to shoot him."

CHAPTER
FOURTEEN

Tommy

AND THAT, BOYS AND GIRLS, IS HOW I BECOME A stalker.

It starts with the path Abby takes to ride her bicycle to the hospital in the morning. I hang around, stationed in the shadows of an alley along the route, just to glimpse her as she passes. A few times a week, at night, I wait across from her flat until the light goes on inside—so I know she's home safely.

When it's too cold and icy for her bike, I sit sentry in an alcove at her Tube station. Sometimes I see her there, looking beautiful but tired, maybe even a bit sad—though that could be my stupidly hopeful, James-Blunt-listening, stalkering imagination running wild. Some days, I don't spot her at all.

But she never sees me. I make sure of it.

I know it's stupid and pathetic . . . I just can't seem to make myself stop.

Until one night, a few weeks later, when my sister Janey comes by my place and corners me. For an intervention.

Janey's the only one in my family who knows that Abby Haddock exists. The only one who knows me well enough to understand that while I said all the right things when I first told her about Abby—that it was casual and no-strings, a fuck of convenience—the fact that I was saying anything at all already meant it was more.

My sister's eyes are a hard, impenetrable wall of light green, without a speck of sympathy. And that's good. Because right now, I'm just barely holding it together—I don't think I could handle her pity.

"Why her?" Janey asks me. "What is it about this girl that you can't shake off?"

It's a good question. One I've asked myself more than once. What is it about a person that hooks the heart and keeps you tied to them even after they've walked away?

And the answer is . . . I don't know.

It's not just one identifiable thing. It's everything—Abby's beauty and intelligence and her refined demeanor. It's her heat and her heart and the vulnerability that she hides so desperately . . . that she's only showed to me.

And it's because at some point, all the parts that make her up— the frustrating fractures and the shy, sweet tender bits . . . it felt like she became mine.

Mine to protect and cherish, to lead and to follow.

And I really fucking liked feeling like Abby Haddock belonged to me.

"You have to let it go, Tommy. She's done with you—that's what she said. She hasn't reached out . . . you have to move on."

I give my sister a nod. And from that point on, I give it a go.

I stop checking my phone like a lovesick twat every ten minutes. I stop finding excuses to venture toward Abby's side of town. I throw myself into work—signing up to guard a Wessconian banker traveling to Dubai for a month, and when I come back, picking up extra hours from Winston guarding at the palace. When I'm not sleeping, I'm working—moving—training the new hires to be extra thorough, completing projects around the shop, staying busy every second of every day.

On the outside I'm all me—cracking jokes, drinking, laughing—all the things I did before.

I start smoking again, and it feels bloody good.

And maybe . . . a bit spiteful.

But inside, in my head, late at night when the quiet wraps its hands around me and strangles—I'm still stuck on her. That doesn't really change.

I think about her, picture her, dream of her—the vibrant silk of her hair, the sharpness of her eyes, the "O" of her pretty mouth when I made her moan and gasp. I toss off to the memory of that sound—the feel of her surrounding me, tight and wet and perfect.

I wonder where she is and what she's up to. I worry that she's sad or lonely . . . and I worry that she's not. I'm able to concentrate on work, focus when I need to—but Abby's always there in the background.

The white noise of my life.

And the cavern where my heart beats—that doesn't change either. It drowns in the same hollowed-out, gutted sensation, every bit as fresh and empty as the day I forced my feet to walk away from her door. The awful ache doesn't ease, and it doesn't mend.

And after the days drag into weeks, and the weeks blend into months—I start to believe it never will.

———— ❖ ————

"Hey, Tommy—that girl over there is looking at you."

Willis is our newest hire. He's a good lad—tough, loyal—if a little on the dense side. It's Saturday night and we're all at Katy's Pub, drinking to him completing his training this week.

I glance over my shoulder at a dark-haired vixen with a heart-shaped red mouth giving me the eyes. And it's like my whole body just sort of . . . shrugs . . . without a scrap of interest.

Fucking hell.

"So she is."

Willis leans forward, his young blue eyes wide and stunned.

"Are you practicing to be a monk or something?"

I chuckle dryly. "Nah—she's just not my type. I'm selective."

I prefer brilliant, frustrating, emotionally stunted redheads with legs for days, heartbreaking eyes, and a pussy that will make you fall to your knees and believe in God.

And my own hand, of course—Righty and I have never been so close.

"Willis," Owen calls, "come on, we're playing darts."

The boy goes off, leaving me and Bea alone at the table.

No one could ever accuse life of being short on irony, that's for damn sure. Because while the only reason they crossed paths was when Abby came to Katy's that night seeking me out, Harry's still in deep with Henrietta and Bea is still hooking up hard with that Kevin guy. I haven't asked either of them for intel on Abby—because they work for me and I refuse to come off like a total fucking simp.

I'm pretty sure Harry is oblivious to the fact that there was anything going on between me and Abby anyway. Henrietta's not the type to tell him dick—that one's strong on the girl-code of silence, I can tell. Kevin's a different story. His sort may be aloof and quiet on the outside, but when he feels like talking, he's going to talk to someone he's screwing.

To Bea.

Her eyes are heavy on me from across the table—in a way that tells me she knows something.

"Kevin said Abby's been working like a beast lately. She's practically living at the hospital these days."

The information prickles at me—like an invisible hand poking a hat pin at my heart.

I take a long drag from my pint.

"Good for her. That's exactly what she wanted."

"He's worried about her."

I shake my head. "Not my problem, Bea. Hasn't been my problem for a while."

We have now moved into the bitter portion of our programming, in case you hadn't noticed.

"I know," she hedges. "But do you think, maybe—"

A shout from the dartboard side of the room cuts off whatever Bea was about to suggest.

"Son of a whore!"

"Shit," I murmur, darting up from the table.

Because Owen and Gus were playing darts with Willis—but they were showing him the version that involves knives. And the handle of one of those knives is currently sticking out of Willis.

Not his hand, mind you—it's imbedded in his fucking chest—about two inches below his collarbone. Way too close to his heart for comfort.

He reaches for the handle, but I grab onto his forearm before he can grasp it.

"If you yank the blade out it might cause more damage than it did going in. And relax your arm—don't jostle about—you don't want to nick an artery."

If he hasn't already.

"Ah, fuckin' hell," Willis groans. "If I bleed to death, my mum's going to be so pissed."

Yeah—I get that.

"Really sorry, Willis," Owen says contritely from behind my shoulder. "That one got away from me."

Gus hands me gauze from the first-aid kit that's no longer behind the bar, and though there's not a lot of blood seeping out, I carefully pack it around the handle to hold it stable.

"You're gonna need a doctor," Gus tells Willis.

"I don't know any doctors," he replies.

And the lovely white noise that's always on the periphery of my thoughts comes roaring to the forefront.

"I do."

———— ✦ ————

Abby

Life after Tommy Sullivan is different than it was before him. Quieter, calmer—grayer. It's like a tree that's faded from summer to winter—the tree's the same, the same branches, same trunk, but it's bare. No foliage to decorate it, to give it color.

I make a concentrated effort to shake off the funk that's shrouded me since the day I kicked him out of my flat. I consider getting a pet—a cat or a pretty bird or a rowdy puppy that will keep me on my toes. But I don't have time to care for a pet properly.

So . . . I buy plants.

Lush, sturdy green plants with vibrant multihued flowers that add a spark of color to my flat. What did Tommy call it? *Lifeless.* Right.

I put the plants on a on a wrought-iron shelf in the front parlor by the window that I bought just for them. I read all the books about them—I water them, feed them, fertilize them, sometimes I bloody sing to them.

And one by one, apparently—I kill them.

No matter what I do, they wither and die and they're not shy about it.

One night after our shift, Etta comes over to my place with a box of wine and stands at the shelf, staring at the vegetation morgue.

"Holy Morticia Adams!" She fingers one crispy leaf. "Are they supposed to look like this?"

"No," I reply. "It's like they came in here and lost the will to live. I don't know what to do about it."

Etta smirks. "Get a sign above your door—'Abandon All Hope—Ye Plants Who Enter.'"

I stick my tongue out at her.

—✦—

With the plant companion plan an epic fail, I try another tactic.

Chocolate.

I eat it with every meal. And I go for long walks in the early evening when I'm not at the hospital to offset the calories. In the hopes of tricking my brain into producing the joyful endorphins that a word or a text from Tommy Sullivan used to inspire so easily.

One evening, just past six, I happened to walk by Paddy's Pub, and glanced through the large picture window totally by chance . . . and Tommy was there. Looking achingly handsome and carefree at the bar, his head thrown back in an easy laugh, not a worry in the world.

And he wasn't alone.

There was a fit-looking man beside him with a petite, obviously pregnant, beautiful woman at his side. I surmised from my past conversations with Tommy that they were his partner Logan and his little wife, Ellie.

But next to Tommy, leaning into him in a familiar way, was another woman—stunning and voluptuous, with bouncy blond hair and a bright, broad smile.

And I couldn't seem to move.

I stood there, watching them, steeped in a dreadful, self-flagellatory, pining pain.

But, as much as it hurt to watch them—because I wanted to

be the one in there beside him—there was a part of me that was glad. Tommy had brought excitement and spontaneity and comfort into my life. And he deserved to be happy.

I stopped going for walks after that.

I refocus all my energy on work instead. Back to the grind—striving to be the best—to be exceptional. I take extra shifts at the hospital—I read more, study harder, go through pounds of chicken's feet every week practicing my surgical techniques.

What I don't do is attend the family brunches at Bumblebridge.

I make excuses, telling them I don't have the time, my schedule is too full. Luke texts me that my parents have covertly texted him—inquiring as to whether it's really work that's keeping me away or if I'm involved with someone. A certain man on a motorbike, perhaps.

But the Dowager Countess isn't the only one who doesn't have the stomach for things. I don't trust myself to see her again and remain civil. While the first rule of being a Haddock is to be extraordinary, civility and composure are absolutely the second.

A few weeks into the start of my fourth year of residency, the hospital hires a new resident—a fifth year, named Riley Bowen. He's an excellent surgeon and movie-star good-looking, with dark blond hair and broad shoulders that get all the nurses chattering.

On his second day at the hospital, he asks me out to dinner.

It's not difficult to turn him down.

While I like him well enough as a coworker, his arrogance rubs me the wrong way. It's so starkly different from Tommy's. His cocky swagger came from a steady, capable, calm confidence that was irresistibly attractive. Riley's egotism feels like a flex of superiority—a need to show off—because he has something to prove.

I wonder if this is how it's going to be now—that I'll compare every man I meet to Tommy Sullivan and find them hopelessly lacking.

For ever and ever, the end.

One evening, I'm at the nurse's desk on the surgical floor, adding some final notes to a patient's chart before heading over to scrub in on a procedure. I hand the chart to nurse Betty and then I look up.

And my whole world stands still.

Because Tommy's here. Really, truly, here. Just a few feet away.

"Hi," he says softly.

"Hello."

It's been so long since I've seen him—except in my dreams. My entire being soaks him up like a parched sponge suddenly submerged in cool water. The scruff on his jaw is thicker, his dark hair a bit longer, there's an intensity in his eyes that wasn't there before—but his face, his hands, the swells of muscle beneath his gray shirt are every bit as perfect as they always were.

I move towards him—smiling.

"How are you? You look . . ." *Terrible. Wonderful. Beautiful.* ". . . well."

"You too." His eyes devour me, up and down. "You look lovely."

He says it like he means it—even though I'm in the middle of a fifteen-hour shift with my hair twisted up into a messy bun, wearing shapeless dark blue scrubs.

But it doesn't feel awkward between us—I could melt into him like no time has passed at all.

The stilted sensation comes from not being able to do that. From having to hold myself back—maybe we both are.

"What are you doing here?" I ask.

He tosses a thumb over his shoulder. "I brought one of my guards to the emergency room."

"What are his symptoms?"

"Bleeding. The boys were messing around. He got stabbed."

I think a bodyguard's definition of "messing around" is different from the rest of world's.

"They say he'll be fine."

"Oh good." I nod. "That's good."

"Yeah." His throat ripples as he swallows. And I remember kissing his throat—the taste of his skin on my lips and tongue. I stare at his mouth, his face—there's nowhere else I want to look ever again.

Tommy starts. "I wanted to—"

But then Riley is there, like a wedge, angling himself between us.

"Dr. Sealing is waiting for us, Abby. We have to scrub in."

"Yes, I know," I snap. "I'll be right along."

Riley glances at Tommy a moment. Then he walks away and I catch Tommy's glaring gaze following his retreating form.

His eyes darken back on me—possessive and questioning.

I shake my head. "He and I aren't . . . there's nothing—"

"Right." Tommy nods sharply. "Well . . . you're busy. I'll leave you to it." His voice goes low and rough. "It was good to see you, Abby."

Then he turns, walking away towards the lift.

Leaving.

Panic claws at my throat and lodges there.

"Tommy!"

He turns back as I rush up to him. I lift my hand to touch him, but stop at the last moment. Because if I touch him . . . I'm very sure I'll fall apart right here in the hall.

"I was abrupt the last time we saw each other. I've regretted that so much." I lick at my lips, buying time, searching for the right words. There's a wet, salty taste in the back of my mouth and a burning in my eyes.

"I hope life is kind to you. I wish that for you . . . every single day."

His jaw goes tight, and he glances down at his shoes, nodding.

"All right."

I give him a small smile, but if feels sad on my lips.

"Take care of yourself."

"You too, lass."

And then the lift door opens and he steps inside—and he's gone all over again.

CHAPTER
FIFTEEN

Tommy

SEEKING ABBY OUT AT THE HOSPITAL WAS NOT ONE OF MY better ideas. Now I'm like a once-sober junkie who fell off the wagon for a night—and my blood has been screaming for another fix for the past week.

It wouldn't be so difficult if she didn't still want me. But she does—I'm certain of it. The way she looked at me, the way she breathed, how her voice trembled—Christ, I could smell the desire coming off her as sweet as the scent of apples on her skin.

I could push her—I'm sure of that too. I could go to her place, just walk in and lock the door behind me. I could kiss her, take her mouth—take any part of her I want—and she would let me.

Or I could bring her to my place—keep her there—tie her to the bed, make her talk, make her tell me what's happening in that twisted-up little mind of hers.

I could make her love it so easily. Have her begging for it—for me.

Don't think I haven't thought about it.

But I don't want her that way. It's not that I mind chasing Abby—I still like the chase. But I've been pushing her, backing her up, breaking her down since the day we met. It's not just about us screwing anymore—it's different now. More.

So I have to know it comes from her. That she wants me,

174

DIRTY CHARMER

needs me, that she feels what I feel all on her own. Not because I've talked her into it, or teased her or fucked her into it—but because she's right here in this with me.

That's the only way it'll ever work between us, the only way it will last.

I shove thoughts of Abby out of my mind, because I need to focus on the here and now. I'm working with Gordon, guarding an international shipping magnate and his wife who've come to Wessco to attend a world economics forum. Tonight they're at a posh banquet hall for the party that caps off the three-day summit. All the bigwigs are here—energy moguls, media billionaires, royalty.

From my position against the wall, I spot Duchess Olivia all dolled up and gorgeous in a shimmery gown beside her tuxedo-clad husband, Prince Nicholas. I was on Nicholas Pembrook's personal detail for a few years before he went to New York and met Olivia Hammond . . . and the whole world changed. I stayed on with them as they dated and were married, and had two little ones—twins, Langdon and Lilliana—only leaving his employ when Logan resigned to be with Ellie and we started our own shop.

Olivia catches my eye and smiles, giving me a wave. I lift my chin and throw her a wink in reply.

Then I return my attention back to my bald-headed mark as he drinks champagne and chortles with the other nobs.

And as I once explained to Abby, I don't listen to the clutter of conversation that surrounds me. What they're saying neither interests me nor matters. I scan the area around my client, eyeing the entrances, the bustling waiters and other guests—searching for anything that my gut says is off.

But then, through the verbal din, I hear something. Two words.

They capture my attention and snap my head around.

"Alistair Lipton . . ."

And I think of Abby in that tub—her skin ashen and her voice small. I see that awful, flat expression on her face and the haunting that was in her beautiful eyes.

I try to shake it off, to let it go—because it's not mine to deal with. *She's* not mine.

And that lasts for all of two seconds.

Then—*fuck it.*

And I'm speaking into the microphone at my wrist that's connected to the piece in Gordon's ear.

"My man's on your six—keep an eye on him. I need to take care of something."

"You what?" Gordon's confused voice surges back, because this is a break in protocol. It goes against all our training—and I can't make myself give a single shit.

"Tommy, what—"

I pull the piece from my ear and slip it in my pocket as I move to the group of five tuxes where the name was uttered. I push my way through to the center, getting right up in his space, nose to nose—I don't know how I know it's him, I just do.

"Alistair Lipton?"

"Yes?" is what comes back—indifferent and disdainful.

He's got the kind of face that's easy to hate, and even easier to break. Translucent skin and thin bone structure, wide-set eyes—like prey—classic but oddly arranged features that hint at a bloodline of inbreeding.

"Do I know you?"

Every muscle in my body is coiled rock-hard and tight, ready to spring. But I'm not in a rage, not out of control.

There's a cold calm that settles over you before you annihilate a man.

Almost a centered sort of peace that comes from knowing exactly what you're about to do and the innate awareness that it needs to be done.

"No. We have a friend in common. Abigail Haddock."

And it's all there on his face—plain as fuck. No one else sees it, but I do. The flash of recognition—the flinch of cornered fear and cowardly guilt—not over the act itself but at the worry of being found out.

He remembers. He knows what he did. He's known it all this time—and he knew it then. And now he knows I know it too.

And that's good.

I want him to understand what it's about. And if it's the last moments of understanding this worthless fuck gets to have on this earth, I want him to know . . . that it's for her.

I swing my arm quick, landing the brick of my fist in the center of his face—feeling the brittle crunch and the wet give beneath my knuckles. He goes down and I go down after him—and time loses meaning.

It all blends together in a symphony of swinging and pounding and punching, splitting skin and shattered teeth, shouts and screams, and pulverizing vengeance.

Rough, faceless hands tear me off him too soon and drag me outside, throwing me on the wet pavement. They twist my arms back and clamp cuffs around my wrists—and I'm hauled into the back cage of a police car.

As I sit there catching my breath, my ability to think normally again returns. At least normal for me.

My first thought is—Lo's gonna be royally pissed. What I did was stupid, and irresponsible, and possibly ruining.

My second thought is—completely fucking worth it.

I've never actually seen the inside of a jail cell. That's not to say I haven't done things to deserve getting locked up in one . . . I've just never gotten caught.

It's not so bad.

There's heat, decent lighting, working plumbing—that's better than a few of the houses around my neighborhood. The wooden bench I'm sitting on is hard, but my arse has sat on worse.

And the company's colorful, to help pass the time. There's Alvin who's in for boosting a car, Forrest who apparently tried to strangle his tool of a brother-in-law, Mickey who got busted for possession, a bloke who calls himself Jinx who reeks of trash and is too drunk to stand, and a poor old gent named Horris whose only offense seems to be talking out loud to several people who aren't there.

They'll release me on my own recognizance in the morning. I'm sure as shit not going to call my mum to bail me out—my present company is much more pleasant. And Ellie's in the home stretch of her pregnancy, so I don't want to bother Logan at this time of night.

When Jinx staggers a bit too close my way, I warn him, "If you vomit on me, mate, I'm going to have to snap your neck."

And he lurches in the other direction.

Then I settle in, tilting my head back against the wall and counting the water stains on the ceiling.

That's when an officer appears on the outside of the bars.

"Sullivan—you're out."

Maybe Gordon and the lads chipped in to spring me.

But when I follow the cop out to the processing desk, it's Prince Nicholas and Olivia who are there waiting for me. I look between them—in their fancy eveningwear—standing out in the downtown police station like a sixth toe on a left foot.

"What are you doing here?"

"What do you mean, *what are we doing here?*" Olivia asks—that hint of New York still clinging to her words. "Did you think we were going to just leave you in here?" She dips her head, her blue eyes dark with worry. "Are you okay? What happened tonight, Tommy . . . that's not like you."

It was always a privilege to guard them—it would've been an honor to take a bullet for them. Not because they're royalty—but because they're good. It's fills them both to the brim, through and through.

"Yeah." I clear my throat. "I'm fine. Thank you."

As the clerk hands me my belongings, Nicholas shakes the police captain's hand. "I appreciate your assistance."

He gives a shallow bow to them both. "Happy to be of service, Your Highnesses."

The driver—one of Winston's palace boys—leads us out the back to the waiting limousine.

Once we're inside and moving, I ask Prince Nicholas, "How much do I owe you for the bond?"

He shakes his head. "No bond. The charges have been dropped."

"How'd you manage that?"

"With a phone call. To Alistair Lipton's father, Sir Aloysius. The man's a full-on prick, but that's how these things work. I promised him a favor, to be determined later, in exchange for his son not pressing charges. So . . . what you owe me is an explanation as to why I had to make a deal with the devil. Why'd you attack Lipton?"

My jaw locks up tight. "I can't say."

Nicholas's gray-green eyes pin me hard.

"That's not good enough, Tommy."

I rub the back of my neck, giving him what I can without betraying Abby.

"He hurt someone I care about."

"Who?"

"I can't tell you that—it's not my story to tell." My voice goes low and solemn. "But I swear to you, he deserved it. I swear to God."

The Prince knows me well enough to understand I don't swear to God lightly. And if I do, it's not just something I say—it's something I mean, body and soul.

He holds my eyes for a moment, and then he nods.

"Are you sure you're okay?" Olivia hands me a cloth napkin filled with ice from the bar for my hand. "It looked like you were locked in there with some pretty rough characters."

I snort—she was always a cute one. Prince Nicholas thinks so too, chuckling sweetly at his wife.

"He *is* the rough character, love. They were locked in there with *him*."

Olivia rolls her eyes at us both.

And then we're pulling up to the curb in front of my building.

Nicholas pauses a moment, recognition rising in his eyes as they're trained on something outside the window behind me. Then he lifts his chin.

"Tommy . . . you have a visitor."

I turn my head, and she's there. Standing outside on the pavement, pale and perfect, her hair a halo of burning gold beneath the streetlamp.

I quietly thank Nicholas and Olivia again and step out from the car, closing the door behind me and giving a nod to the driver before he pulls away.

Then my eyes are on Abby and her alone.

The wet mist clings to her wool coat, glittering like a dusting of diamonds. She gazes at me long and a little desperately—like she's trying to absorb the image of me—keep it for later.

"What are you doing here, Abby?"

"News travels fast. News about Alistair Lipton getting beaten to a bloody pulp travels at warp speed."

I nod.

"You did that for me?" she asks softly. "You hurt him . . . for me?"

My throat aches with the weight of words, with all the things I feel for her.

"I wanted to kill him for you."

Her breath shudders as she inhales and her green eyes shimmer with wetness.

"But why? We're not together, if we ever were. We're finished now."

I shake my head, drifting closer.

"See, that's the thing—we don't feel finished. Not to me." I splay my hand on my chest, over my heart. "Not in here."

Slowly Abby smiles even while a tear spills over, slipping down her cheek. She picks up my hand, stroking her thumb gently across the bruised knuckles like she wants to smooth the hurt away.

Then she dips her head and kisses me there, whisper-soft and infinitely tender.

"We don't feel finished to me either."

And that's when I know. That's when I'm sure.

Me and Abby . . . we're never going to be finished.

CHAPTER
SIXTEEN

Abby

INSIDE TOMMY'S BEDROOM, HE KISSES ME SLOW, cradling my face and stroking my cheek.

How did I ever go so long without this? Without him.

Our clothes are unbuttoned and skimmed away gently. And it all feels new—a wondrous discovery of warm skin and soft touches—and yet beautifully remembered. I relish the sharp intake of his breath that I know will come when I run my tongue across his throat and slide my hand down his abdomen.

A long moan seeps from my lips when he moves behind me, pressing his chest to my back and coasting his lips across my shoulder, scraping and nipping at the sensitive skin.

We fall to the bed, molded together, all kissing and whispering and sliding caresses. Every nerve ending is awake and alive and pleading.

Yes, there.

Please, like that.

Don't stop, never stop.

And the need weaves around us both—the craving for closer and deeper and more. To take and keep, ruin and wreck, forever and always.

My back arches from the bed when he glides his thick fullness inside me. It's been so long, but there's no pain—only the snug, pressing surge and the thrill of being filled and connected to him in every way.

My breasts tingle where they rub Tommy's chest as he moves above me, over me, steadily stroking the swollen pleasure points within me. I lift my hips, rotating in that matching rhythm; I grasp at his back, holding him tenderly, and press my lips into his hair.

"I missed you," I whisper, my voice reedy. "I missed you so much."

Tommy straightens his arms, drawing my eyes to his, keeping the smooth pace of his pushing and retreating hips. And his face is filled with such affection—so much tender, sweet adoration— my vision goes blurry with tears.

Because no one has ever looked at me like that before. No one has ever made me feel all the things he makes me feel. My heart pounds and my breath races with the joy of it. Of being cherished and wanted—and I know he sees those same emotions reflected in my eyes.

The swells of Tommy's arms tighten with exertion and his thrusts turn more demanding. I run my palms down his biceps— because they're beautiful—*he* is beautiful like this. Lost in the moment, in the thunder of this passion.

I scrape his waist with my nails, making him groan, and the pure masculine sound makes my muscles contract, squeezing around him.

And I feel it building inside me, heavy and full and blindingly good.

"So good," I pant, "so close . . ."

But I don't have to tell him; he already knows. He feels it too.

Tommy dips his head and takes my mouth—harsh and ravenous—devouring my lips. I grip his sides and angle my hips for his pounding thrusts. I press my knees against his rib cage and lock my legs around his lower back—pulling him in—needing more and more and all of him.

With a final push, he plants himself in deep and the dam breaks. Waves of wet, white pleasure crash over us, through us. I go limp, drowning in the ecstasy, letting the current take me. Tommy tilts his head back, his perfect face twisting with carnal rapture, rasping my name like a hallowed prayer.

"Abby, Abby, Abby . . ."

———✥———

The next morning, after the deepest, deadest sleep I've had in three months, I open my eyes to the sight of Tommy Sullivan gazing down at me. His smile is tender—making him look young and handsome and boyish, like a lad who got exactly what he was wishing for all year for Christmas.

"Hi."

"Hi."

I reach up, scratching my palm against the morning bristles on his jaw. Then I tell him the truth, and nothing but the truth.

"My grandmother's going to try and ruin you. That's what she said—why I kicked you out that day."

I cover my face with my hands. "God, saying it out loud makes it sound like some bad reinterpretation of a Shakespearean tragedy."

I relay the whole conversation to him, how she came to my flat, how I tried to sway her but couldn't manage it.

Tommy stares down at me, processing all I've told him.

"So you ended things between us . . . because you were trying to protect me?"

"Yes, I did. Are you angry?"

He snorts. "No—I think it's sweet."

"Sweet?"

"Adorable."

"Tommy—you're not taking this seriously."

He rolls over onto me, nudging my legs apart and settling his hips between my thighs—rubbing that thick, relentless hardness against me.

"You feel that? I told you before, I take my hard-ons very seriously."

"But—"

"Abby, look at me."

I lift my eyes to his as he strokes my hair with the pads of his fingers. "Except for my sisters, no one's ever wanted to protect me before. That's usually my job. And it means something that you did—it means a whole lot."

He kisses me softly, slow and sweet.

Then he shifts us to our sides . . . and smacks my arse. Hard.

Whack.

"Ow!"

"But you should have told me. Instead of leaving me marinating in misery for the last three fucking months."

I narrow my eyes at him. "I don't think you were all that miserable."

"You'd think wrong."

"I saw you . . . through the window at Paddy's. You were with your partner and his wife. But there was another girl there—blond and pretty—you had your arm around her."

Tommy maneuvers to his back, pushing a hand through his hair. Then he holds up a finger to me and reaches for his mobile. He puts it on speaker as he makes the call, and a moment later an energetic, chirpy voice answers.

"Hey, Tommy-Tommy."

"Hey, Ellie. Sorry to call so early."

There's a laugh in her voice. "Early does not exist in the house anymore—time is an infinite loop. Logan's already wrestling with Finn in the den and it's not like baby St. James #2 is letting me sleep. What's up?"

"Do you remember when you and Lo and Marlow and me went to eat at Paddy's when she was here visiting from the States?"

"Yep, I remember."

Tommy glances towards me as he speaks. "In all the time we've known each other—how often have Marlow and I hooked up?"

"Ha! Like, in reality or in Marlow's dreams?"

"Reality."

"Ah . . . never. When you first met, Marlow and I were still in high school and by the time she was a legal-beagle, you were thinking of her like one of your sisters."

Tommy nods. "Exactly."

"You want to tell me why you're asking?"

"I'll fill you in another time. Thanks, Ellie."

They end the call and Tommy tosses his phone to the floor. Then he turns my way, tugging the sheet down. He traces a tickling, taunting line with his finger down the center of my breasts, across my stomach, circling my navel and back up again.

"Like I said—fucking misery."

I nod, my breath hitching as Tommy rolls my nipple between his thumb and forefinger—before leaning his head down to bring his lips and tongue into the mix.

"What are we going to do about my grandmother?" I ask.

Though she's the last damn thing I want to be discussing. Because Tommy's mouth is magical—and I'd rather be focused on that.

"I can handle your granny, Apple Blossom." He kisses around

my breast, my neck, shifting back on top of me, enveloping my mouth in consuming openmouthed kisses. "Don't worry your pretty head—or any of your other pretty parts—about it."

And when he says it like that and surrounds me like this—every inch of him strong and protective and certain—it's impossible not to believe him.

Because Tommy Sullivan can handle anything.

Everything.

I can't remember now why I ever doubted it.

The first step in Tommy's plan to "handle" my grandmother involves bringing him to the Bumblebridge estate for brunch so I can officially introduce him to the rest of the family.

And so the Dowager Countess can get to know him better. He's under the impression that since he can charm me out of my knickers anytime he likes, he'll be able to charm the nastiness out of her just as easily.

I have my doubts about that part, but I trust him, so I follow his lead.

We're the first to arrive that Saturday—me in my simple beige sheath dress and sweater and Tommy looking devastatingly handsome in his dark gray suit and sharp black tie. As I gaze at our reflection in the gilded mirror while we wait in the grand foyer . . . I realize something.

I don't want Tommy to simply entice my grandmother into changing her mind about our relationship. I want her to understand clearly that we would be together regardless of her approval, that it's not her decision to make. I want her to know that her thoughts and threats don't matter—that I am not a puppet on a string. At least . . . not anymore.

It's like osmosis, like Tommy's surety and boldness have seeped into me. And here, now, with him in my life again, I'm strong enough to tell my grandmother exactly what I should have said from the very start.

And I don't just want to do it, I *need* to.

For him and me—and very much for myself.

"I'm going to have a private word with my grandmother before things gets started."

Tommy glances hesitantly in the direction of the library. "You're certain? I could come with you."

"No, I'll just be a moment. It'll be fine."

He nods and kisses me sweetly on the cheek.

I enter the library without knocking, closing the door behind me.

"Grandmother."

"Abigail," she says from behind her rosewood desk. "How nice that you've decided to grace us with your presence. I wondered how long you'd carry on with your temper tantrum."

I see she's as pleasant as always.

"Yes, about that—Tommy is here with me."

One sharp, damning brow reaches for the sky.

"Excuse me?"

"He wanted to meet the family and it seems fitting to introduce him . . . with him being my boyfriend."

The brow inches even higher, paired with an appalled drop of her jaw.

"Boyfriend?"

"It's not as juvenile as it sounds," I explain curtly. "It's serious between us. The term 'lover' is a better fit, but I was trying to be mindful of your delicate sensibilities."

Her lips press into a thin line of irritation as she stands.

"Abigail—"

But she's already had her say—it's my turn now.

"I'm not you, Grandmother. My choices belong to me and me alone. No one gets to take them away."

There are no raving dramatics, no shouts of hysteria—I'm perfectly composed—my words are simple because they're sincere and weighted with finality.

"If you try to harm him in any way, I'll never forgive you. I'll never come back here. I'll never speak to you or think of you or admire you ever again. I honestly don't know if that matters to you, but if you care about me—even just a little—you will let him be. Let *us* be."

She looks into my eyes for several beats and I stare right back, refusing to be cowed this time. Because this family means everything to her, there is nothing she wouldn't do for it; that's what she said. And that's what I'm counting on.

The Dowager Countess releases a long, vexed sigh, then she lowers her dark green eyes. And she nods—it's stiff and begrudging, but I'll take it.

Tommy

Brunch with Abby's family explains so fucking much.

I'd read up on each of them, from the report Amos and Stella compiled all those months ago. But seeing them together in one posh dining room really drives home the idea that the apple doesn't fall far from the tree—and the Haddocks are an orchard of straitlaced oddness.

They're formal when Abby introduces me and when they greet each other—reserved and as bland as the walls in Abby's flat. Even the two young nieces are strangely subdued.

Possibly medicated.

I don't have much experience with the whole bringing-me-home-to-mum-and-dad thing. The women I dated before Abby veered towards the wild side and tended to have issues with their families. Or the relationship crashed and burned before we ever got to that point. But I've been dealing with the peculiarities of the wealthy and titled my whole adult life—so I'm dead-on sure I can win these crusty crumbs over.

As we move to take our seats, I offer my hand to Abby's father and mother, giving them my best gentlemanly smile. "It's an honor to meet you both."

Abby's dad is tall—studious and bow-tied—the type who's more of a thinker and contemplater before he considers being a doer.

Abby's mum is strikingly similar to her. Not just because they share the same porcelain skin and exquisite features—but because of the silent, observant way she looks at me when she shakes my hand. Like she's dicing me up into slide-sized pieces in her mind to be analyzed later.

I intercept the Dowager Countess on her way to the table, dipping my head respectfully.

"It's a pleasure to see you again, Your Ladyship." Then I give her a wink. "And don't worry about that whole trying-to-strong-arm-Abby-into-kicking-me-to-the-curb thing . . . you were only looking out for her. I can respect that."

Abby's father pauses midway to his seat.

"What's this now? I didn't catch that."

I wave my hand. "Nothing worth repeating. Water under the bridge." My look to the Dowager Countess is heavy with meaning. "Isn't that right, madam?"

Her lips pucker, like a lemon is stuck in her mouth.

"Yes. Nothing of consequence."

Once we're settled, brunch is served.

And even the way they eat is bizarre. As if they're bird–human hybrids—pecking and nibbling like they're trying to make each bite last as long as possible.

If I'd tried eating like that growing up, I would've bloody starved to death before age five.

The butler places a butter dish in front of Abby's grandmother. "Thank you, Grogg."

A laugh barks from my throat. "*Grogg*—that's a good one."

Because I figure it's a joke—only a twisted bastard would stick a moniker like Grogg on a boy. It'd be like naming him Beer.

Then I get a look at his face.

"Oh, shit, that's you're real name? Sorry, mate."

"Mummy," the twin niece on the left whispers, "Auntie Abigail's friend said the naughty poopy word."

I grin at her across the table and try to redeem myself.

"I'll watch my mouth more carefully, sweetheart." I slip a coin from my pocket and dance it across my fingers. "Do you want to see a magic trick?"

What child doesn't enjoy a good magic trick?

This one, apparently.

Her face scrunches into a mighty frown . . . it must be genetic.

"Magic isn't real."

"Of course magic is real. "

I bet they don't believe in Father Christmas either. What kind of nightmare house is this?

"Mummy," the niece whispers again, "Auntie Abigail's friend is telling lies."

Wow. Tough room.

I toss the coin up, snatch it from the air and move to slip it back into my pocket. Before I do, Abby's sharp-eyed older brother, who's built like a tank, takes notice of the bruising scabs across my knuckles.

"What happened to your hand, Mr. Sullivan? Some sort of accident?"

The thing about lying is, if you're going to do it, it's always best to stick as close to the truth as possible. That may not have made it into the Bible, but it's still a golden rule.

"It had a run-in with a man's face. In my line of work, physical altercations are an occupational hazard."

"What is it you do?" Abby's mother asks.

And I get the distinct impression this is the most conversation these walls have heard in years. Maybe decades.

"Tommy owns a personal protection firm—the same firm that guarded us last year when Father was at trial. It's how we met the second time," Abby says. Gazing my way with this soft, adoring kind of expression that makes my cock stand up and take notice.

And I can't help but think how delectable she would look stripped bare and bent over this lovely antique dining table.

"The second time?" the Dowager Countess inquires.

Abby sips her juice. "Yes. We met in the hospital the first time when Tommy was recovering from an injury. He woke up, just sort of grabbed me and kissed the daylights out of me."

"Grabbed you?" the waifish sister asks, wide-mouthed and appalled.

When you're not used to talking, you forget that some things sound better in your head than they do out loud.

"It was a good grab. Just like a fairy tale," Abby jokes.

They don't get it.

The funny bone seems to have skipped a Haddock generation. Or all of them.

So I elaborate—might as well put it all out there now. In for a penny, in for a pound.

"She grabbed me back, of course. Then she smacked me

across the face." I give Abby a warm look. "It was a nice shot—knocked the hell out of me."

"Mummy, Auntie Abigail assaulted her friend."

Well, that one's just a little tattletale, now, isn't she?

"That reminds me," Abby's father says, removing his glasses and cleaning them with his cloth napkin. "My partner's son was in an altercation several nights ago."

My voice is loose and steady. "You don't say?"

"It seems he was attacked at a private affair. A random sort of thing."

"What are the odds?" I click my tongue regretfully. Sorry I didn't have time to break every bone in the bastard's body.

"The world is a dangerous place." I shrug. "More dangerous for some than others."

And with that, the Haddocks appear all conversationed out. They resume their reading and planner-writing, food-pecking and phone-scrolling—as if they're in the same room, but separated into solitary worlds by invisible cubicles.

It's hard to hold on to the anger I've been carrying around for them. These people who planted seeds of unworthiness and insignificance in Abby's perfect beautiful head. It's clear that they don't mean to be malicious or indifferent.

Well . . . perhaps the grandmother does.

But the rest of them—they're just fucking clueless.

They care for her, I suspect they care a lot . . . they just have no damn idea how to show it.

——————✦——————

Showing has never been a problem for the Sullivans.

If anything, life would go smoother if they managed to keep a few things to themselves once in a while. Abby gets a front-row seat to the showing when I take her to my parents' place for supper the following Sunday.

She stands on the pavement, looking like an angel in a cream floral dress and heels, staring up at the house like it's going to reach out and bite her.

"I'm not certain this is a good idea."

I walk around the car and take her hand.

"It's going to be fine."

A ruckus of laughing voices comes from inside, then a crash.

"Perhaps I could meet your parents alone? At a nice quiet dinner, just the four of us. And then the rest of your family afterwards. Slowly."

I chuckle. "At that pace it'll take you years to get through them all." I tug her along the path to the door. "My family is like the deep end of a cold swimming pool. It's better to jump in with both feet. You try inching it, you'll just end up freezing your balls off."

"Tommy, I—"

I pull her in, hands on her hips, and I swallow her worries in a deep, slow kiss. I don't let up until that little moan is purring from her throat and her nervousness has melted away.

And it's all going to be all right. The day will be different for Abby—loud and unfamiliar—but she'll see how it's supposed to be. What it's like to belong to a living, breathing family. I already know how they'll react to her.

My brothers will tease—asking what a nice girl like her is doing with a reprobate like me. Bridget will be chatty, Janey will be standoffish but not for long, Fiona will admire her dress and poise. Mum will test her, then she'll warm up and put her to work. Dad's going to adore her on sight.

And once they get to know her . . . they'll love her. I can't imagine anyone not loving Abby once they know her.

A blast of loud hits us when we walk in the door. Dogs

barking, strings of children weaving between clusters of chatting, chuckling adults with drinks in their hands. The air is filled with the scent of warming food and the sounds of music coming from speakers in the back garden.

"*This* is your family?" Her big, pretty eyes are so wide they may actually fall out of her head.

"Aye." I give her hand a squeeze. "I guess a few couldn't make it; it's usually more crowded."

We're greeted in quick succession as we move through the house—to where the alcohol is—that's key.

There's my brother Arthur and his friendly, beady-eyed wife, Victoria. My weirdest cousin, Robert, whose claim to fame is a record-breaking collection of decorative socks. There's my never-married twin aunts on my dad's side, Bertie and Lois, who can finish and start each other's sentences. And on and on it goes—an assembly line of introductions:

Have you met Abby?

This is my girl Abby.

Say hello to Abby.

"My head is spinning," she exclaims when we finally make it to the back. "This is worse than medical school—I'm never going to remember who's who."

I lean in close and press a kiss to her hair. "We'll make you flash cards, and have study sessions that rely heavily on flashing."

Abby laughs out loud. And it's now officially my very favorite sound.

But then she angles her head, her brows scrunching in confusion at someone across the room.

"Tommy—I think that girl just ran her finger across her neck at me. Like the sign for slitting a person's throat."

I glance over. "Yeah, that's Mellie. She lives next door—she's got a bit of a thing for me."

"Wow." The corners of Abby's magnificent mouth turn upward. "Should I be worried?"

"Probably." I wink. "Stay close to me. You'll be all right."

And she's laughing again.

Over her shoulder I spot my dad behind the bar, with my mum in her apron beside him, and I lead us over.

"Dad, Mum—this is Abigail Haddock. Abby, these are my parents, Rupert and Maggie."

I gave my dad the inside scoop on Abby a few days ago.

"Welcome, Abby." He comes out from behind the bar, shaking her hand first and then hugging her. "It's so nice to meet you, lass."

And she glows, blooming beneath the light of his warmth like I knew she would.

"It's a pleasure to be here, Rupert, thank you. I'm happy to meet you both as well."

"You're every bit as lovely as Tommy said you were."

Hands on her hips, my mum's gaze darts from my father to Abby and back.

"*Tommy said*, did he? He hasn't said anything to me."

My dad pats her arm. "You were busy, my pet."

"Oh, this is for you." Abby lifts a bakery box from the shopping bag in her hand and passes it to my mother—with a banoffee pie inside that she stopped to purchase on the way here.

My mum turns the pie this way and that like a food critic or a health inspector searching for nits.

"Store bought, how fancy. You don't bake your own?"

"No," Abby confesses, "I'm afraid I'm not much of a baker."

"She's a surgeon, Maggie," Dad announces—already so proud.

"Hmm, I see." My mum smiles in that derisive, snooty way that's not really a smile at all. "I'll just take it to the kitchen for later. Thank you."

"You're welcome, Maggie."

My mother continues to smile—sweet as arsenic.

"You may call me Mrs. Sullivan."

Right. Fucking grand.

Things go downhill from there pretty quick.

With a beer in my hand and a soda in Abby's because she's on call, we claim a comfy corner and talk to my uncle Bardan about the goings-on at the harbor where he's a dockworker.

From the corner of my eye, my sister Janey approaches Abby on her right. While Bardan goes on about the installation of the new pilings, I hear Janey's voice, low and lethal.

"Hurt him again and I'll hurt you."

My head snaps around.

"Lay off, Janey. It's not necessary."

But Abby lifts her chin and doesn't shy away from my sister, which is good—if you ever go up against a raging mother-bear it's best not to show fear.

"I understand."

After Janey moves on, I try to put Abby at ease.

"Don't pay her any mind. If she didn't like you she wouldn't bother threatening you."

Janey makes a liar out of me when Logan and Ellie arrive—hugging Ellie warmly and taking chubby-cheeked Finn from her arms.

And that's how it goes the rest of the day.

The extended relatives are kind enough to Abby, and she and Ellie really hit it off, chatting long and easy. But my sisters—they ignore her. Blatantly. Nastily. And I have no clue why.

Once I catch Bridget and Janey and Fiona whispering and giggling in Abby's direction—like mean girls in fucking school. The only reason I don't blow like a firecracker is because she didn't notice, and I don't want to embarrass her.

A few hours later, out in the back, my niece Rosie comes

running over excitedly, displaying her mud-coated little hands. She stumbles, but Abby catches her—and ends up with two perfect mud handprints on the front of her dress.

"Hey, Tommy," Andy calls from the grass where he and my cousins are playing football. "Lionel's gotta run. You wanna fill in for him?"

I start to turn him down, but Abby interjects.

"You should play." She gestures to the stain on her dress. "I have to get some cold water on this anyway. Then I'll come right back and watch you."

And she says it in a way that makes me think she'd like to watch me do other things. Naked things.

Or maybe I just enjoy connecting Abby to naked every way I can.

"All right." I nod, jogging across the yard as she heads into the house.

But about ten minutes later when Abby still hasn't come back, I bow out of the game and go looking for her. I find her coming out of the kitchen—almost colliding into me as I was about to go in.

"There you are. I was just—"

Her eyes are too shiny, her mouth too taut, her skin a shade too pallid.

"What's the matter?"

"Nothing." Abby shakes her head—lying to me. "I've been called into the hospital—I need to head out."

"I'll drive you."

"No, don't be silly." She puts her hand on my chest. "You should stay here with your family. I'll take a taxi. It's fine, Tommy."

But it's not fine. Nothing about her right now is fine. She's skittish and devastated—a sad little bird who can't fly away fast enough.

Outside, I hail a cab for her. Standing in the open door, Abby reaches up, pressing goodbye lips to mine.

"Ring me when you're home," I tell her.

She forces a smile for me, then climbs in.

I watch her drive off and then I turn back towards the house—like a volcano ready to spew. My blood is hot, livid—not just about the mean-girl bullshit from my sisters and mum, but at myself.

Because whatever cut into Abby, it happened on my watch.

And that shit does not fucking happen on my watch.

When I walk into the kitchen, they're all there—cackling like witches around a cauldron. My voice is deceptively level but sharp as a blade, shutting their mouths the second I start speaking.

"I thought you knew me. I thought you knew me well enough that I didn't need to tell you she means something to me—that bringing her here already said that loud and clear. But apparently that's not the case, so I'm saying it—she's fucking important to me."

I jab a finger at Janey, where she's sitting lock-jawed stubborn at the table.

"You fuckin' knew that more than anyone."

"Mind your mouth," my mother bites out.

Janey's eyes drop to her hands on the table, telling me if she doesn't feel badly already, she will very soon. Bridget and Fiona have the heart to look contrite as well.

My mother, on the other hand, stands straight and unrepentant, and I know that she was the ringleader—that my sisters were unwelcoming to Abby because she told them to be. And whatever nasty swipe sent Abby running, it came from her.

"What did you say to her?"

She dries her hands on a towel and shrugs. "Only the truth—that she's got no business being here with you. That the two of you are just wasting your time."

I want to put my hand through the goddamn wall.

"You don't even know her. You have no idea how hard it was for her to come here today, but she did it. She did it for me."

Because I promised her it would be fun. I told her this is how real families are, what they do. *Fucking Christ.*

"You're a working man, Tommy—you'll be one until the day you die. A working man's life is only sorted when he's got balance. When he's got a partner taking care of all the demands that need doing that he doesn't have time for because he's out working himself to the bone. You think it's easy? Running a house, raising a family, making a home. It takes grit and sweat . . . and that girl doesn't know the first thing about it. She's all about herself, her career—she's not for you, lad. Her type can't even boil water and they have no desire to learn."

I scrape my teeth against my lip, trying to keep in the harsh words that are busting to get out . . . that I won't be able to take back.

"You know, Mum—I always knew you were hard. Tough. But I never thought you'd be small." I shake my head. "That is truly disappointing."

I throw up my hands, disgusted with the lot of them. And then I walk out the door.

Bridget calls after me, "Tommy, wait."

"Let him go," I hear my mother say. "When he sees reason, he'll come back."

The next afternoon I meet up with Abby on a bench outside the hospital on her break. It's a sunny day, clear skies, but chilly. Her cheeks are freshly pink from the cold and she's looking sexy and sweet in light blue scrubs, a puffy coat and a knit cap on her head.

I kiss her soft lips and hand her one of the two cups of tea in my hands. We sit comfortably side by side for a while, watching a horny squirrel chase the playing-hard-to-get object of his affection in frantic circles before disappearing into a bushel of secluded branches up a tree.

He's like my spirit animal.

"Your mother hates me," Abby states in a matter-of-fact sort of way.

I take a sip of my tea.

"It's not personal. She was going to dislike anyone she didn't handpick herself."

Abby nods silently.

"And I don't exactly blend with your family either," I add. "Though I'm betting they're too dignified to say it, I don't imagine they like you with me."

"No," she says quietly, "I don't imagine they do."

Then she reaches down, putting her hand over mine where it's resting on my leg, threading our fingers together and holding on tight.

"But I like you with me."

And I'm so fucking proud of her. This is all new, hard territory, but she's facing it headfirst—holding her ground, holding *our ground.*

"I figured as much." I smirk. "Especially the other night—you seemed to like you with me a whole lot when I pulled you up onto my face and you gripped the headboard and I did that thing with my tongue . . ."

She starts blushing fiercely and bumps my shoulder, but I go on.

"And you moaned so loud I think you scared the life back into those pitiful plants. What did you do to them, anyway?"

Abby's laughing now, shy and giggly.

"Shut up, Tommy."

The sunlight's all around her, making her hair shimmer with gold and her long-lashed eyes a seafoam green—so damn pretty it tugs right at my heart.

I lean towards her, smiling, brushing her nose with mine . . . because how can I not.

"Make me."

She doesn't disappoint. Abby presses her sweet lips against mine, playful at first, then delving and stroking—making it wet and hot and messy.

Shutting me up in the very best way.

She rests her forehead against mine, breathing out a little sigh.

"Our families are kind of the worst."

"They are." I look into her eyes. "It's going to have to be just you and me, then."

"Just you and me . . ." Abby smiles. "Yeah."

CHAPTER
SEVENTEEN

Abby

TIME GOES ON, AS IT TENDS TO DO. AND LIFE CHANGES—the good, slow, building sort of change that's only decipherable months later when you gaze backward and realize your past existence is unrecognizable to you now.

Tommy insists on buying me a television and installs it on the wall of my front parlor.

I resist at first, but as deftly as its irresistible installer did, it lures me in, seducing me completely. And before I know it, we're wrestling for control of the remote and spending lazy afternoons on the sofa, snuggling and kissing, while I point out the inaccuracies of an otherwise riveting medical drama.

One day I insist on reorganizing the closets and cabinets in Tommy's flat—because it's a bloody miracle the man can find anything in the chaos of their shelves. He doesn't just let me, we do it together.

I get used to the sight of him coming home on days when he's been guarding a client—how he slips out of his suit jacket, all broad shoulders and thick arms, and removes his gun from its holster and stores it in the bedside table drawer. He picks up my habit of sparing the lives of spiders and other crawly things that have wandered inside, setting them free outdoors instead of splatting them with a shoe.

And our lives weave around each other—a beautiful mismatched quilt of laughter and sex, sleeping and rushing around, silly chats and soul-stripping conversations and perfect unforgettable moments.

My fourth year of residency melds into the fifth—challenging and demanding and amazing. S&S Securities grows larger, expanding their operation and reputation. Sometimes our schedules keep us apart for days, but the reunion is blissfully worth it.

Ellie St. James gives birth to her and Logan's second child—a chubby-cheeked cherub of a boy they name Declan—and just four months later, she's pregnant again with their third.

We don't avoid our families out loud, but we're not chomping at the bit to see them, either. There's the occasional awkward brunch at Bumblebridge, and it's not Tommy's presence that makes it awkward—it always was, I see that now—I don't think my family knows how to be any other way. But it's his presence in my life that allows me to admit it.

There's the unavoidable birthday at the Sullivans' here and there. Tommy's sisters warm to me, his brothers are endearing and his father is a delight. But Mrs. Sullivan remains cold and unhappy—going out of her way to make me uncomfortable in those small, subtle ways some women are so skilled at.

On Christmas Eve, Tommy meets me for dinner in the hospital cafeteria during my shift. It snows on Christmas Day and we use that excuse to not step a toe out of bed.

On Easter Sunday, he's in London for work, so I take the train and surprise him when he's off the clock, wearing a lace, pastel lingerie confection that Etta helped me pick out. It ends up shredded on the floor of his hotel room before the night is through.

Being in a relationship with a bodyguarding man is thrilling and beautiful—but never boring.

Nothing exemplifies this more than the night I'm called down to the emergency room for a consult and find Tommy bleeding from a bullet wound to the thigh and being dragged in by Logan and James under each arm.

"What happened?" I gasp, guiding them to a gurney.

"It's a long story," James explains.

Tommy's eyes are glazed and his smile is loopy.

"I got shot," he tells me.

"All right." James shrugs. "Maybe not so long after all."

The wound isn't fatal, but he needs surgery.

Hospital policy and common sense force me to pass him into the care of Riley Bowen—the talented but still snide doctor who never quite got over the insult of my turning him down for dinner last year.

He reviews Tommy's chart and checks the wound, clicking his tongue. "These things can be unpredictable. Let's hope he makes it."

I realize he's joking, that he thinks he's being funny.

But Tommy's rubbed off on me more times than I can count, and in a variety of ways.

"If he doesn't make it, Riley, I'll cut your heart out and feed it to your mother."

Tommy grins up at me from the gurney.

"You're so romantic, Abby. I think you might like me . . . just a bit."

I cup his jaw tenderly, smiling soft. "Just a bit."

Tommy breezes through the surgery fine and dandy. His recovery is another matter entirely. Whoever said doctors make the worst patients clearly never encountered a bedridden bodyguard. They're the worst—and it's not even close.

In the early days of his recuperation, he's sullen and cranky and itching to argue.

And then I master the art of the striptease and the careful lap dance to keep him compliant. And "blow jobs"—those always cheer him right up—so it's a win for us both.

----◆----

If I pick up the ins and outs of being in a relationship with a bodyguard, Tommy catches on quick to what it's like being in one with the daughter of an aristocrat. Which means mandatory attendance at various charity functions several times a year. We haven't encountered Alistair Lipton at any of the previous events—it's possible he's dropped off the face of the earth or left the country, but I don't care enough to find out.

Tonight, it's a black-tie gala in support of an organization that specializes in congenital heart condition research that's particularly dear to the Queen, and to my family. I emerge from my bedroom in a slinky dark green gown with a cleavage-revealing neckline and beading throughout the snug bodice. My heels are high, my hair is down, shiny and curled at the ends, and I feel good—even pretty.

But when Tommy's gaze slowly coasts down, caressing me, and he lets out a long, highly appreciative whistle—I feel absolutely stunning. Like a mythical magical fairy-tale mermaid who's emerged from the ocean and enchanted the handsomest man in all the land.

"Outstanding. You clean up nice, Apple Blossom," he says roughly.

I wink—a gesture he's passed on to me that never ceases to delight him.

"I get dirty even better."

A deep chuckle rumbles through his fine, tuxedo-clad chest—making me go deliciously warm and tingly between my legs. Tommy's laugh and smile and that hungry tender look in his eyes are the very best aphrodisiacs.

The first time we attended an affair together, I was surprised that Tommy is such a skilled dancer, though I shouldn't have been. He's already proven beyond doubt that he has an infinite talent in all things physical—the ebb and flow and rhythm of his body's movements.

He's equally capable in making polite conversation, chatting with an earl or a duke as easily as he does with the boys at his shop.

At the moment, we're standing in the grand banquet hall, swathed in the glow of the glittering chandelier above our heads and radiance of the golden candelabras on every table, speaking affably with Prince Nicholas and Duchess Olivia.

Just behind us, my father converses with Queen Lenora, their voices carrying over to us as he tells her of my brother's traveling ways and how he wishes Luke would come home more often.

"But the boy simply refuses," Father says.

"Children," the Queen laments, "always so certain they know everything."

"True," Father agrees. "But were we really so different at their age, Your Majesty?"

"Well . . ." Queen Lenora considers his question.

And then she answers.

"When I was young I was sure I knew everything . . . but it turns out I was right, so that's not the same thing at all."

We all hear it, our eyes meeting and laughing in unison.

Prince Nicholas shakes his head in affectionate exasperation.

"She's right on brand."

The night goes on, and while these sorts of things are typically stuffy affairs, with Tommy beside me it's different—a whirl of laughing and champagne drinking and heated glances and one lovely dance after the next.

Later, Tommy walks with me from the ballroom down a secluded hall in search of the lavatory. And we encounter Wessco's
other prince—the now heir to the throne, Prince Henry, and his
wife, Princess Sarah.

They have two children at last count, nearly four-year-old
Princess Jane and three-year-old Prince Edward. But when they
step out into the hall—from the door of what appears to be a
broom closet—it's apparent they're still mad for each other.

"Oh, hello," Princess Sarah says to Tommy and me, immediately flustered and blushing a blazing bright pink. "We were just
. . ." she gestures to a framed landscape on the wall " . . . admiring
the lovely artwork."

Henry Pembrook has had a reputation for being a rascal his
whole life—and marriage hasn't tempered that a bit.

"We were making out," he confesses.

"Henry!" Sarah gasps.

"Oh, look at their faces—they knew you were lying. You're
rubbish at it."

He loops a possessive arm around her shoulders, turning her
towards him.

"We're going to have to work on your game face, sweetheart.
For instance, you can practice saying you're not hopelessly, desperately infatuated with me—until you're able to declare it believably."

Sarah grins, looking up at her husband with adoration in her
big brown eyes.

"I don't think I'll ever be that good of a liar."

Henry dips his head, whispering breathlessly, "Good."

Tommy takes my hand and we slip discreetly past them—not
that the future king and queen would notice.

They're already making out again.

Tommy

A month after the royal charity gala, Abby and I get sloshed. Shit-faced. Not two sheets to the wind—but three. The kind of intoxicated where the corners of your vision take on that mellow pleasant haze and your joints are liquid and it's impossible to keep your hands off each other.

The scene of the drunkering is Katy's Pub, where we met up with Lo and Ellie, Henrietta and Harry, Kevin and Bea, my sister Janey and some worthless twat she's been spending time with, for a melding of the friend groups.

Abby doesn't see as much of Kevin and Etta around the hospital these days, as they've each branched off into their surgical specialties—so they spend time catching up and drinking more rounds than I can count of some fruity cocktail that I can taste on her sweet breath. Lo, Janey and I get into a shot contest that starts off friendly but escalates into a battle royale for shit-talking rights. Ellie—the poor lass—is the designated driver, though she doesn't seem to mind, because she's ecstatically knocked up.

Again.

When the night is done, she and Lo drop us at Abby's building, where the two of us rush randily up the steps to her flat as quick as our flying-high feet will take us. We make it just inside the door—barely slamming it shut—before we're wrapped together so close you can't see where she begins and I end.

Our mouths slide together, wet and moaning. And fuck, I'm so gone for her. My luscious, lovely girl—it's like I have amnesia—and any time before when I didn't crave her, want her body and soul, has been wiped from my memory.

And all that's left is her and this and us.

I press Abby back against the wall, sucking at the skin of her petal-soft neck and earlobe—grinding the granite pipe of my cock right there against that spot where she loves it and needs it. Abby's chin lifts and her mouth opens and I slide to her lips, breathing in the same air, pumping harder against her.

She tugs at my hair and pleads against my mouth.

"If you don't get inside me, I'm literally going to die."

And we're laughing together because she read my mind.

I sweep us to the sofa because the bed is just too bloody far.

And we pull at the abomination of the clothes that stand in the way. When she's wearing nothing but bare soft skin, I want to slow down and savor and lick up every inch of her.

But she won't let me.

She's fire in my arms, lashing and burning for me.

I guide her to her back on the sofa, spread her legs and hook one arm under her knee. Holding her hooded eyes with mine, I suck at the pads of my fingers and stroke her pussy, slipping inside and coating her with the added slickness.

Not because she needs it—she's already dripping—but because it's dirty and hot and she likes watching me do it.

I withdraw my fingers and bend my knees, sliding the head of my cock between her folds—then I surge in fully with a single thrust. She's perfect and slippery and so clenching tight my eyes roll back in my head.

Abby moans my name.

And I growl, "Christ, you feel good."

Three pumps later, the small non-pickled portion of my brain wakes up and kicks me. Pointing out just why Abby feels so damn good.

It's because I'm not wearing a condom.

Shit.

And she's not on the pill—it gives her migraines.

Double shit.

I freeze.

"Wait," I pant, raking in air to my starving lungs. "Wait, wait, fuck, wait . . ."

But her hips buck and a sob breaks from her like I've broken her heart.

"No, don't stop."

I grasp her thigh, holding her still.

"I need to get a condom, love." I lean over her, kissing deep and stroking with my tongue, promising, "Then I'll come back here and fuck you into oblivion, I swear."

Abby stares into my eyes—and her green orbs are clearer, heated yes, but conscious and aware of what she's about to say.

"I don't want you to get a condom. I want to know how it feels . . ."

She squeezes her pussy deliberately, clamping down hard like she's trying to trap me inside.

Her hips lift slowly, rotating and rubbing against me. And her words are liquid silver, nitroglycerin temptation.

"Don't you want to feel it with me, Tommy? Just you and me and nothing in our way?"

I laugh. Painfully.

It's ridiculous question—asking a man if he wants to go raw is like the grand-prize jackpot of fucking. No one in his right mind, or not, would say no.

But still, I run my thumb over her cheek and draw her eyes to mine. Because I have to know she means it, that this is what she wants. I need to know she's certain now and she'll still be certain tomorrow.

It'll break us if she's not.

"Are you sure?"

Abby bites her lip—a tantalizing sex goddess who owns me in every way. Keeping my gaze, she drags her hips up and down slowly, hugging my cock in a scorching embrace and rubbing her clit against my pelvis.

"I'm sure."

I climb up her body, spreading her hips wide and driving into her hard.

Abby lays back with a sigh and a smile on her perfect fucking mouth. Her eyes are closed, her arms are raised and her hips are high—giving herself over completely to the pleasure.

Completely to me.

I ride her just like that for several moments, pumping steadily in and out—relishing the feel of her and the scent of sweat and sex that rises up between us. Loving how her beautiful tits sway in time to my movements.

I look down where my cock stretches her tight, slick flesh—and I love that too.

And too soon that exquisite pressure coils tight, building low and surging, making my balls heavy and my blood hot.

I rise up to my knees and my fingers dig into Abby's hips, yanking her to me as I thrust forward again and again. The obscene wet slap of our skin echoes in the room, mingling with gasps and moans.

"I'm going to come," I groan. "I'm going to fucking come so hard."

And Abby's right there with me—writhing and reaching for me. Keening, jagged pleas pour from her lips, driving me mad.

Yes, come.

Yes, inside.

Let me feel it.

Please, Tommy, please.

Please, please, please . . .

Her words are wild, filthy, gorgeous rasps, and I can't hold back.

I jerk her to me one last time, and then I'm spilling and pulsing inside her, my body strung tight. She comes at the same time, and I can feel every beautiful bit of it around my cock—each spasm and sweet contraction of her roiling release.

Later, in the bed, we go at it again.

It's lazier the second time around, less frantic but still intense.

And when Abby slides up over me, straddling my waist, I can see my come glistening on her thighs. When she sinks down on me and I feel her filled and sticky wet from me—it's the hottest fucking moment of my life.

We fall asleep meshed together, with her splayed across my chest and my arms holding her. And everything is right and perfect in the world.

Until five weeks later . . . when Abby wakes up puking her guts out.

CHAPTER
EIGHTEEN

Abby

*S*TUPID, STUPID, SO DAMN STUPID.

That's the mantra that repeats in my head as I set the pregnancy test on the bathroom counter with shaking hands. Tommy went out to purchase it early this morning—right after I woke up sick and retching and we looked at each other and thought the same thought at exactly the same moment.

That night. That wild, beautiful, stupid night that I'll remember for the rest of my life.

And I may have a whole other reason to remember it now.

I was so close, I was almost done. Well, not really—even after surgical residency there are years to still prove yourself, specialized instruction and training to be considered the top in the field, but still . . . how could I have been so *stupid?*

The answer is simple. Happiness makes you careless. Joy breeds recklessness. When everything is good and wonderful, it's so easy to slip into the illusion that it will always be that way. That nothing could possibly go awry.

I step out of the bathroom pale and nauseous and face Tommy where he sits on the edge of the bed with his elbows braced on his knees, an alien expression of seriousness clinging to his handsome face.

He stands and moves to take me in his arms.

"It's going to be all right, sweets."

But I squeeze my eyes and shudder, turning away from him.

"No, it's not."

This is going to change everything. It already has for me.

I sit at the edge of the far end of the bed. And my grand-mother's voice joins the chorus of stupidity ringing in my ears.

Choices must be made. Sacrifices. And for women and wives and mothers—the sacrifices will always fall on us.

"If it's positive, would you get an abortion?"

My head whips up. Because Tommy Sullivan is a Catholic boy—a crooked-haloed angel—through and through. But there's no judgement or coaxing in his tone—he's not trying to sway me in either direction—he genuinely just wants to know where my head is at.

"Would you want me to?"

"No," Tommy says—quick and definite.

Then he swallows harshly, and looks at some spot beyond my shoulder.

"But if that's what you wanted, I would understand. You won't lose me over it."

My answer is already set. I know it through and through, down to the marrow of my bones.

"I wouldn't have an abortion, Tommy."

And it's the ramifications of that truth that has my throat nar-rowing and my heart trying to crash out of my chest.

Tension releases from his shoulders and a long, relieved breath slips from his lips.

"Good. That's good."

And he gazes at me gently—almost happy now.

I'm not.

However this turns out—whatever the little stick of chaos proclaims—there is no happy outcome for me.

Sixty seconds later, Tommy disappears into the bathroom. When he emerges, he sits beside me and takes my hand—his expression sweet and his words soft.

"It's negative. You're not pregnant, Abby."

And there it is.

The crush of relief . . . and the vise of disappointment. A sadness over what could have been and a strange, out-of-body confusion at the planted seeds of new wants.

New dreams.

It's an altering that sends my thoughts tumbling.

Because once upon a time I had a plan. A straight line and clear path to get to where I wanted my life to go. Perhaps I wasn't precisely happy, but I was satisfied.

Then Tommy Sullivan came along . . . and he changed all my plans.

And now he's doing it again. I could see that life with him. I can taste it—babies and a home, the scent of dinner cooking in the air and the sound of laughter and little feet.

Is that who I am now? Is that what I want?

And if so, when?

How?

"Could you . . . could you go for a bit, Tommy? I need to be alone for a little while."

Confusion pulls at the corners of his mouth. He leans over to comfort me because that's who he is—that's what he does.

But his touch and his scent and the sheer presence of him muddles everything.

It always has.

I dart up from the bed and step back, not meeting his eyes.

I sense it when he rubs a hand down his face and when he speaks, there's pain in his voice. I hate that I've put it there.

"Don't do this, Abby. I'm begging you, don't do this."

"And I'm begging you to leave. Please. I just . . . I just need to think."

I hate this. The short breaths and swirling panic and sickly spin of not knowing what I want or how I feel.

"To think about fucking what? It's negative! It's fine—we're fine."

It's the first time he hasn't been careful with me.

Because he doesn't understand.

Every space Tommy occupies he controls—he runs the room. He's confident, sure—in himself and his wants. Always. He makes decisions in a snap and it's done. Nothing controls him, nothing sends him spiraling, nothing makes him falter.

But I don't work that way. I never have.

I need time and distance and quiet—just a little.

"Come on, Abby. Just talk to me. Tell me what you're thinking."

I push out the first thought that's front and center in my mind.

"I don't want to end up like Ellie."

Or maybe that's exactly what I want. Why I'm so flustered. It's strange—the confliction. This tearing of desires that stem from the same beginning—like the end of a branch split in two.

"What the fuck is that supposed to mean?" Tommy bites out.

He's insulted now—defensive—and I don't blame him at all.

"Do you know that she'd planned to go to graduate school? To become a psychologist? And then she met Logan and all that got put aside. And now she's home, having babies, one after the other."

"You have no clue what you're talking about. Ellie's mum was murdered when she was young—family is everything to her. She's staying at home with the boys because it's what she wants—what she chose! And if the day ever comes that she wants something different, Logan will break his back bending over to give her that."

"Do you want that? Children?" I ask.

He straightens up, resolute and unapologetic.

"Yeah, I do. Someday."

I stare at the floor, trying to pull myself together and organize my thoughts. But I just end up saying stupid things out loud.

"We were raised differently. We're different people, you and I. If I was with someone like Riley Bowen who understood what my career—"

"You wanna date Reilly fucking Bowen? Is that really what you're saying to me?"

"Yes. No—I mean not how you think; I'm not explaining this right."

I shake my head, rushing out haphazard words to clean up the mess I'm making.

"Someone like Riley would understand the disruption a child will cause to my career. That it's something separate to be planned with care."

"Do you hear yourself? You can't carve your life up into boxes, Abby. A box for your career, a box for me, a box for children. Life is all just one messy fucking box . . . and that's what makes it beautiful. Can't you see that? Can't you try?"

He rakes a rough hand through his hair, like he wants to rip it out. Because he's too hurt and frustrated to see that I *am* trying.

And then he's muttering to the floor.

"Jesus Christ, you're hard to love sometimes."

My eyes jerk up, stunned at hearing those words from him— here and now and for the first time.

"You love me?"

Tommy goes still as a shocked statue.

"Are you insane? What the hell do you think has been going on between us for the last year? That last five years! Of course I love you."

"You shouldn't."

I don't know why I say it. I don't mean it—not even a little.

Stupid, stupid, stupid.

Tommy flinches, stuttering back a step away from me—like I've sliced him open and ripped his guts out. Then his jaw goes to granite and his eyes turn glacial.

And he rips my guts out right back.

"I was wrong. You're not so special. You're scared—no different than anyone else in the fucking world."

Then he turns and walks out the door, slamming it shut behind him.

Leaving me, just as I asked him to.

Tommy

Talk about a kick in the balls.

The priests always say our sins will catch up to us eventually. That there would be consequences.

Welcome to Judgement Day.

And my arse has landed square in the center of purgatory.

I've always thought purgatory was the shittiest of deals. You can't move up, you can't go down, you're just . . . stuck.

Christ, this fucking girl.

I can't decide if I want to shake her until some sense falls out or hold her close and promise it will all be okay.

I want to do both—and apparently, she doesn't want either. The only thing she wanted from me was to get gone.

And it's bloody hard. Because as frustrated as I am with all that she is . . . I still fucking love her.

Her stubbornness, her fire, and how it blends so perfectly with her fragility.

She's a designer drug—cut just for me. Those qualities had me hooked from the very beginning, kept me coming back and back for another fix. And now they've got me strung out. Scraped raw over her.

It's completely pathetic. And I don't do pathetic. Bad poets, they do pathetic—not a man like me.

I walk across town in the early morning light. I don't go back to my place and I sure as shit don't go anywhere near my mum's. I can't speak a word of this to Janey—she'll never let Abby forget it if we make it through.

But I need to get my head on straight. I need to shed this anger and sadness, molt it off like a pitiful snake.

So I head to the gold standard of relationships—Lo and Ellie's.

They're both in their kitchen, at the stove, when I lumber through their back door, moving slow, like my veins are filled with lead and my muscles weigh a few hundred pounds each.

I hear the happy, high-pitched chatter of Finn and Declan through the monitor, but even that can't pull a smile out of me.

Logan doesn't say a word, but I feel his gaze—assessing and probing and understanding. I lower myself into the oak chair at their kitchen counter and Ellie slides a cup of tea in front of me.

"I think this might be it. It might really be over," I tell them. "Abby says she's going on a date with that doctor she works with."

All right, she didn't say that directly—but it was implied.

So just in case, I tell Logan, "We may have to take this guy out."

He knows I'm not serious.

Well . . . he knows I'm only half serious. Three-quarters, tops.

So he shrugs. "Okay."

Ellie's not so sure.

"No. No, there will be no *taking out* of anyone."

She pushes playfully at her husband's shoulder as he moves past her to the stairs to get the boys.

And then I tell Ellie everything, because she's easy to talk to—kind and smart and a steel safe of a secret keeper. I tell her about my toxic mix of a morning—about us thinking that Abby might be expecting and her freaking out. And then I tell about how we confirmed that she's not—and Abby freaked out even more.

When I've finished speaking, Ellie takes a slow breath, nodding to herself.

"There are two kinds of people in the world, Tommy. People like you and me—we're like . . . driftwood floating on top of a wave. Easy, light—we go where the current takes us and nothing really pulls us down. And then there are the Abbys—the Logans. They're more like . . . anchors. They dig in deep and get settled. They like consistency and steadiness—because they know they're the only thing keeping shit from crashing together or sailing off course."

Ellie taps the counter with the tips of her pink nails.

"But when that sea floor shifts and things change big time— it uproots them and it sends them spinning. And they need time to dig back in and settle in a new spot. A new normal."

Ellie smiles gently.

"Abby will settle and she'll settle on you—I know she will. You just have to wait her out."

Foreign bitterness burrows in my stomach, like a nasty alien. It crawls up my throat and speaks words from my lips.

"And what if I'm tired of waiting, Ellie?"

Her blond head tilts sympathetically.

"Are you?"

It only takes a moment for me to snort like it's ridiculous. Because it is.

"No. I don't think I'll ever get tired of waiting for her. And it's fucking awful."

All the movies they make about love . . . the books and songs about the transformative joy and beauty and peace of finally finding that one person who really does it for you.

They leave out the other side—the terribleness of having your heart and happiness chained to someone else's.

Knowing somewhere down deep that if you lose them, you'll never feel like a whole you ever again.

Yep . . . still fucking pathetic.

CHAPTER
NINETEEN

Abby

THE MOMENT TOMMY LEAVES, I WANT TO RUSH AFTER him, pull him back in and take back what I said.

Because obviously I'm a complete mess.

But I don't do any of that.

Because that wouldn't be fair to him.

My stomach purges twice more and I suspect I may have the flu. Though the symptoms of influenza and heartbreak are shockingly similar—everyone knows that.

For the first time in my career, I call in sick—because even if I wasn't, I'd have no business being anywhere near an operating room.

For a day and a half, I don't leave my flat. I sleep some—a tossing, restless slumber—and when I wake a terrible worried weight sits on my chest that I've ruined us.

I text with Luke and speak with Etta on my mobile. If I'm being honest, "speaking" is an exaggeration. Mostly it's just crying, with an occasional word making it through here and there.

As my grandmother said, my practicality is my greatest talent. So I sit on the sofa and try to sort it out. What I want, how I feel, to set new goals. How to become the top-notch surgeon I want to be, and love Tommy like he deserves—with the new added craving of a life with him and a home and a dozen beautiful dark-haired rascal children.

I try to make a list. Lists are helpful.

But I end up staring at the page, seeing that last look on Tommy's face—the anger and hurt that I put there—and the devilish smile that was achingly missing because I took it away.

And I keep waiting for it to pass—this awful hollowness in the center of my chest. But it just gets worse—with every hour—more painful with every tick of the clock.

Because I miss him. I miss him so damn much, I can hardly breathe.

A knock comes at the door. I set my not-a-list on the table, and for the first time the ache lessens just slightly. Because I think it might be him.

But when I open it, I'm surprised to find my parents standing there instead. My father in his tweed jacket and gray bowtie, and Mother wearing a black pencil skirt, red blouse and pearls. Both of them looking dignified and polished . . . and concerned.

And I'm suddenly aware of how I look—in my two-day-old nightclothes, with my hair in a bedraggled bun, my face blotchy-red and my eyes puffy.

"Hello. What are you doing here?"

I can count on one hand the number of times they've dropped by—and never without ringing me first.

I open the door wider and they file in.

"We were having lunch near your father's office when Luke rang us," Mother explains. "He suggested we check on you. He said you've been ill."

"Are you all right, Abby?" Father asks.

"Yes . . . no, I . . ." I gaze back and forth between them as a burning pressure rises behind my eyelids. "I . . ."

And I completely fall apart in front of them.

Covering my face, sobbing into my hands, laying out the sordid mess in fractured sentences and sniffling hiccups.

Once I start, I can't seem to stop. We migrate to the sofa and I tell them everything—things that a year, a month, a week ago I would've cut my tongue out before confessing to them.

I tell them how Tommy and I began with an arrangement of convenience that grew to something more. Something deep and precious. I tell them about Grandmother's threats and how we overcame them, about Tommy's mother and how she hates me, and I point my finger at them and rage that I know they both dislike him as well—and that they're total and complete arses for it.

I tell them about the short chaotic moments when I thought I was pregnant—and the bizarre mixture of joy and stark terror I felt at the prospect.

And I tell them the aftermath—the way I pushed Tommy out the door and the horrible, stupid way I tried to explain myself. I tell them of the regret I've felt every moment since.

I tell them that I'm a fool. That I can't believe there was a time I worried that Tommy would be a distraction. That being *without* him is the worst distraction of all.

But with him beside me, next to me, holding my hand—I can face anything.

Everything.

"Well, that's . . . quite a bit of information," my father says stiffly.

And then he frowns.

"Where did you get the notion that we dislike Tommy? Your mother and I happen to like him very much."

I look up at him with watery eyes.

"You do?"

Father hands me his handkerchief, nodding.

"He's a good man—hardworking, direct. And I like the way he looks at you."

My heart squeezes with a piercing pain.

"I like the way he looks at me too," I whisper.

Right before I burst straight back into tears.

After the second wave subsides, Mother presses a cup of tea in my hand and I'm able to swallow a few sips.

"I'm sorry about this," I tell them, because at this point I'm just completely pitiful.

"I'm sorry I'm not more like Sterling and Athena—I've tried to be, but I can't. And I'm not going to try anymore. I just want to be me. I like me, and Tommy likes me—or at least he did. I'm sorry if that's a disappointment to you."

"A disappointment?" My mother gapes. "Where the devil did you get that idea from?"

Father leans forward. "Your mother and I have always been so proud of you, Abigail. I'm sorry if we've been remiss in telling you. We assumed you knew."

Mother nods.

"I used to worry about Sterling and Athena, that they would be successful . . . but not happy. But you, Abby—dear girl—I was never worried about you. You have such a spark inside; you always did. And when you ran down to Tommy at Bumblebridge that day, and climbed on the back of that dreadful motorbike—your face, Abby, was so full of life. I knew then that you had found your happiness, and you would hold on to it with both hands and never let it go."

I shake my head miserably—and say aloud what I already know.

"But I did let it go, Mother. I've messed things up terribly with Tommy."

"Well, you get that from your father," she says dryly. "He mucked things up with me dozens of times before we were finally settled. Back and forth, up and down we went."

"It's true." Father sips his tea. "But admitting you've mucked it up is the first step. Now you just have to fix it."

"What if I can't? What if . . ." The words catch in my throat. "What if he's finished with me? What if I've broken his heart?"

My mother's smile is gentle.

"Then it's a good thing you're a remarkable cardiac surgeon. If you've broken the lad's heart, you'll know just how to put it back together again."

Those words—those words from her—are just what I need to hear.

Because I don't need to sort out anything—it's already sorted. As long as Tommy and I have each other, we'll be able to face, and have, and love whatever life has in store for us. Together.

"I need to go," I blurt out, standing. "I need to go see him right now."

And I fly out the door . . . in my slippers, nightshirt and robe. I make it halfway to the road before I realize it.

When I come back in, my parents are not surprised to see me.

"I forgot to put on clothes first."

As I head down the hall, I hear Father tell Mother, "She gets *that* from you."

CHAPTER
TWENTY

Abby

SOUND DECISIONS ARE ALWAYS ACCOMPANIED BY A pushing sense of urgency. It's human nature that once a solution has been found, you want to enact that solution as soon as possible. The urgency is fueled with determination and at times—carelessness.

Run, run as fast as you can . . .

That's why I take the stairs down to the first floor of my building, instead of waiting for the lift.

That's why outside—clothed now—I trip over nothing but my own feet and almost stumble into the road as I hail a taxi, bathed in the bright yellow of the unusually sunny day.

It's why I blurt out the address of S&S Securities to the driver too quick for him to understand, and he looks over his shoulder with a garbled, "What's that now?"

And I have to repeat the destination a second time.

Because the fog of confusion has lifted and my thoughts are a rushing river of apologies and heartfelt declarations.

The words that I'll say to Tommy the moment I see him—the words that will make everything perfect and good between us again. I'm not afraid or hesitant. Tommy won't reject me, or even if he does at first—I'm resolved to come back again and again until I can make it right.

The only possible ending for us is a happy one. I've never been so sure of anything in my life. I can do this. *We* can do this.

I'm so stuck in my own head, I don't realize I've left my coat behind until the stark chill of the leather taxicab seat seeps into my skin, making me shiver.

I'm so fixated on how the scene of our reunion will play out, seeing it in my head, I don't notice how fast the taxi is flying through the streets—too fast—until we take a turn so sharply, my shoulder smacks up against the door and the safety belt cuts into my collarbone.

I open my mouth to tell the driver to slow down—but my voice breaks when I see the glass bottle of whiskey rolling to and fro on the center console.

The *empty* bottle.

"You can let me off here," I say.

But he doesn't respond.

I tap his arm, the words coming louder and commanding.

"Stop the car. I want to get out now."

And the whole world slows down into snapshots of micro-seconds. Like a nightmare where the air is gelatinous and every movement is sluggish, requiring an all-consuming effort.

The driver turns his head my way and I see what I was too hurried to detect before—how his mouth is slack and his eyes are clouded beneath heavy, half-closed lids.

The light in front of us is bright red.

There's a silver car stopped perpendicular in the intersection, coming closer and closer.

I rear back and squeeze my eyes closed and raise my hand. But it renders no effect.

An ear-piercing scream of steel against steel rents the air. My head jerks to the left while my body is thrown forward so force-fully the air gushes from my lungs. The vivid blue sky spins on a wheel going beneath me, then above, and beneath again, and the stench of gasoline burns in my nose.

And as the blackness creeps in to consume me whole, I hear the words I couldn't wait to tell Tommy—all the words I'll never get to say—echoing in my ears.

CHAPTER TWENTY-ONE

Tommy

I SHOULDN'T HAVE PUSHED HER.

Not then, not like I did.

It's the recrimination that haunts me all the next morning when I'm supposed to be focused on training at the shop. That and the tortured, terrified look in her eyes when she pleaded with me for time—just a little.

And I didn't give her that.

Because I was all twisted up inside. About what she was thinking, feeling.

Because I liked the idea of seeing two blue lines on that test. Maybe not yesterday—but one day. That Abby and I could create a whole new little person together, who would have the best parts of each of us. Her adorable quirks and magnificent mind and my indomitable personality.

Yeah . . . I liked that a whole fucking lot.

And then the horror slammed in that Abby might not ever want that with me.

And I wanted to know, needed to hear her say it.

So I pushed and pushed until she fucking broke.

Of course she did.

I know Abby—*I know her*—how her heart beats and her soul sings and the way her puzzle-solving mind sorts things out. It's why I fell for her. Why I'll never love anyone as insanely as I love her. Her strength and weakness and tenderness and beautiful vulnerability that makes her trust so fucking precious. A gift.

A gift she's never given to anyone . . . except me.

And I pushed it back straight in her face.

"All right, lads, that's enough for today."

I walk away from the startled looks of the new hires—because it's only early afternoon and we're supposed to go until evening. But Lo's boys have colds and he's home with them today.

And I can't do this now. It's so unimportant it's almost comical. None of this matters—and if I don't get things straight with Abby, none of it will ever matter again.

I head into my office for my wallet and keys. Then I'm going to the hospital and planting myself outside a surgical suite all fucking day if that's what it takes.

Until I can see Abby and tell her it's all right—she can have her time.

Yes, I'm going to hunt her down and corner her—to tell her she can have all the space away from me she needs. It may not seem to make a lick of sense . . . but it makes sense for us.

"Hey, Tommy." Celia sticks her head through my office door. "There's an accident down on the corner—looks pretty bad. Emergency services are on their way, but Gordon and a few of the boys are going down to see if they can help."

I nod, snagging my keys and wallet and heading down to the corner to see if I can help as well.

Halfway down the block I can smell the smoke, acrid and oily. In the distance, there's a crunched heap that used to be two separate cars but is now molded into one metal monstrosity.

And there's a pushing at my shoulders. A cold, panicked spark streaking up my spine that says something is wrong. And I need to move faster, to get there.

To get there *now*.

My heart pounds and the blood rages in my ears and there's a pulling pain deep inside, like a hook in my soul.

I start to run. Sprinting.

When I reach the car, I see the unmistakable smear of copper strands against cracked windowpane, glinting in the sun.

And something between a roar and a wail comes out of me.

Because Abby's in there.

In all that sharp, twisted, burning metal.

God, please, please—fucking please.

The driver's seat is empty—I don't know if the driver crawled away or was thrown from the car—and it's just Abby inside. Alone. And the bent door won't open, so I grip the metal and pull with everything I have. To tear it apart, to get to her—to get her out. The car shakes as I yank and strain, but it doesn't fucking move.

Inside, Abby jostles with my efforts—her skin terrifyingly pale, her eyes closed, lips still.

This can't be happening. Not now. Not after *everything*.

It can't end like this.

It can't end at all.

I hear the echo of the last words I said to Abby and all the words I've wanted to say since, and it's like I'm fucking dying inside. Like I'm already dead.

Ashes to ashes, dust to dust.

There are so many things I have to tell her. So many words she needs to hear.

In the edges of my vision, I see movement—the lads working around the other side. And I smell the black smoke, the heat, the fire.

"The car's burning, Tommy. The whole thing's gonna go. We gotta move," Gordon tells me in cold, clear tones.

Because that's how we work best. When we're tactical. Detached. Assessment and risk. That's what we do.

But this is different.

I punch at the glass of the window—not feeling a thing as the slivers stab into my knuckles, splitting skin and drawing blood. When it doesn't break, I shift to jabbing with my elbow.

Come on, come on, you bastard.

"Tommy! Gotta move, gotta move."

And it's all so clear. So simple, as the nanoseconds of precious time tick by. The kind of truth that's settled in the deepest recesses of my being. And I know without question that I'm not moving from this spot. I'm not going anywhere.

That if Abby is going to burn . . . I'm burning with her.

I kick and smash at the window like a madman, a jumble of curses and prayers tumbling from my mouth.

And at last—at fucking last—the glass gives.

Chunks and shards of sharp glass rain over Abby, but my hands are on her. Wrenching the safety buckle out of the seat. Lifting. Pulling her through the shattered space, tucking her against me to shield her, turning and running.

As the pop and hiss slashes the air behind me like a vicious snake, and the car—the seat where Abby was just lying and the spot where I stood—is consumed in flames.

I fall to my knees on the pavement and turn her in my arms, brushing her hair and bits of glass from her face with my bleeding hands.

"Abby. Abby, love, wake up. Wake up and look at me."

Her golden brows wrinkle and draw together as she whimpers.

Then Abby's eyes open. And she stares up at me for the longest moment and her words come on a soft, airy whisper.

"Is this heaven?"

And my vision, my whole fucking world, goes blurry with the relief. I choke out a laugh, as wetness seeps from the corners of my eyes.

"It is now."

She smiles weakly, her green eyes shimmering with her own tears. She reaches up with one hand and strokes my cheek.

"I'm sorry, Tommy. I didn't mean—"

"Shhh, it's fine. None of that matters now. Don't try to talk."

"No." She clenches my shirt in her one hand. "You have to listen—I have to say this."

She licks at her lips, swallowing.

"You were right—I was afraid. Afraid of wanting so many things at once. But it wasn't about you. I love you, Tommy. I wasn't unsure of that. I love . . ." Her voice catches, breaking, and she tries again. "I love you. I'm never, ever going to not love you. I want the whole messy box with you, Tommy."

I chuckle gently as her words wash through me—a smooth, soothing, healing balm.

"And I don't want us to be apart anymore. Not ever again."

I hold Abby closer, brushing my lips against her forehead.

"Then we won't be. Not ever again. I swear to God."

Tears streak down her sooty cheeks as she nods, smiling and crying at the same time as she nuzzles into my arms. The shriek of the ambulance sirens gets louder, closer, until paramedics arrive and I have to force myself to let Abby go so they can tend to her.

There are more things to discuss and plans to make.

But for now, this is enough.

This is everything.

CHAPTER
TWENTY-TWO

Abby

A WEEK LATER, I'M IN MY FLAT AT THE DINING ROOM table, hunched over a red grape that's stabilized with forceps, painstakingly suturing the delicate split skin back together with a needle and thread in my left hand.

Because I was wrong. Doctors actually do make the worst patients. And a surgeon with extra time on her hands runs the risk of being especially petulant.

In addition to a smattering of minor cuts and contusions, the accident left me with a concussion and a Grade 2 strain of the scapholunate ligament of my right wrist—which means I'm home from the hospital for two weeks and banned from the operating room for a month.

There was a time when such a delay would've caused my whole world to fall apart.

But my world is bigger now.

And having a gorgeous man with a devilish smile taking extra good care of me—who enjoys being naked more often than not— has definitely pillowed the blow.

That doesn't mean I can't put my recovery time to productive use, however.

That's where the grape comes in.

I've been working on developing the dexterity and skill in my nondominant hand. My right forearm is encased in a black stabilizing splint, but I'm able to use my fingers to tie off the thread in the now stitched grape. The sutures aren't pretty—the grape looks like the fruit incarnation of Frankenstein, but still . . .

"Not bad," I say out loud to myself.

But a moment later when Tommy walks through the door, it's not just myself in the flat.

I feel my skin grow warm as I watch him approach—how the lines of his impressive physique stand out as he moves and his hair falls over his forehead in that careless way that makes my fingers twitch to run through the thick strands.

Then that warmth penetrates deep, turning to a swelling tenderness inside my chest that always comes when I'm gazing at him.

Because I love him.

And I'm so grateful, so happy that he's here and mine and I'm his.

He stands beside me, the heat of his thigh against my arm, glancing down at my handiwork.

"How's the patient, Dr. Abby?"

"He'll live." I smile.

"Excellent." Tommy plucks a grape off the vine from the bag on the table, tosses it in the air and catches it in his mouth with a smooth, effortless grace. "Then I came home just in time."

He gave notice on the lease of his place and moved in here with me—not just to take care of me while I recuperate, but for good.

"You deserve a reward," he says in a teasing tone. "And so do I."

Then he proceeds to unbutton his black shirt. Slowly.

And I put down the suture needle.

"Since you were so generous with the stripteases when I was on the mend, I thought it was time I return the favor. If you're feeling up to it."

He strips his shirt off his arms—revealing deliciously warm, tan muscles—leaving him in black trousers that cling in all the best places.

"I'm feeling all sorts of things at the moment."

His grin is wicked and his voice is a low, decadent promise.

"Don't get too worked up, lass. We're going to have to go extra slow—I'm even thinking about tying you down . . . just to be sure you don't hurt yourself."

My head goes pleasantly light—drunk on him—and my breasts are heavy and tingling for his touch.

Tommy scoops me up, cradling me against the smooth heat of his chest, my hair swinging long and loose behind me in a way I know he adores.

"You are a dirty, dirty man. And I am a lucky, lucky girl."

He dips his head, his mouth drifting close.

"And you love me."

It's not a question, but a declaration, because he adores that too—saying the words, hearing the confirmation out loud of all that we feel for each other.

I lean in, kissing him softly and tracing his bottom lip with my tongue.

"I really, really do."

The following Sunday afternoon, we're at Tommy's parents' house to celebrate his niece Matilda's second birthday. The house and back garden are filled to the brim with his loud and plentiful family and I sit on a blanket on the grass beside Tommy's youngest sister, Fiona, and the birthday girl herself.

Matilda's little face is scrunched with seriousness as she puts the new toy doctor bag Tommy and I gave her to good use—tapping the diaphragm of the brightly colored stethoscope against my chest and listening intently at the eartips that disappear beneath the baby-blond braids on either side of her head.

"Hmm . . ." she hums thoughtfully, and it's so adorable I smother a laugh.

Then she nods, quite seriously. She drops her stethoscope into the bag and carefully sticks an oversized electric-blue adhesive bandage to my splint.

And then she hands me a lolly.

"Why thank you, Dr. Matilda! I feel so much better now."

She giggles in that magical, high-pitched way that makes anyone who hears it smile along with her, and then she toddles to her feet, gathers her bag and rushes off to see her next patient.

A moment later, Tommy is dropping to his knees on the blanket next to me, handing me a plate of crackers and cheese.

"Thank you." I smile up at him. "Though I really could've gotten it myself—my wrist is sprained, not my leg."

He shrugs, then bends his head to smack a kiss on my lips.

"Now you won't have to get up—you can sit back and watch me and Lionel kick Andy and Arthur's arses all over the yard."

He's going to play football with his brothers—a common pastime at Sullivan gatherings, which can go from playful to deadly in a hot minute and usually does. Sullivan boys are competitive.

Tommy kisses me again, then heads off—telling his sister as he passes, "Keep Abby company, Fi."

No sooner is he out of earshot than his youngest sister wonders, "Would you write a prescription for birth control for me if I asked you to?"

I cover my eyes with my good hand. And groan.

"Why me? Why do you ask me these things? You have three older sisters and a mother who loves you incessantly."

By "these things" I mean questions—generally sex related—for the past few months.

At first I thought she was doing it to tease me or purposely make me uncomfortable . . . like her naughty brother before her.

But now I think it's something else. That Fiona's looking for someone to talk to, someone who won't judge her, someone she can trust.

While that someone is absolutely me, it doesn't mean I have to be happy about it.

"Have you met my mum?" Fiona gives me an inane look. "I could never talk to her like this. She'd lock me in my room until I was thirty."

I look across the grass to the lady of the house—Mrs. Sullivan—pointing and giving directions and orders like a drill sergeant gunning for a promotion. I've come to realize that handing out tasks is her way of showing affection—of saying she likes you enough to want your contribution and has faith in you to do it correctly.

The woman's never asked me to even pick up a bloody spoon.

"Sometimes mums and dads can surprise you," I tell Fiona.

Mine did.

After our heart-to-heart at my flat that day, and then the accident, things changed between me and my parents. Don't misunderstand me—they're still stuffy as all get-out—they don't know how to be anything else. But they've gone out of their way to have lunch with me each week and there's a closeness, an honesty, a realness to our conversations that wasn't there before.

"My mother will never surprise anyone," Fiona insists. "She's as stubborn as a stone in a five-hundred-year-old castle."

"Be that as it may, this is still a discussion you should be having with her. Or your regular physician."

Fiona leans forward.

"But if I didn't want to discuss it with either of them—would you do it if I asked?"

I take a breath, and I think about it only for a moment.

"Yes, I would."

"What if Tommy didn't want you to?" she asks.

"The prescription wouldn't be for him, so it's not really any of his business, now is it?"

"What if he was angry about it?"

My gaze finds Tommy across the way—his eyes dark and intense, his hair clinging damp to his forehead and a smudge of dirt on his cheek, making him look rough and rugged and so handsome it sears my heart.

"He wouldn't be. Nauseous more likely at the thought of his baby sister having sex, but not angry. Above all he would want you protected."

After a moment of thinking it over, Fiona nods.

"For the record—I'm not asking. But it's always good to know." Then she reaches over and hugs me, quick and sweet. "Thank you, Abby."

After an aunt calls Fiona over, I find myself looking over at Mrs. Sullivan again.

She's standing on her own now, arms crossed, watching her four boys play ball with just a hint of a smile on her face. And speaking of discussions that should be had . . .

I stand up from the blanket, brush my beige trousers off and walk straight over to Tommy's mum. She doesn't acknowledge that I'm standing next to her at first—but I tell her what needs to be said anyway.

"I love your son, Mrs. Sullivan. It'd be easier for him if you liked me, but it doesn't truly matter if you do. I'm not going anywhere." I look across the grass at Tommy, then back to her again—and now I've got her attention. "He's the best thing that ever happened to me. And I'm going to spend the rest of my life making sure he feels like I'm the best thing that ever happened to him."

She doesn't say anything for a bit—she simply stares back with an unreadable face.

Then she turns her gaze to the game—to Tommy—and sighs slowly, before nodding.

"All right, then. I'm heading to the kitchen to get supper served. Tommy says you're talented with a knife. Would you like to carve the roast, Abby?"

And it's like I'm glowing from the inside—alight with a wonderful contentment that spreads down my limbs to the tips of my fingers and toes.

Because this is a peace offering. A start.

"I'd be happy to help, Mrs. Sullivan."

"Good." She picks up a wayward plate from the table behind her, before turning back. "And you can call me Maggie. Or Mum if you'd like . . . everyone in the family does."

With that, she walks off ahead of me. And I just sort of stand there—stunned.

I feel Tommy's eyes on me, because he always knows where I am. When I look at him, he lifts his chin towards his mother—silently asking if I'm all right.

I give him my biggest, brightest smile.

Then he's smiling back, sending me a sexy wink just because he can.

And life isn't just perfect . . . it's extraordinary.

EPILOGUE

Tommy

7 years later

PERSONAL SECURITY HAS BECOME NOT JUST A NECESSITY for the wealthy and privileged, but a status symbol of sorts. Like a private jet or an overpriced ugly handbag—anyone who thinks they're someone wants to have it.

Which means for S&S Securities, business has been booming. We have our regular, serious clients who truly need guarding and a fancier set who just enjoy knowing a trained professional has their back.

But we don't fuck around—we protect them all the same.

The firm expanded so much, Lo and I took on another partner— James Winchester. The three of us always did work well together, and it's been smooth sailing ever since James hopped on board.

I've hung up my guarding boots and only rarely take a shift with a client—sticking to training and supervising day to day. Because I've come to appreciate Abby's penchant for a consistent schedule and reliable routine.

Especially once our son was born.

We named him Oliver and he's almost three years old now. He's got my hair and Abby's eyes—he's a holy terror and a blessing in one—exactly the kind of lad my mum says she always wished on me.

Ollie's favorite pastime is roughhousing with his uncles and Logan's boys. He's tough and quick-witted and gives back as good as he gets. When his uncle Luke comes to town he teaches him chess, a game Oliver's picked up with fascinating ease. He also takes piano lessons—at the Dowager Countess of Bumblebridge's insistence—because she swears he's a regular Haddock prodigy.

But to me and Abby, he'll always simply be the most perfect thing we've ever done.

I take him to the shop with me every day I can. But six p.m. is closing time.

"Get your shoes on, Ollie—time to go," I call to where he's wrestling around in the rink with Lo's brood.

Lo and Ellie took a break from popping out kids like there's going to be a shortage after number four.

Their third, Izzy, wags a finger at Oliver when he doesn't get up fast enough.

"Are you deaf, Ollie? Your dad said it's time to go. Move it."

At six years old, Izzy is a fucking hilarious combination of Ellie's tiny stature and Logan's personality. She's the only girl in the bunch and she runs the rest of them ragged.

My boy rolls his round eyes to the ceiling—but then he gets his shoes on and scurries over to me. I lift him onto my shoulders and carry him there as we head to the hospital to pick up his mum. He pelts me with adorable questions the whole way.

Why are the walls of the Tube station blue?

Why does the hospital have so many windows?

When will I be big like you?

And *why* and *when* and *how* and *why* again. He keeps me on my toes, and there's not a single thing about it that isn't amazing.

We come out of the lift on the surgical floor and Abby's there at the nurse's desk, her delicate brows drawn together and her pouty lower lip trapped between her teeth in concentration over a chart. She's wearing dark green scrubs that she still manages to make gorgeous, and her hair is up in a copper bun, with a few wispy tendrils escaping to frame her lovely face.

And the sight of her and all that she is to me kicks me right in the gut—every time.

When she senses us, she looks up—smiling stunningly—which sends a surge of hunger straight to my cock.

That happens every time too.

"Hello, my loves," she says—pressing her mouth softly against mine, then peppering Ollie's little outstretched hands in devoted kisses. She takes him from my shoulders and holds him close, and he rests his face against her neck with a happy exhale.

"How did it go?" I ask her.

"Splendid—without a hitch."

I rub her shoulders, because she did a heart transplant today and I know her neck is probably stiff.

"Tired?"

"Not so much."

Abby's been hinting she'd like to start trying for a little brother or sister for Oliver, and the hot little grin she sends my way tells me I'll most definitely be getting lucky tonight. Twice—at least.

When Ollie was on the way, we moved out of Abby's flat into a rowhouse with more space and a perfect pretty garden. For a long time, I didn't think a man like me would get off on domestic activities like making dinner and bath times and bedtime stories.

But life is funny like that—how it spins you around and shakes you out into something more beautiful than you ever could've imagined.

The thirst for a challenge—for an adrenaline rush—that used to drive me is now quenched by other, infinitely better quests.

Like the joy that punched through me when I slipped a band

of gold on Abby's finger and she whispered "I do" beneath a banner of white roses in front of our friends and families.

Like the thrill of seeing her complete the gauntlet of her last year of residency—watching that dream come true for her.

Like the excitement that spiked in my veins—that felt like I was having a bloody heart attack—when Abby was two days past her due date and her green eyes looked up into mine and she told me it was time to head to the hospital.

And like the indescribable exhilaration that pounded in my chest the very first time I held my son.

When Ollie is down for the night, Abby takes a bath and then slips between the sheets into my arms—bare and beautiful and every inch of her mine.

The only chasing I'm interested in these days is after our rowdy boy—or after my wife when she's feeling especially frisky.

And it's all so damn good.

Because I already caught the most precious prize in the world—Abby's tender heart, her rapturous body, her sweet soul, her love.

And along the way of that mad merry chase . . . she caught mine right back.

The End

ABOUT
THE AUTHOR

New York Times and *USA Today* bestselling author, Emma Chase, writes contemporary romance filled with heat, heart and laugh-out-loud humor. Her stories are known for their clever banter, sexy, swoon-worthy moments, and hilariously authentic male POV's.

Emma lives in New Jersey with her amazing husband, two awesome children, and two adorable but badly behaved dogs. She has a long-standing love/hate relationship with caffeine.

Follow me online:

Twitter: twitter.com/EmmaChse
Facebook: www.facebook.com/AuthorEmmaChase
Instagram: www.instagram.com/authoremmachase
BookBub: www.bookbub.com/authors/emma-chase

Subscribe to my mailing list for the latest book news, exclusive teasers, freebies & giveaways!
authoremmachase.com/newsletter

ALSO BY EMMA CHASE

Keep reading for a free sample of

ROYALLY ENDOWED

PROLOGUE

Logan

SOME MEN THINK WITH THEIR COCKS.

You know the type. Quick smooth-talkers, shifty eyes always scanning for a nice pair of legs, a set of full tits, or a tight arse they can pant after.

Other blokes think too much with their brains. You know that type too. Annoyingly careful, slow-moving, constantly parsing their words like they already know whatever they're saying is going to come back and take a bite out of them.

I'm not either of those.

I always go with my gut. When it clenches with a warning, I act—no hesitation. When it tugs and nudges, I pause and reevaluate. When it twists and writhes, I know, guaranteed, I've cocked up big-time.

My gut is my best friend, my conscience, my most lethal asset.

And it has never let me down.

It's my gut that drags me to her door. That roots me in place as I knock. That gives me the words—pleading, unfamiliar remorseful words—I'll gladly say to make this right.

To get her back.

Because while my gut is brilliant, sometimes I can be a real fucking idiot.

Yesterday was one of those times.

"Ellie. It's me—open up, we need to talk."

I sense movement on the other side of the solid oak door—not in sounds or shifting shadows beneath it, but more of an awareness. I can feel her in there. Nearby and listening.

"Go away, Logan."

Her voice is tight, higher-pitched than usual. Upset.

"Ellie, please. I was a twat, I know . . ." I'm not keen on begging from the hallway, but if that's what it takes . . . "I'm sorry. Let me in."

Ellie is difficult to anger, quick to forgive; she just doesn't have it in her to hold a grudge. So her next words fall like an axe—cutting my legs right off from under me.

"No, you were right. The princess's sister and the East Amboy bodyguard don't make sense—we'll never last."

Did I actually say that to her? What the fuck is wrong with me? What I feel for her is the one thing in my life that makes sense. That matters.

But I never told her that.

Instead . . . instead, I said all the wrong things.

I brace my palm against the smooth wood, leaning forward, wanting to be as near to her as possible. "Elle . . ."

"I've changed my mind, Logan."

If a corpse could speak, it would sound exactly like my Ellie does now. Flat, lifeless.

"I want the fairy tale. I want what Olivia has . . . castles and carriages . . . and you'll never be able to give me that. I would just be settling for you. You'll never be able to make me happy."

She doesn't mean that. They're my words—the insecurities I put on her—that she's hurling back in my face.

But God, it fucking hurts to hear. Physically hurts—stabbing deep into the pit of my stomach, crushing my chest, grinding my bones. I meant it when I said I would die for her . . . and right now, it feels like I am.

I grab the doorknob to walk inside, to see her face. To see that she doesn't mean it.

"Ellie—"

"Don't come in!" she screeches like I've never heard her before. "I don't want to see you! Go away, Logan. We're done—just *go!*"

I breathe hard—that's what you do when pain wrecks you, breathe through it. Then I swallow bile, straighten up, turn around and walk down the hall. Away from her. Just like she wants, like she asked. Like she screamed.

My brain tells me to move faster—get the hell out of there, cut my losses and lick my wounds. And my heart—Christ—that poor bastard's too battered and bloody to express anything at all.

But then, just over halfway down the hall, my steps slow until I stop completely.

Because my gut . . . it strains through the hurt. Rebels. It shouts that this isn't right. This isn't her. Something's off.

And even more than that . . . something is very, very wrong.

I glance up and down the quiet hall—not a guard or a maid in sight. I look back at the door. Closed and silent and still.

Then I turn and march straight back to it. I don't knock, or wait, or ask for permission. In one move, I turn the knob and step inside.

What I see there stops me cold.

Because whatever I was expecting, it sure as fuck wasn't this.

Not at all . . .

CHAPTER ONE

Logan

Five years earlier

"Y OU WANTED TO SEE ME, PRINCE NICHOLAS?"

Here's a confession: when the powers that be first offered me a position on the royal security team, I wasn't interested. The idea of following around some self-important aristocrats who were in love with the sound of their own voices—and the smell of their own arses—didn't appeal to me. The way I saw it, guards were only a step above servant-boys—and I'm no one's servant.

I wanted action. A blaze of glory. Purpose. I wanted to be a part of something that was bigger than myself. Something noble and lasting.

"Yes, Logan—have a seat."

I'd distinguished myself in the military pretty quickly. And Winston—the head of Palace Security—had taken notice. They were looking for very particular qualities in Prince Nicholas's personal team, he'd said. Young lads who were quick on their feet, loyal and ferocious when required. The type who'd be just fine bringing a knife to a gunfight—'cause he wouldn't be needing a fucking knife or gun to win.

After only a few weeks, I had a different take on the position. It came to feel like a calling, a duty. Important men make things happen, get things done—they have the power to make life easier for the not-so-important people.

I protect them, so they can do that.

And the young prince sitting across from me, behind the desk in the library of this luxurious penthouse suite—he's an important man.

"How old are you, Logan?"

"My file says I'm twenty-five."

If Saint Peter was a fisher of men, I'm a reader of them. It's a skill that's essential to this occupation—possessing a gut feeling for what someone else's intentions are. The ability to read a man's eyes, the shifting of his feet—to know what he's capable of and just what kind of man he is.

Nicholas Pembrook is a good man. To his core.

And that's a rare thing.

More often than not, important men are prime scumbags.

His mouth twitches. "I know what your file says. That's not what I asked." He's also not a fool—and he's been lied to enough in his life that he's got an ear for things that don't ring true.

"How old are you really?"

I look him in the eye, wondering where he's going with this.

"Twenty-two."

He nods slowly, massaging his thumb into the palm of his other hand, thinking. "So you signed up for the military at . . . fifteen? Lied about your age? That's young."

I shrug. "They weren't real discerning at the recruitment office. I was tall, solid and good with my fists."

"You were still a child."

"I was never a child, Your Highness. Any more than you were."

Childhood is when you're supposed to muck up, figure out who you are, what you want to be. You're given permission to be a jack-arse. I didn't have that privilege; neither did Nicholas. Our paths were set before we were born. Opposite paths, sure—but whether you grow up in a shack or a palace, the expectations and demands of those around you tend to snuff out innocence pretty damn fast.

"Why'd you leave home so young?"

Now it's my turn to smirk. Because I'm not a fool either. "You know why. That's in the file too."

I'm good at identifying scumbags because I come from a long line of them. Criminals—not especially successful ones. Petty, scrounging, desperate enough to be dangerous—the kind who'll smile to your face, pat you on the back, then stab you as soon as you're not looking.

My grandfather died in prison—he was in for murder committed during an armed robbery. My dad will die there too, hopefully sooner rather than later—he's in for manslaughter. I've got uncles who've done stints for a whole range of criminal activities, cousins who've been killed in broad daylight in the middle of the street and aunts who've pimped out their daughters without a second thought.

By the time I was fifteen I knew if I stayed in that shit-hole, I'd start to stink. And then I'd have only two options: prison or the cemetery.

Neither one of those worked for me.

"What's this really about? All the questions?"

It's always better to cut to the chase, deep and quick.

His gray-green eyes focus on me, his face probing, his shoulders slightly hunched, like an elephant's sitting on them.

"Now that I have Henry in hand, the Queen wants us back in Wessco, in two days. You know this."

I nod.

"I want to bring Olivia home with me, for the summer."

For a time, I was on the fence about the pretty New York baker. She put ideas in Nicholas's head, made him reckless. But she's a good lass—hardworking, honest—and she cares about him. Not about his title or his bank account. She couldn't give a shit about those and probably would prefer him without them. She makes him happy.

And in the two-odd years I've worked with the Crown Prince, truly happy is something I don't think I've ever seen him be.

"Is that wise?" I ask.

Olivia Hammond is a sweet girl. And the Palace . . . has a knack for turning sweet to sour.

"No. But I want to do it anyway."

And the look on his face—it's raw and exposed. It's yearning. From the outside looking in, you'd think there's nothing a royal could want that he can't have. Nicholas has private planes, servants, castles and more money than he can spend in a lifetime—but I can't think of a single instance when he did what he wanted, just for the hell of it. Or when he let himself do something he knew he shouldn't.

I admire him, but I don't envy him.

"Olivia wants to come, but she's worried about leaving her sister alone for the summer. Ellie's young, still in school and . . . naïve."

She's got a wild streak in her too. As bright as the pink in her blond hair, which has been joined by blue, then green, during the two months we've been in New York.

"I could see her attracting trouble," I comment.

"Exactly. Also, Ellie will have to run the coffee shop on her own, with just Marty for help. Olivia's father is—"

"He's a drunk."

I'm good at spotting them too—can smell them from a mile away.

"Yes." Nicholas sighs. "Look, Logan, you've been around long enough to know that I don't trust easily, or often. But I trust you." He pushes a hand through his black hair and meets my eyes. "Which is why I'm asking you. Will you stay in New York? Will you help Ellie, watch over her . . . make sure she's safe?"

She seems like a decent girl, but I already said I wasn't a servant—and

I'm also not a nanny. Protecting the royal family is a duty I've chosen; keeping tabs on an American teenage girl is a fucking headache waiting to happen.

Nicholas glances out the window. "I know it's a lot to ask. It's not your job; you can say no. But there's no one else I would choose . . . no one else I can depend on. So, I'd consider it a personal favor if you say yes."

Ah . . . hell.

I have a brother. To say I wish I didn't would be an understatement. And not in the same way Nicholas wishes his royal snot of a brother would grow the hell up, or how Miss Olivia seems put out by her younger sister at times. The world would be a better place if my brother weren't in it—and that's a stance shared by others.

But if I had a choice, if I could assemble a brother from the ground up, I would build the man sitting across from me right now.

Which is why, even though I'm going to bloody regret it, it takes only a moment before I give him my answer.

"James has a boy back home—about a year old, so he'll want to go home with you. Tommy'll be happy to stay—the Bronx is like his own personal harem. Between the two of us, and two more men, Cory and Liam maybe, we'll keep the girl out of trouble and the business afloat for the summer."

Nicholas's face splits into the biggest smile and relief lights up his eyes. He stands, holding out his hand to shake mine, pounding my shoulder with gratitude.

"Thank you, Logan. Truly. I won't forget this."

If nothing else, this summer will be . . . different.

To continue reading, purchase at your favorite online retailer.

CPSIA information can be obtained
at www.ICGtesting.com
Printed in the USA
LVHW111002180520
655911LV00001B/137